BURNING BRIDGES

What Reviewers Say About
Lesley Davis's Work

Playing With Fire

"Strong, mature characters embracing their feelings (good, bad and indifferent). An awfully attractive African-American MC, Takira Lathan. Dealing head-on with stereotypes. Good chemistry. A lovely relationship wherein the MCs talk to each other about themselves, their insecurities, their feelings and even what they like sexually. This book has a lot going for it."—*Reviewer@large*

"First of all, this book is a total geek dream. …This book was packed with tropes, like seriously all the best ones, and had everything from references, to cute moments inspired by making sure we all believe in a little bit of magic. It was uplifting and just added a little something extra to this story, like the right ingredients in a secret sauce."—*LESBIreviewed*

Raging at the Stars

"*Raging at the Stars* is a very entertaining and engaging read. The alien invasion storyline—with a twist—is very original and the plot is very well developed. The two leads are very likeable and the supporting characters are equally interesting. The author's style of writing is very engaging, especially the witty dialogue."—Melina Bickard, Librarian, Waterloo Library (London)

"A sci-fi book with a side of romance and a hint of aliens (Or is there really a hint? What else could be going on?). Anyway, it's basically my perfect book, and I thought it was totally awesome."—Danielle Kimerer, Librarian, Nevins Memorial Public Library (MA)

"I am 800% here for this book. It reminded me of a fun mashup of *X-Files* and *Independence Day*, with lesbians, and honestly, I can't think of anything cooler at this moment. ...I'll definitely track down more of Davis's titles. Definitely recommend."—*Kissing Backwards: Lesbian Book Reviews*

Playing in Shadow

"*Playing in Shadow* is different from my typical romance reading, but at the same time exactly the same. I loved the two main characters and the secondary characters. The issues they all face were realistic and handled really well. ...I do not often read LGBT romance, but thus far every time I have I have been thrilled with how fantastic the writing is. I guess I need to read more!"—Sharon Tyler, Librarian, Cheshire Public Library (CT)

"Overall this was an amazing read, great and engaging story, and as it progresses adding layers to the characters and the complexity of their struggles it starts to consume a little bit of your heart making you wish this was a Saga and not just one story."—*Collector of Book Boyfriends*

"The story is emotional and feels very honest. You won't miss out on the romance either, with equal parts of 'Awe, that's so sweet!' and 'Whoa, Steamy!'"—Katie Larson, Librarian, Tooele City Public Library (Utah)

Starstruck

"Both leads were well developed with believable backgrounds and Mischa was a delight. It was nice to 'run into' Trent and Elton from the author's previous book."—Melina Bickard, Librarian, Waterloo Library (London)

"*Away with the Faeries*" in Women of the Dark Streets

"Wondrous three-way duel between vampires, werewolves and faeries. The ending had me bowled over and howling with laughter. Grandiose!"—*Rainbow Book Reviews*

Truth Behind the Mask

"It is rare to find good lesbian science fantasy. It is also rare to have a deaf lesbian heroine. Davis has given readers both in *Truth Behind the Mask*. In her tightly wrapped novel, Davis vividly describes the feeling of the night wind and the heat of the fires. She is just as deft at describing the blossoming love between Pagan and Erith, two of her main characters. *Truth Behind the Mask* has enough intriguing twists and turns to keep the pages flying right to the exciting conclusion."
—*Just About Write*

Playing Passion's Game

"*Playing Passion's Game* is a delightful read with lots of twists, turns, and good laughs. Davis has provided a varied and interesting supportive cast. Those who enjoy computer games will recognize some familiar scenes, and those new to the topic get to learn about a whole new world."—*Just About Write*

Pale Wings Protecting

"*Pale Wings Protecting* is a provocative paranormal mystery; it's an otherworldly thriller couched inside a tale of budding romance. The novel contains an absorbing narrative, full of thrilling revelations, that skillfully leads the reader into the uncanny dimensions of the supernatural."—*Lambda Literary Review*

"[*Pale Wings Protecting*] was just a delicious delight with so many levels of intrigue on the case level and the personal level. Plus, the celestial and diabolical beings were incredibly intriguing. ...I was riveted from beginning to end and I certainly will look forward to additional books by Lesley Davis. By all means, give this story a total once-over!"—*Rainbow Book Reviews*

Dark Wings Descending—*Lambda Literary Award Finalist*

"[*Dark Wings Descending*] is an intriguing story that presents a vision of life after death many will find challenging. It also gives the reader some wonderful sex scenes, humor, and a great read!"—*Reviewer RLynne*

By the Author

Truth Behind the Mask

Playing Passion's Game

Playing In Shadow

Starstruck

Raging at the Stars

Playing With Fire

In The Spotlight

Playing Love's Refrain

Burning Bridges

The Wings Series

Dark Wings Descending

Pale Wings Protecting

White Wings Weeping

BURNING BRIDGES

by
Lesley Davis

2025

BURNING BRIDGES

ISBN 13: 978-1-63679-872-1

This Trade Paperback Original Is Published By
Bold Strokes Books, Inc.
P.O. Box 249
Valley Falls, NY 12185

First Edition: September 2025

CREDITS
Editor: Cindy Cresap
Production Design: Susan Ramundo
Cover Design By Tammy Seidick

Acknowledgments

Thank you to Radclyffe and all at BSB for everything you do in the publishing world. I'm proud to have twelve books flying under your flag.

Sandy Lowe, thank you for checking in on me and prodding me along! This story was done a lot quicker with your encouragement.

Thank you, Tammy Seidick, for a wonderfully dark and moody cover!

Cindy Cresap, thank you for your awesome editing style, enthusiasm, patience, and your geeky genius!

Thank you to all my readers, I hope you'll enjoy this one.

Pam Goodwin and Gina Paroline

Kim and Tracy Palmer-Bell, (Kim, thank you for always telling me your favourite parts. x)

Cheryl and Anne Hunter

Sean Lidynia

Annie Ellis and Julia Lowndes

Donna and Jools Chidley-Gosling (Donna, thanks for the many hours of laughter as we game upon the mighty seas!)

Natalie Sussenbach (for joining me down every rabbit hole!)

And Cindy Pfannenstiel for listening as the ideas form, for beta-reading the result, and just being there.

Dedication

For my gamer buddies, Natalie and Donna,
for casting light upon my darkest days.

Chapter One

The Missouri River, longest of all America's rivers, refused to reveal any of its secrets to a casual eye. Silt deliberately colored and hid whatever lay beneath the water. Clancy Madsen steered her inflatable boat back and forth upon a stretch of it, keeping a steady pace as she marked out a grid for her search. She diligently watched her screen. The small monitor affixed in the bow displayed side imaging from the boat's sonar. It afforded her a view of seventy-five feet out from port and starboard. She could see everything, from the underwater structure of the dock nearby, the river's overgrown banks, down to a school of fish swimming about. Lit in an eerie glowing orange tone, the depth took on an otherworldly view. The screen also had a down imager that detailed precise depths and heights so, if anything was found, Clancy would know how far down it lay or how tall a structure it was. From that she could deduce if it was a car or something else. If it was a car, she hoped it was one linked to her list of missing people. She had a growing case file with the names of someone's loved one feared lost within the water's cold embrace.

This waterway wasn't anything like the clear waters of Florida. If the Missouri had things to hide, it hid them exceptionally well in a dark, unforgiving shroud. Sonar scanning was the only saving grace.

Clancy's eye caught something and, for a second, she held her breath. There was an anomaly on the riverbed. She stilled the boat and kept her gaze fixed on the foreign object.

"Is that a car?"

Inez Wilson's hopeful voice sounded out loudly over the radio, startling Clancy. Clancy realized she'd been radio silent for almost an hour while charting her course. She'd been listening intently to the sound of the water. The purr of the boat's engine had become nothing more than white noise pushed to the back of her mind. Clancy tried to tune it all out. She needed to single out a specific sound amid a cacophony. She used to be able to lose herself in a pocket of blissful silence when all around was roaring. It was just getting harder to attain, the more stress she put upon herself. She shook her head to return to the present when Inez asked the question again.

Clancy stared at the object outlined on the riverbed. "I don't think so, but let me come at it from another angle just to be sure." She turned the boat around slowly, her eyes never leaving the screen. She heard the disappointment in Inez's voice as the broken bow of an old rotting boat became more obvious.

"Sorry, Inez, false alarm."

Clancy could picture Inez watching the sonar findings back at their RV nearby. Inez shared the same dedication Clancy had for the job. She felt safe knowing Inez was also monitoring a separate feed running a live stream recording from the GoPro camera Clancy wore attached to her life vest. She never left shore without it when traveling alone on the water.

She never wanted someone to have to come searching for *her*.

Clancy hoped what they were uncovering on these missing person cases would never dull the bright smile and cheery disposition Inez shared with the world.

It had worn Clancy's soul down to barely a sliver.

Clancy and Inez had started the journey together following the mighty Missouri River. They were charting every inch of it, having started in North Dakota, working their way through South Dakota, and then into Iowa and Nebraska. The Kansas-Missouri boundary was their current location.

"Has Evan graced us with his presence today?" Clancy was thankful Inez couldn't see her amusement.

"No, not yet, thank goodness." The relief in Inez's voice was palpable.

Clancy hated not having a permanent secondary diver on her team. She'd lost her last one literally the day before the Missouri River job landed in her lap. Not even the generous amount the Chicago unit was paying her and her team was enough to make Peter change his mind. Clancy couldn't begrudge him moving across the country for the sunnier skies and surfing spots in Florida, but it left her scrambling to find a replacement on such short notice.

They'd had to have a new diver, sometimes two or three switching around, in each state so far. Evan Green was signed on to do the last leg of the river and came highly recommended. He only needed to turn up when Clancy required help with the diving. However, he seemed quite enamored with Inez and made all manner of excuses as to why he needed to be there when Clancy was just cruising the river.

Clancy was just thankful she could conduct the searches her *own* way without too much interference, prying eyes, or curious ears. The job was hard enough without someone who kept asking what she was doing.

The warmth of the morning sun made Clancy tug a little at her life jacket. It was getting increasingly hotter with every hour. She looked down at the water. The Big Muddy wasn't her idea of a refreshing dip, but it was looking more inviting with every hot minute. She picked up her map and checked again the three circles drawn on it.

Five-mile radius from her house. Five miles from her place of work. The last location where her phone pinged off a cell tower and then was gone. Everything pointed to here.

Quietly, Clancy began to speak. "Joanna Drysdale, are you out here?"

Only the splash of water against the boat answered her.

"Joanna, your family is waiting for you. Please, let me help you." Clancy reread the missing person's report. It was just habit. She already knew it by heart. Joanna Drysdale had last been seen five months ago at a gas station near the hospital where she worked. CCTV showed her paying for her fuel and picking up an expensive bottle of wine. Then she left, never to be seen or heard from again.

She joined the growing number of women who had disappeared in the same way over a period of two years.

Clancy had been tasked to find as many as she could. Joanna was still on the list.

"Joanna? If you can hear me, call to me. I'm here to set you free."

A chill snaked its way through Clancy's bones. It made her shiver, despite the warmth of the sunshine. In the finite moment between Clancy taking a breath in and breathing it back out, time slowed, then ground to a halt around her. The water stopped flowing. The birds stopped singing. Not a bee buzzed or a wing beat the air. The boat stilled upon the water. The world paused, *waiting*.

Clancy also waited, ears straining in the hopes of hearing a reply.

"Hello?"

Clancy breathed out in relief. Her surroundings began to move again in slow motion as her attention was pulled farther up the river. As soon as Clancy was pointing in that direction, everything snapped back to normal. The returning birdsong was almost deafening after the moment of utter silence.

"Hi, Joanna. Don't be afraid." Clancy kept her eyes on the screen to make sure she didn't miss anything as she piloted her boat forward into unmarked territory.

Within five minutes of traversing farther up the river, Clancy saw the undeniable shape of a car, half buried, deep in the water below. She stopped the boat directly above it. A coiled length of rope, a bright red buoy tied to one end and a heavy magnet on the other, lay on the bottom of Clancy's boat. She carefully lowered it over the side into the water, aiming it to land on the car's roof to mark its location. She watched on her screen its slow descent into the murky water to find its target.

"Who are you?"

Clancy gave the rope a tug, satisfied the line was secure. The buoy bobbed on top of the water. X marks the spot.

"My name is Clancy."

"Why are you here?"

Clancy smiled down into the depths of the water.

"I'm here to take you home."

CHAPTER TWO

Clancy safely secured the last fastening on her wet suit then padded through the long length of her behemoth Grand Design RV. It was currently parked on the dock where Clancy had been trawling.

The base of operations Inez manned took up the largest space inside. It was a professional looking office with a bank of monitors, desks, and laptops all within easy reach. It seated two very comfortably, but Inez had made the space undeniably *hers*. Colorful crystals were artfully placed in every corner, courtesy of Inez's Wiccan mother. A bejeweled suncatcher cast rainbows across a stack of files. It brought a welcomed splash of light to the darkness of the work they were involved in.

Beyond that lay a small kitchen area with a compact dining table should Clancy ever feel civilized enough to eat there. Farther down the length of the vehicle was a comfy sofa seating area with a large TV, where Clancy usually ate off a tray. Two decent-sized bedrooms were situated toward the back. Inez had made her home in the spare one once she joined Clancy for the Missouri River trail. A compact bathroom afforded the promise of a warm shower after a dive in cold waters. Finally, rear compartments kept all Clancy's diving equipment securely locked away. It was the most perfect office/home environment Clancy could have dreamed of. The thought of having a sedentary life chained to a white picket fence existence scared her. She needed to keep moving.

Attached behind the vehicle was a combo trailer that racked Clancy's precious adventure bike, her Triumph Tiger 900 motorcycle. To Clancy's never-ending embarrassment, Inez's dinkier bright pink Vespa nestled beside it. The trailer also carried the RID, the blue rigid inflatable boat Clancy employed for her work. Hitched to the front, a sturdy silver Ford pickup towed the whole lot.

Clancy wandered back to where she could see Inez sipping a coffee. Studious and bright, twenty-year-old Inez ran the multi-screens with ease, recording every inch of the river that Clancy sailed upon. Inez also had a direct line to their bosses, a special branch of law enforcement in Chicago, that would immediately dispatch officers from any state concerning anything Clancy found. It was they who had asked for Clancy's involvement. Inez called them the Men in Black. Clancy knew they were way more mysterious than that.

"Where'd you get the coffee?" Clancy's frown soon dissipated when Inez held one out to her. Clancy took a deep drink, savoring the bitter taste on her tongue. She was going to need the caffeine boost.

"Evan treated us." Inez rolled her eyes and held up a bag, shaking it gently. "You also get a cookie when you're back on dry land."

Clancy reached out to grab the bag but Inez pulled it back.

"No cookie until you're out of the water and the job is done."

Clancy sighed. "You act like I'm going to run my tank down and drown myself while trying to recover a body."

"I wish you wouldn't joke about it. I'd be blind not to see how depressed you've gotten with each body you've recovered. I told you that you were pushing yourself too hard getting back to work so quickly after we found that body in Iowa. You need to decompress more between searches. Too much staring into the face of death darkens your spirit." Inez's eyes were kind, but they burned through Clancy's soul with the look of someone way older than her tender years.

Clancy let out an exasperated groan. She'd never admit that Inez might be right. "Why your mother felt I needed an empath by my side twenty-four/seven I'll never know."

"Because she knows how hard this work is on you and because she loves you. And I love you too. Every time you step into that water,

I'm going to be here on the bank showing you a reason to come back out."

Clancy sighed and hugged Inez tightly to her, grateful for her presence and her wisdom.

"I hate it when you use your mother's tone on me."

Inez snuggled her face into Clancy's shoulder, hugging her tighter. "I know, that's why I do it."

"Just save me a couple of those cookies for when I get back, Agatha Harkness," Clancy grumbled, letting Inez go.

"I'm telling Mom you called me a bad witch." Inez ripped open the bag and pulled out a large chocolate chip cookie for herself.

"You should be flattered. Kathryn Hahn is a hottie."

Inez laughed at her. "No one uses 'hottie' anymore, *Aunty* Clancy."

Clancy grimaced at the honorific title she was proud to have bestowed on her but hated hearing. It irritated every butch nerve she possessed. Inez laughed even more at her discomfort.

"Sorry, but you know Mom wouldn't let me call you Uncle, no matter how butch you are."

"Clancy is just fine and you know it." She glared at Inez. "Do not eat all my cookies, brat."

Inez took another cookie out for herself then hid the bag in a drawer.

The sun was blinding when Clancy stepped out from the RV. She slipped her feet into her flip-flops to head back to her boat. Evan was dutifully waiting beside it with the rest of her gear. He was excellent at his job and very respectful. His surfer boy physique, blond hair that fell dangerously close to his eyes, coupled with his barely restrained exuberance, made Clancy think of a golden retriever desperate to jump in every puddle. He was twenty-five and Clancy was ready to dump his body in a patch of water so deep never to be found if he made one wrong move toward Inez.

"Thanks for the coffee and cookies." Clancy turned to let Evan settle her scuba tank on her back. The weight grounded her in a multitude of ways. She put on her hood, then her full-faced mask, and tested all her gear one more time. Inez stood watching nearby and Clancy flashed her a thumbs up when she was satisfied. Inez disappeared back inside and Clancy switched on the camera mounted to her mask. She flashed two separate lights at Evan who nodded that they were working. Inside the helmet was a communications device so that Clancy and Inez could talk while Clancy was underwater.

"Can you hear me?" Clancy said.

"Loud and clear, Rubber Ducky."

Clancy smiled at the call name Inez had stuck her with since she'd been big enough to watch Clancy dive beneath the water.

Clancy picked up her flippers and did one last run through, tapping everything on her suit to make sure she had all she required. Satisfied she was set, she patted Evan on his arm.

"Time to see who's out there."

That first step underwater was both exhilarating and terrifying. Clancy watched as the water closed over her head. She remembered the first time she'd deliberately immersed herself in a body of water. She recalled the fear she felt as her lungs screamed for air and her eyes stung from the cold. The water had dragged on her clothes, making them feel like lead weights, and she'd sunk quicker than she had imagined she would. The pressure of the water shut out the noise from above, and for a moment she had finally felt peace.

"Clancy?"

Inez's voice in her headset broke whatever peace Clancy was remembering. She swore that kid could read her mind whenever her thoughts turned brooding.

"Just to remind you, you're looking for a Chrysler Neon, midnight blue." Inez rattled off the license plate and kept up a one-sided dialogue.

Clancy knew damn well all the details of what she was looking for but recognized Inez's chatter for the distraction it gave before she would reach the car. Her camera was recording the slow descent down through the murky water. Inez was with her all the way.

"Geez, that water is gross. It looks like you're swimming in root beer," Inez said.

Clancy hated that the river was so hard to see in. She was thankful for the rope guiding her down to the car. She'd never have found it if she had just dived down herself. Evan sat in the boat above her, wearing his own wet suit, just as a precaution. Rivers were unpredictable. Water itself even more so. Dirty water especially.

Clancy reached the end of the rope and directed her lights onto the buried car. She'd have to work to get the silt-covered roof to show her even a patch of paint she could identify. She rubbed at the closest piece of metal. The car was still intact but wedged into the riverbed. After a few minutes digging away, Clancy finally uncovered enough of the metal to see a blue spot that caught her light.

"Confirming blue exterior," Clancy said. She felt her way along the side of the car to find its trunk. "Trunk closed, back window on driver's side closed, rear window still intact." Clancy was thankful for small mercies. Closed windows meant evidence was tucked safe inside. She felt her way down to try to find the license plate. Her gloved fingers were bulky and clumsy around the thin tin plate, but Clancy needed it for identification and she wasn't returning topside without it. She took out a knife from her belt and pried at the metal. It loosened and with a sharp tug, Clancy managed to rip the license plate free. There was detritus all over it. She started painstakingly brushing everything off until the license plate revealed its numbers. Clancy read them off and Inez gave a restrained "yes!" that spoke of respect but also relief.

Clancy kept the license plate safe as she maneuvered around the trunk to check the passenger side window. "Passenger window closed." She then pulled herself all the way around to shed some light on the driver's side. The hood of the car was partially wedged in the silt, keeping the car in place and well hidden. Clancy reached out a hand to wipe at the driver's side window.

"Driver's window closed."

The current picked up suddenly, threatening to pull Clancy away. She quickly clung to the car door until it settled and she could get back into position. The bright lights on her mask fell upon the filthy glass. She steeled herself for what lay inside.

"Joanna?" Clancy called.

The violent slam of a skeletal skull against the glass made the car shudder. Clancy tightened her grip on the door handle and grabbed for the shattered side-view mirror to keep her balance and stop from floating away. The scared voice in her head screamed for her to swim away as far and as fast as she could. This was the worst part of her job. It was never easy finding a dead body but, to make matters worse, Clancy's *talent* gave her a front row seat to her own private version of hell.

The skull hit the window again as if ensuring her attention. It twisted, turning to look at Clancy with deep, empty, eye sockets. The jaw dropped open dramatically and Clancy bore witness to the last soul-destroying screams and pleas of a woman fighting for her life. The fear in that voice shook Clancy to her core.

The rest of the skeleton began reattaching itself, like some grotesque Ray Harryhausen stop-motion creation. It formed a bone frame to hang the bloated body upon. Clancy couldn't look away as rotted flesh gruesomely reattached itself. She needed to watch, to catalog every stage that passed before her. Lividity colored the skin then shifted and changed hues as a semblance of life began to be breathed back into the corpse. The shape of a woman appeared, her long hair matted with blood. Her skin, deathly pale, morphed into a vivid array of black-and-blue bruises. Her face was battered and bloody. A vicious cut across her throat, so deep it all but severed her head, left Clancy in no doubt what the killing blow had been. Each body she'd found so far had its own particular finishing move. Each had shown a growing escalation in violence. Lifeless eyes stared out at Clancy as the moment of life leaving the body was revealed to her.

Clancy had seen enough.

"Show me your true form," she said.

Joanna Drysdale shuddered violently. She lost the battered shell of her former self as easily as if shrugging off an old coat. Clancy smiled when she saw the beautiful woman underneath. She was unblemished, radiant. She was imbued with a light that came only from escaping earth's brutal grasp.

Intelligent eyes stared around the car's interior and realization dawned upon Joanna's face.

"He killed me."

Clancy nodded. "What was his name?"

"Trevor Craven."

Clancy repeated it aloud. She waited while Inez checked their data.

"No surprise there's no match with the others. Dammit, he's so random in his choice of false names. I wish all his aliases had horror film connections so he'd establish some kind of pattern."

Clancy stayed silent. Inez dutifully filled her in.

"Wes Craven, *A Nightmare on Elm Street*? *Scream*?"

"You know I don't watch scary movies." Clancy didn't need them. She had more than enough horror from what she dealt with daily. She turned back to Joanna. "I need everything you can tell me about what happened that night and how you met this man. Will you help me find him?"

Joanna nodded.

"I also need to get your car out of the river. Your family needs closure. They need to know you've been found."

"I want to talk to them."

"I can help you with that. You'll get to say your goodbyes, I promise." Clancy began to prepare for her swim back up to the surface. She held out her hand. "Come with me?"

Joanna hesitantly reached out a ghostly hand. She looked surprised when it passed right through the car door. Clancy held onto her though with a firm grip, pulling Joanna free from the car and propelling her upward as Clancy swam.

"You can touch me like this? How?"

"Honestly, I have no idea."

"Don't let go."

"I won't, I promise. You're safe now. You're free."

Clancy swam up along the line until she finally saw the welcoming glow of daylight rippling atop the water.

"Inez? Contact Detective Chandler, please. Tell her Joanna Drysdale has further information for her."

Clancy surfaced beside the boat and handed over the license plate to Evan. She tugged her helmet off and handed him that too, then held onto the side of the boat and let him pull her back to shore. Joanna sat inside the boat with her face tilted toward the sky. She looked as if she was welcoming its warmth after being consigned so long to the river's cold clutches.

Clancy's eyes never left the shoreside. A man stood beside her pickup, dressed all in white. Joanna looked down at her.

"Who is that?"

"He's a friend who's going to keep you company while I deal with the authorities."

"No one else can see me though, can they?"

"No. But they know you're here."

"But I can't stay, can I?"

"You can, for a little while. We need your help and you need to get your own closure. Then, when you're ready, you can move on."

"I thought I'd never be found. He tried his hardest to make sure I wouldn't be."

"I wasn't the first, was I?"

Clancy shook her head. "No, and you won't be the last if we don't find a way to stop him."

"I'll do all I can."

"And I'll do everything I can to help you finally find peace."

Chapter Three

"Still no word from your friend Mia?"

Jude Patterson looked up from her phone guiltily. She shook her head at her boss, Jackie Vee, who had come into the bar without Jude realizing it. Jude was supposed to be cleaning the bar ready for the night's customers, but she was distracted as hell. She needed to keep her job so she put her phone back in her pocket and made a more concentrated effort to wipe the countertop spotless.

Jude had been back home in downtown Kansas City for two months. She'd been honorably discharged from the navy where she'd served as a diver, maintaining and repairing ships. Not the most glamorous of roles, but she'd enjoyed its physicality and purpose. Jude had barely stepped foot into her new apartment before her neighbor, Mia Murray, had greeted her with a plate full of cookies and a welcome to the neighborhood smile. They had zero in common, but Mia was friendly and not overly intrusive.

It had been Mia who had pushed Jude to interview for the bartender job in Gentleman Jackie's, the local lesbian bar. Jude had been lucky to get the job on the spot. She knew it wasn't due to her meager skills at mixing drinks, a skill she'd quickly learned on the job thanks to the other bar staff. Instead, it was for the fact she was a five-foot-ten unashamed butch woman, muscular and heavyset, and perfect as a part-time bouncer should the need arise. Very few customers dared to try her patience twice. More than a few had tried their feminine wiles on her instead. She gave both the same stony face she'd perfected in the navy and went about her job with a quiet diligence. She didn't want to pick up a woman in her place of work. That never went well if there was a breakup and the offended party kept coming back to stare daggers at the ex. Jude wasn't a "girl in every port" kind of sailor. She was way more circumspect. Mia argued Jude needed to take more risks, put herself out there, live a little. Just like Mia was doing after going through a particularly nasty divorce.

Jude checked the time again. She hadn't heard or seen anything from Mia in three days. It wasn't like they lived in each other's pockets, but Jude was used to a text throughout the day, a call to come over for take-out, or an endless stream of memes that Mia thought hysterical but Jude didn't get the humor of. If Mia was going anywhere out of town, she always enlisted Jude to water her plants and feed her cat. Jude hadn't thought much of it the first day. Mia worked as a hospital receptionist and would cover shifts for others to get the extra cash. By day two, Jude was aware just how uncharacteristically quiet Mia was so had sent her own messages and left a voice mail on Mia's phone. It was now day three and Jude was growing concerned. Unfortunately, she'd lost most of the day to a migraine. It had only eased and finally let her get out of bed an hour before she was due to work. Jude had been thankful she hadn't had to call in sick. She'd been preoccupied rushing to get ready and not be late for her shift. It was only later she checked her phone again and there was *still* no contact from Mia. Jude made a mental note to go check Mia's apartment the next day in case she was sick at home and was trying to tough it out on her own.

Satisfied she had a plan of action, Jude busied herself with her tasks before the doors opened and customers poured in. She didn't check her phone again. Mia was thirty-five, only five years younger than Jude. She wasn't a child that needed constant attention. Jude would see her tomorrow and they'd catch up then. No doubt Mia would tell her more about some new guy she was seeing and what future she saw ahead for them both. And, like the dutiful older lesbian friend she was, Jude would try to feign interest in the boring sedentary life Mia seemed to think would be so heavenly.

Jude had no idea what she wanted in life now that she'd left the military. Her future was a blank canvas and she was waiting for inspiration to strike.

Her first customers of the night poured in noisily through the doors and made a beeline for the bar. Jude would take one day at a time, make one drink at a time, and let fate decide what it had in store for her.

"Good evening, ladies. Welcome to Gentleman Jackie's happy hour. What can I get you all?"

For now, this would do until life showed her real purpose again.

❖

The three-story apartment building was nondescript. Each apartment even had the exact same door as the next. Jude tried not to look shady, standing outside Mia's apartment in full view of the neighborhood. She'd rung the bell, knocked, and had tried to peer through the window, but the blinds were shut. She'd phoned to tell Mia to open the door, but her call remained unanswered. Jude huffed in annoyance and held up a door key. The new shiny key with a Hello Kitty fob on the keyring jogged her memory. Mia had given her the spare key to her apartment in case of emergencies. This certainly was beginning to look like one. Jude put it in the lock and swung the door open.

"Mia?"

The pitiful mewling of a cat came from the bedroom area and Smokey Joe, Mia's big black fluffy cat, came running toward her. He head-butted her legs, meowing the whole time.

"Hey, Holy Smokes, where's your mom?" Jude bent down to pet him.

Jude closed the door behind her and walked through Mia's home, diligently checking each room. Smokey Joe was glued to her side. Nothing looked out of place. It was tidy. There was nothing missing that Jude could discern. Everything was as it should be.

Except Smokey Joe's food dish and water bowl were empty. Jude immediately saw to them and watched as Smokey Joe gobbled his food down as if he were starving.

Mia hadn't been home to feed her cat.

"Where the fuck are you?" Jude said as she checked every room again to be sure and, even though she felt weird about it, opened closets and cabinets, afraid to find something inside. She couldn't shake a sense of foreboding as she searched for anything that gave a clue as to where Mia was.

Jude found a list of numbers for the hospital pinned to a board in the kitchen. She picked the one that corresponded to Mia's role and waited to be put through to a human voice. The on-hold music was tinny and annoyingly jolly once Jude had jumped through hoops picking through the endless department choices. Finally, someone picked up.

"Hi, this is Jude Patterson. I'm trying to locate my neighbor, Mia Murray?"

"Oh, you're the naval officer, right? She's mentioned you. Jude, she hasn't been at work since last Friday. We've been trying to get in touch with her. I'm Angela, by the way. I work with Mia three days a week. I've been worried about her. She always calls in if she's sick."

Jude's stomach fell. This was the news she'd been dreading. "Does anyone there know where she might have gone? Her apartment looks untouched, her cat hasn't been fed for days, and I haven't heard from her at all."

"Let me check, honey."

The on-hold music blasted once again into Jude's ear while she waited for Angela to return. Jude prayed Mia was with someone and had lost track of time. Or she was somewhere in the hospital itself after a dumb accident and had been trying to call but had lost her phone and forgotten Jude's number. Jude didn't care where Mia was as long as she knew she was okay. Jude wished her heart would stop pounding with a foreboding fear the longer she waited for someone to come back to the damn phone.

"Sorry to keep you waiting. Alice says she thinks she remembers Mia was going out with one of her boyfriends. He'd surprised her, wanting to meet up with her early, so she left work to go meet him somewhere. That was last Friday."

"Do any of you know who he is? Do you have a number for him?"

"There's a Stan, or was it, Dan? No, she'd broken up with him. There was this new guy. She was keeping him very hush-hush though.

Mr. Mysterious. Some of us were worried he was a married man with all the secrecy, but she assured us he wasn't."

Jude was exasperated. "Do you have even a name? Anything?" She heard the question being shouted out around the room. None of the women knew his name.

"Maybe he swept her off her feet to elope and they are on a honeymoon somewhere," Angela said, squealing a little in excitement at the thought.

"Here's hoping she did, but she's explaining to her cat why she left him starving," Jude said. She'd be livid if that was what had happened, but it was better than where her thoughts were starting to turn. She and Angela exchanged numbers with a promise that whoever heard from Mia first would inform the other.

Jude looked around the room and spotted Smokey Joe watching her. Jude sighed. "Guess I'm getting a roommate until we know where your damn fool mother is."

Jude gathered enough food for a few days, grabbed his bowls, brushes, and grimaced at his litter tray. "Dude, next time knock on my wall and I'll come around to save you from this smell." She cleaned the tray out swiftly, gathered new litter, and then searched for Smokey Joe's cat carrier. He stepped in it with little fuss. Jude grabbed his bed, his favorite toy, and treats. "Holy Smokes, you're lucky I know where your mother stashes all your best bites." Satisfied she had everything the cat would need, Jude tried to carry it all out onto the landing so she could lock the apartment back up.

"Don't worry, I'll send your errant mother a text saying I've kidnapped her cat and holding him for ransom. How many muffins do you think you're worth?"

Jude knew it wasn't like Mia to leave Smokey Joe alone. Jude had become chief cat sitter for her much loved pet. Mia didn't like leaving him for her to go to work. It was unimaginable she'd leave him alone for days.

Jude unlocked her own door and bundled everything inside. She placed Smokey Joe's stuff in the same areas in her apartment as Mia had them placed in hers. Having cookie cutter apartments was a blessing when babysitting a cat used to his own space. Jude let

Smokey Joe out and left him to wander around and get used to her apartment like he did anytime he had to stay with her. It wasn't long before he jumped into her lap while she sat on the settee. Jude petted him and listened to him purr.

"If your mother isn't back tomorrow, I'll go to the police. She wouldn't leave you unattended. You're her baby."

Smokey Joe head-butted her chin in agreement then settled himself in to sleep sprawled across her.

Jude picked up her phone again and typed a message to Mia. She took a picture of Smokey Joe fast asleep and sent it off. Then she switched to Google to find where the local police station was and saved its location.

"What the fuck am I going to tell them? She's been gone for three days, we think. Yes, she has a new boyfriend, but no one knows his name, or where he lives, or even if he exists. No, I don't listen to her when she's listing off her 'swipe right for Mr. Rights.'" Jude grimaced. "Maybe if I'd listen more like a friend should then I'd know who he is." Jude ran her fingers through Smokey Joe's fur. "Your mother isn't very discerning who she dates, Smokes. I've lost count of the dates she's gone on since I've known her. But I get it. She's desperate not to be alone."

Jude couldn't remember the last time *she'd* had a girlfriend. She'd had one serious relationship fifteen years ago. Since then, there'd been women who had never lasted long enough to become anything more serious.

A lot of the time it had been *Jude* who hadn't stayed.

"Maybe I should get a cat?" She patted Smokey Joe who opened one eye at her, trilled, then went right back to sleep, safe in her care.

Jude could only hope wherever Mia was, she was safe and sound and blissfully unaware her friends were worrying about her.

Chapter Four

Clancy lay spread out on her settee. Her arm across her eyes blocked out as much light as she could manage. She had her headphones on, blasting Charlotte Wessels's "The Obsession" as loud as she could stand it. The hard rock and symphonic metal music kept the voices at bay. It was supposed to stop her from having to think for a while.

But the thoughts kept seeping in like an annoying trickle that threatened to explode like a Yellowstone geyser.

Clancy couldn't stop remembering the sight of Joanna's car being dredged out from its watery grave. Water streamed from the chassis as it hung from the chains that dragged it out into daylight. The wrecked car, Joanna's tomb, was brought to the surface and placed back on dry ground. Her remains had been found in the passenger seat, left there with no remorse.

Clancy's Zoom call with Joanna's family went the same way they all did. They had been highly skeptical of Clancy at first until she began to relay direct messages from Joanna to them. She felt their grief, their angry disbelief. Then watched as a dawning realization struck them all as Joanna told Clancy what to say that finally made them believe. No matter how many times Clancy spoke for the dead, it was never easy. The sorrow of the family left behind. The mournful wails of a mother finally realizing that her child was truly lost to her. The ghostly tears wept by the spirit saying her goodbyes to a family she hadn't meant to leave. Closure was supposed to be a blessing for a family of someone missing. It didn't make their loss any easier to bear.

Clancy's week had been a heavy load placed on already bowed shoulders. Thankfully, the removal of the car had been smooth thanks to the people the Chicago unit sent as their agents. They answered all the questions the local PD had, leaving Clancy to call in a tow truck and direct the car's removal herself as she preferred.

Then she'd had to direct a three-way conversation between Detective Daryl Chandler—who was Clancy's go-to gal at the unit—herself, and Joanna. The Man in White was a friend of the detective's, Clancy guessed. He arrived every time Clancy found a body. Joanna had been the eighth. Eight women murdered and left in the Missouri River, and he'd come to meet them all. Clancy knew enough to recognize when something was *not* of the earth. And he was definitely *not* human, even though he looked like a man. A man, dressed in a fancy white suit, sporting a huge pair of white wings. He had ushered Joanna aside, shielding her beneath his wings as they worked to raise her car. He also stood by her side while she told Clancy and Detective Chandler everything she could about the man who'd romanced her, promising her the world. The same man who brutally murdered her then dumped her in the river.

The details were all too familiar. Clancy's interviews with the previous victims all told the same story. A pattern was forming, an evil modus operandi of a serial killer haunting the river's banks. Clancy desperately hoped that was his *only* dumping ground.

Today, Clancy had finally watched Joanna leave, taken away by the angel. Joanna had been grateful that Clancy found her. Now she was ready for her next journey to begin. Clancy watched her be guided toward the light. She remembered how it felt. How the light radiated with the warmth of the sun on a sleepy summer's day. How the light soothed your senses like a lullaby. How easy it felt to just let yourself drift toward it and leave the world behind.

The angel had stared at Clancy as if he could read her mind. He looked disappointed and shook his head at her until Clancy felt chastened like a child. Then he wagged his finger at her as a further no-no, and mouthed something very clearly to her.

"Not yet."

He'd never done that before. He'd never acknowledged her at any of the other retrievals. But then, Joanna was the first one Clancy had felt the need to stay and watch leave.

She'd brought herself to his attention. He'd seen into her heart. He'd *admonished* her.

In truth, he'd totally freaked her out, laying her deepest, darkest, wish out for them both to see and be horrified at.

She'd sought the solace the RV afforded her and tried to make sense of the horrible feeling she'd fallen drastically short in his expectation of her.

An hour later, Clancy was still deafening herself with her music on repeat. Anything to distract herself from the fact she was sure she'd just been royally told off by an *angel*. And not just any angel. One who guided souls toward *the light*. A *reaper*.

Something touched Clancy's arm and she startled so hard she was certain she jumped a foot off the settee. She flung her arm off her eyes and glared at Inez who sat on the floor beside her, grinning like an idiot at scaring her.

"For fuck's sake, Inez! You nearly had me following Joanna to the other side!" Clancy shifted to sit upright and roughly pulled her headphones off.

Inez grimaced when she heard how loud the music was. "I don't know how you can listen to that music so loud."

"It helps me think."

"It makes me think you'll be deaf before you're forty." Inez handed Clancy a drink of water and a pill. "You're making your migraine face. Take this."

Clancy did so without question. "What does your mother put in these things?" Clancy hadn't had to buy any pharmaceuticals since she'd met Wendy "Rainbow" Wilson. Whatever magic it was that Rainbow possessed, it never ceased to chase off Clancy's psychic headaches. It was just one of Rainbow Wilson's many talents.

"Do you want to go over the transcript of the interview with Joanna?" Inez held up her iPad.

"Not tonight. Save it for our road trip in a few days when we get to go camp out in Kansas City. I just need to finish this last area of water then we can switch locations." Bone weary, Clancy leaned her head back on the settee cushions and closed her eyes. "I want to take a week off when we get there. We're long overdue and they've paid us enough that we can slack off a little."

Inez punched the air. "Yes!"

Clancy cracked open an eye to look at her. "I'm only doing it because you're getting cranky."

"I am not cranky. *You* are so close to a burnout it's not funny. So yes, let's take a proper break before you resume searching." Inez flicked a screen up on her iPad and began typing.

"What are you doing?" Clancy peered over Inez's shoulder.

"Finding you the best restaurants where you can eat, drink, and be merry." Inez studied the screen, then let out a squeal.

"Let me guess, you've found a tech store?" Clancy teased her.

"No, something even better. I've found you a lesbian bar." Inez held up the screen for Clancy to read.

"Gentleman Jackie's? What the hell kind of name is that?"

"You'd get its meaning if you'd managed to stay awake long enough past the first three minutes of the show," Inez said. "It's only a few blocks from where we'll be parked at the police station. Who knows, maybe it will be a place you can relax a little. It has dancing too." Inez held the screen up again and began to sway. "A lesbian bar, loads of women dancing. Maybe you can find someone nice and—"

"Will you quit channeling your mother!" Clancy bristled at Inez's laughter. "She's always at me to find a nice girl, settle down, get some turkey baster children popped out."

"You'd make an excellent mother," Inez said. "After all, you helped raise *me*. You showed me how to play baseball, taught me to ride a bike, how to curl my fist right to punch a guy in the nose if he pissed me off. How to kick him in the balls if he still didn't take the hint." Inez added in a hopeful tone, "You'll take me to get my first tattoo..."

"Hell no. Your mother will hex me for my next ten reincarnations. You're on your own, kid, for that one."

"You deserve happiness, Clancy. Whether you find someone here or not to spend forever with. She's out there. The one who will accept you for all of you. The one who'll make you want to *stay*."

Clancy heard the meaning behind her words loud and clear.

"And you think this bar with the weird-ass name will be the answer to all my dreams?"

"If not, it should have enough of a clientele that you can find a girl just for fun right now. Put yourself out there. Find someone who rocks your world for a night. Fuck someone in the seedy bar's bathroom. You said you needed a break. Go see what downtown Kansas City has waiting for you."

Clancy considered her for a moment. "Since when did you become my one-night stand cheering squad?"

"Since you need to relax in more ways than one. Go get laid. The river will wait. The *dead* will wait."

Clancy knew that was true. The dead weren't held to the living world's quickly ticking clock. They had all the time in the world. For now, she needed time away from them. Time to herself. Time to live a little.

"So," Clancy drawled, settling back in her seat. "What kind of tattoo are you considering getting…"

Inez cheered.

"…when you're *forty*," Clancy said with her best stern voice.

"Now *you're* channeling my mother!" Inez huffed while Clancy snickered at her, unrepentant.

Chapter Five

Jude's perfunctory perusal of the menu was just habit; she ordered the same food every time. The highlight of her working week was coming to Elle's Enchiladas and ordering two beef and cheese sanchiladas. Nothing came close to that mix of sancho and beef enchilada, smothered in enchilada sauce, and topped with cheese.

"Same as usual for you?" Amber George, the newest bar recruit, pored over the menu for something new to try.

"I'm a creature of habit," Jude said. She gave her order to the waitress and Amber quickly came to a decision and did the same. Jude looked around the busy restaurant. There were only a few seats left, but they'd soon be snatched up by the hungry midafternoon crowd.

Jude's wandering attention was immediately caught by who came through the door next. She couldn't stop herself from staring at the older of the two women.

Oh my God, she's gorgeous.

Jude didn't often feel like she'd been struck by lightning when it came to women. But this one was all her deepest fantasies come to life. Jude knew she attracted femmes, especially femmes expecting a *daddy* to cater to their every whim and spending spree. But Jude had always been drawn to a more masculine woman. One just like herself. The woman who had just walked in was tall, dark, and handsome personified. Jude wanted her.

"Oh my God, isn't she beautiful?" Amber gasped beside her.

Jude had to stop herself from warning Amber off.

I saw her first.

"She's so pretty with all that red hair tied up in a cute ponytail. How old would you say she is? So many young girls today look like they're going on thirty once they put on the makeup and designer clothes. I don't want to be weird. Tell me, does she look like a kid to you?"

Jude reluctantly tore her gaze away from the woman of her dreams and spared a look at the younger female accompanying her. She was very attractive, if you were drawn to the young, slender, pretty girly-girl types.

"She kinda looks like that chick from *Stranger Things*," Amber mused.

Jude considered that. "The one that was in Taylor Swift's 'All Too Well' video?"

Amber laughed. "I'll never get over you knowing Taylor Swift."

"I was in the navy, Amber, not living under a rock," Jude grumbled.

"I know but you're so much older than me…"

"Am I going to like where this comment is going?"

Amber continued, regardless. "Aren't you supposed to be singing to Melissa Etheridge or Cris Williamson?"

This drew Jude's attention away from the door. "You're what? Twenty-two? How the hell do you know Cris Williamson?"

"I dated an older woman last summer. Older than you even. 'The Changer and The Changed' was on repeat every time we got down and dirty."

Jude grimaced at the mental images she'd never erase. "Way to take the beauty out of that album." She looked back toward where the women had been waiting for a server to seat them and found them gone. She quickly scoured the room and was relieved to see them a few tables across from her.

The older of the two was directly in Jude's eyeline. Jude unabashedly stared, memorizing every inch of her. She was taller than the girl with her, but no more than an inch or two shorter than Jude. She had the kind of stocky body that Jude loved to worship. She liked it when she didn't have to count the ribs visible on a lover.

The woman's dark brown hair was styled in a distinct wolf cut, short layers on top, longer layers in the back. She pushed back her side-swept bangs with ease of habit. Jude wanted to brush back that hair, to run her fingers through it, to tug on it. To tip her head back and expose her vulnerable neck for Jude to lay passionate kisses upon, nibble a little, leave her mark on. The woman's jaw was strong, her face handsome in a boyish way that Jude found *very* attractive. Jude guessed she was in her thirties by the fine lines crinkling at the corner of her eyes when she smiled. Jude swallowed hard at the roguish grin that was being directed at the girl. It did curious things to Jude's insides. She wondered what it would feel like to be on the receiving end of that look. Jude quickly scanned the woman's attire. She dressed casually, black jeans and a black-and-white-striped shirt. Her sleeves were rolled up enough to show off a beautifully inked Celtic knot design that wrapped completely around her left wrist. The knots looked like they were made of shiny steel while the background was in watercolor rainbow hues. Jude loved tattoos and was impressed by the Celtic artistry displayed. She knew enough to know that the Celtic knot design represented the endless cycle of life, death, and rebirth and how all things in the natural world interconnected. She hoped the addition of a rainbow theme meant that the woman was a lesbian and all those handsome *boi* looks weren't wasted.

"She looks like you do," Amber said, jolting Jude out of her perusal.

"What? Handsome, debonair?" Jude asked, trying to pay attention to her friend and not keep looking across the room.

"Butch as fuck. A dyke on a bike kinda gal. The kind my mom warned me never to bring home."

"So, you went hunting for sugar mommies instead?" Jude knew Amber's penchant for older women. *Way* older women.

"Once I'd seduced my mom's best friend it became a hard habit to break. My school friends' moms were an endless smorgasbord." Amber sat back, smiling as she drank from her beer.

"You're terrible, you know that?" Jude shook her head at her.

Their meals came and Jude gratefully tucked in. She looked back across the tables though at every opportunity. She committed the woman's looks to memory for when she was alone in her bedroom and needed a fantasy lover to ease her loneliness. Something told her this woman would easily fulfil her every desire. Jude wished she had the nerve to get up and go over to her, state her intentions, offer her body, mind, and soul. She scoffed at her fanciful thoughts. Since when did she envisage more than a one-night stand? She was usually the last to want any kind of entanglement.

Jude snuck another look across the room. *She'd look sexy as fuck tangled in my bedsheets though.*

❖

"Don't look now but there's a very striking butch watching you from across the room," Inez said, making room on the table for all the food Clancy had ordered.

Clancy continued eating her beef burrito, delighting in every taste that tantalized her taste buds. She tried not to be too loud in her appreciative murmurs. She was in Mexican food heaven.

"Aren't you at least going to look?" Inez kicked her gently under the table to get Clancy's attention off her food.

"You told me not to. You specifically said 'don't look now.'" Clancy loved winding Inez up. It had been her favorite thing to do from the moment Inez had been old enough to talk back.

"You think you're so funny," Inez said, not in the least impressed. "Quit being an asshole. Two tables across, one back."

Clancy shot her a grin and dutifully looked up and across. Her whole body stilled.

"She's got someone with her," Clancy said.

"Yeah, the obvious lesbian lothario who's been checking me out since I walked through the door. I'm way too young for her and way too straight."

Clancy nodded, only half hearing what Inez was saying. The woman Inez had pointed out to her was the perfect woman. Tall, built like a brick wall, with arms that could hold you tight and never let you go. Clancy tried not to be obvious in checking her out. The blonde was wearing a gray tank top, paired with blue jeans. The tank top showed off her muscular arms to perfection. On her left arm was an elaborate tattooed sleeve. Clancy really wanted to get a closer look. From what she could see from her seat, it looked to be a nautical theme. She could make out a lighthouse, its yellow light the only splash of color amid the black-and-gray design. A huge kraken had one tentacle wrapped around the tower and another around a ship it was dragging under the waves. Clancy wanted to know the story behind the powerful depiction of the sea and the violent creature. She felt pulled toward the woman, and not just because she was a total butch wet dream. There was something about her, something sparking more than Clancy's dormant desires. She loved the woman's resting bitch face. Clancy wanted to see if she could coax a smile onto those lips. She knew they would be firm but would feel so good pressed against her own before marking a trail down to other places. She shifted in her chair. Desire, like she hadn't felt in a long time, made itself known.

"No, she's got someone *else* with her," Clancy said, lowering her voice. "The apparition isn't fully formed though."

"Oh, that's not a good sign," Inez said, looking over, trying to see what only Clancy could see.

Clancy tried to will the veil to drop so she could see who or what she was dealing with. It was no use.

"Whoever is with her doesn't know they're dead yet or refuses to admit it. How intriguing." Clancy looked away when her phone buzzed. She wiped her fingers off so she could tap the screen to read the message.

"That had better not be work related," Inez said.

"Well, would you believe it? Evan got us tickets to a Kansas City Current game. You're the women's soccer nerd in this family. Wanna go?"

Inez reached for Clancy's phone excitedly to see for herself. "Yes, I wanna go! I'll need to go back to the RV and change into my soccer shirt first. I can't go dressed like this."

"Yeah, the preppy nerd look needs to switch into soccer jock." Clancy gestured to the over-attentive server and explained they needed the food boxed up because they had a soccer game to attend.

He hurried to do their bidding while someone else attended to their bill. Clancy paid, gathered up the boxes that she would enjoy feasting on over the next day or so, and hustled a very excited Inez out to the parking lot. At the door, she looked over her shoulder at the blond woman and her ghostly companion.

"Here's hoping fate will bring you back to me, beautiful stranger. As for your ghostly companion, may they find their eternal rest."

❖

"Have you ever wondered why I never made a pass at you?" Amber asked, leaning forward to draw Jude's attention back to their table.

Jude had never thought about it. "I guess I'm not your type? More muscle than money?"

Amber smiled at the sly dig and shook her head. "No. You never once looked at me with a look in your eyes like you have shining for that butch over there. *That's* why."

Jude stuffed her mouth full to stop herself from answering.

"Woman up. Go ask her out," Amber said.

"She's obviously with someone." Jude tried desperately not to scowl at the thought.

"I don't think they're together like that. They don't have that vibe."

Jude snorted. "What, your gaydar not pinging?"

"For the butch? Fuck yes, ringing loud and clear. But the pretty miss? No, alas. Besides, the way their male server is hovering to jump the second she looks up and smiles in his direction I'd guess she's sending off strictly hetero pings."

"They're probably just tourists, dropping in for a meal while they sightsee KC." Jude tried not to sound despondent. "We're destined to be mere ships not even passing in the night."

"So, you like a bit of butch-on-butch then?" Amber spoke inelegantly around a mouth full of food. "No wonder none of the girls in the bar have stood a chance. We do draw a more feminine crowd."

"It would help if the bar wasn't some homage to a British lesbian in a top hat, of all things." Jude finished off the last bite of her meal and sat back with a gratified sigh.

"It's Suranne Jones, Jude. *Suranne Jones*." Amber argued the point fervently.

"Whoever she is, I bet she wore that top hat to stop people from seeing that weird fucking hairdo she had."

Amber let out a loud "Ha!" that was clearly audible over the sound of the restaurant's piped music and the chatter of the other customers. She had the grace to look embarrassed at all the eyes that turned to stare at her, but she still pointed a finger at Jude. "I knew you'd watched the show!"

"Not by choice. Smokey Joe was sitting on me and I couldn't reach the remote without disturbing him. Apparently, it's an unwritten law; you don't move when a cat is on your lap."

"How long have you had him now?"

Jude mentally counted the weeks off. "It's been over a month now."

"And he has a thing for British period drama?"

"It must be the accents."

"Please, go ask that butch for her phone number before you sink into sad cat lady oblivion."

Jude looked over but the table was empty. She'd missed her chance. The chance to say hello to the woman who'd made her heart race and her lips yearn for the promise of a kiss. Jude turned back to Amber with a sigh.

"Guess me and Smokey Joe will be binge watching *Bridgerton* this weekend."

CHAPTER SIX

Clancy lost herself to the beat of the music blaring out the speakers in Gentleman Jackie's disco lounge. The room still bore the remnants from a wedding party that had taken place there. Streamers hung from the ceiling and a helium balloon was floating out of reach bearing the lucky brides' names. Clancy didn't care. She was there to dance until she dropped, not to critique the bar's sense of décor.

She focused entirely on the music as she danced alone. She'd had a few women join her, trying to start a conversation, but it was obvious Clancy was there to just dance. She also was working at ignoring the otherworldly whispers starting around her. They were becoming intrusive and irritating. As they rose in volume, like white noise coalescing, Clancy looked up to find a woman standing before her, a brunette in a sparkly evening dress. She smiled and Clancy smiled back politely but continued to dance. The woman joined in. Her movements were out of place to the beat playing, but she found her own rhythm. She danced as if hearing a different song.

"I haven't seen you here before."

Clancy forced herself to make conversation and play nice. "I'm new in town. This is my first time at the bar. Have you been coming here long?"

The woman laughed. *"Seems like forever. My friends and I come here every Friday night and dance our heels off."*

"Are your friends with you tonight?"

"No, they stopped coming."

Clancy watched the woman's face lose its joy. The skin under her eyes grew shallow and dark, her limbs lost their vitality. Her arms were a bruised battlefield of needle marks and her sparkly dress spilled traces of white powder all over the floor.

"You don't have to stay here," Clancy told her. "You can leave at any time."

"I loved it here. I met my lover here."

"Where is she now?"

"Buried six feet deep under a shopping mall because she couldn't pay our supplier. She's still sore about that and won't come here with me to lighten up."

The woman's skin returned to normal as her past disappeared. *"And so, I dance and whisper warnings in any woman's ear who even dares to snort a line in the bathroom.* She stopped dancing abruptly. *"I'm tired though. I'm tired of dancing alone."*

Clancy understood. "If I sent a friend for you, would you let him escort you home?"

"I'd rather you send a she."

"I'll see what I can arrange." Clancy stopped dancing. "I need a drink. It's been a pleasure meeting you…?"

"Tammy Jones. I'm on the notice board behind the bar. All the opening night patrons were in a group shot. Those were happier times. It's nice to see I'm still remembered somewhere. It's been a pleasure meeting you, Clancy Madsen. Your reputation precedes you and they weren't joking when they described you as a handsome heartbreaker."

Tammy leaned closer to her. *"I'll give you a warning too. Be careful in those waters, Clancy. Not only the dead swim there."* She pressed an icy kiss to Clancy's cheek and disappeared.

"Now I *really* need a drink," Clancy muttered to herself and walked off the dance floor. She studiously ignored the growing malevolent whispers from the other spirits lining the room, all looking at her like she was going to bust them from their favorite haunt.

Clancy had headed straight to where the music was playing when she'd arrived at the bar earlier that evening. Now she was hot, sweaty, and in desperate need of refreshment. She made her way to the bar, weaving her way around people who stood talking, ignorantly blocking her path. Clancy grabbed onto the bar top as if it were a lifeline when she finally reached it.

"What can I get you?"

Clancy brushed her damp hair back from her face and looked up, straight into the eyes of the woman she had seen a few days ago at the restaurant. The woman's eyes widened. Inez had been right. It would seem this woman recognized her too.

"A Coke, please. The largest you have." Clancy knew it wasn't the most sophisticated drink to order, but alcohol played havoc with her abilities. She'd found out the hard way that being intoxicated smashed her psychic barriers to smithereens and every ghostly Tom, Dick, and Haunting Harriet rushed in, demanding attention. Their badgering made a hangover fifty times worse. Soda and water were now her sober choices if she wanted to keep her sanity in check.

"Do you want lime or lemon in that?"

Clancy dragged her gaze away from the woman's mouth. "I'll take it neat, please." The woman's lips quirked at Clancy's lame wit. That tiny smile bowled Clancy over.

"I'm Jude, I'll be your bartender for the evening. Do you want to start a tab?"

Jude. *Jude.* The name suited her. Clancy shook her head at the question and took a sip from her glass to quench her thirst. She ended up downing half the glass in seconds under Jade's amused gaze.

"It's nice to meet you, Jude. I'm Clancy. You pour a mean cola. Forgive me for chugging it like I'm tailgating at a football game."

Jude took someone else's order, but her attention didn't stray far from Clancy. "That's an unusual name you've got."

"It's Irish. It means 'son of the red warrior.'"

"And are you?"

Clancy shook her head. "I hate to disappoint, but I strike out on all accounts."

"This is on me," Jude said, topping up Clancy's glass. "I doubt you could disappoint anyone, Clancy."

Smooth, so smooth, Clancy thought, loving how low Jude's voice dropped with the compliment and how intent her eyes were. Butch flirting at its best. Direct and to the point. "You were at the

Mexican restaurant the other day." *I know you were looking at me there.*

"Yeah, I saw you too." Jude deliberately looked around. "Is your...*friend* here with you?"

Clancy shook her head. "I left her playing *Call of Duty* with her buddies."

"Is she your girlfriend?" Jude pitched the question in a deceptively conversational tone, but her eyes never left Clancy's as she waited for her answer.

"Fuck, no, I'm old enough to be her mother." Clancy shuddered at the thought. "No, she's my best friend's daughter. I changed her diapers, for fuck's sake! But we work together. She's a total computer wiz."

"Really? What line of work are you two in?"

Clancy didn't hesitate giving the safest answer. "Salvage." She quickly turned the tables. "The woman you were with? Is she *your* girlfriend?"

"Fuck, no! I'm not her type at all, nor she mine. She's just a colleague here. She's running the disco tonight. She's been spinning your tunes."

Clancy wondered at the relief she felt hearing Jude's clarification. There was something about her that Clancy was inexplicably drawn to. Suddenly, sharing one night with Jude was Clancy's goal. Life was too short. Clancy had learned to take risks when it came to getting what she wanted. One-nights were Clancy's easiest option. Besides, no one stuck around long once Clancy's psychic side revealed itself.

"To be honest, I couldn't keep my eyes off you in the restaurant. You're absolutely gorgeous and built like a dream. I understand, if I'm not your type—"

"You're exactly my type," Jude interrupted her.

They stared at each other for a long moment, as if they were the only two people in the bar.

"Do you dance, Jude?"

"On occasion."

"Will you get a break tonight?"

Jude checked her watch. "In an hour, yes."

"Would you dance with me?" Clancy held her breath, nervous for the answer that she felt could break her heart either way.

Jude smiled. A proper smile that lit up her blue eyes and made her look even more breathtakingly handsome.

"I'd love to."

Clancy snagged a stool someone vacated and quickly sat on it. "Then I'll just sit here and keep you company until that time."

"Are you sure you don't want to dance some more? An hour's a long time."

"Dancing alone suddenly doesn't have as much appeal as dancing with you does. I'm in no hurry. I can wait all evening for you."

Another customer caught Jude's attention. Once they were served, she returned to Clancy.

"You know, I've never accepted a dance with a customer before," Jude said.

"Then I'm glad you're breaking your rule for me. It makes me feel special."

"You are. What is it about you, non-Irish Clancy? Do you normally walk into a bar and sweep the bartender off her feet?"

Clancy shook her head. "You're the only one I've attempted to, so what is it about *you*, Jude, that makes me so bold?"

"I don't know. Maybe we can find out the answer to that together."

"I'll drink to that," Clancy said, tipping her glass in salute to the most beautiful butch bartender she'd ever laid eyes on.

Clancy was grateful for Jude's decision to have them dance together at the back of the room. They were out of the glaring spotlight of the disco ball and away from prying eyes.

"I'm guessing, by all the surprised looks you dragged me away from, your customers aren't used to seeing you interact with anyone?" Clancy was still breathless from the workout she'd had to a very energetic song. Now she was slow-dancing with her arms around Jude's neck, relishing the touch of their bodies pressed together. Jude's strong hands were holding tightly to Clancy's hips, rocking her lazily to the beat while keeping her close.

"No one else has interested me enough to step out from behind the bar," Jude said.

Clancy loved how serious Jude was. Short and to the point. Almost brutally blunt at times. The hour they'd spent talking on and off while Jude served hadn't been enough. Clancy wanted to know more.

"You really are the most handsome butch I have ever seen," Clancy said, running her fingers through the hair on Jude's nape. Jude wore her hair longer on top but the short bristles at the back were drawing Clancy's fingers like a magnet.

"Now I know you aren't drunk because I've been pouring your drinks all evening. So, I'm going to say you're too kind and remind you that as breathtaking goes, you stole mine away in the restaurant on first sight. I've been struggling to catch a breath ever since."

Jude's lips were very close to Clancy's ear. It was the only way Clancy could hear her over the music. It was also sending shivers down her spine every time Jude spoke to her. And she knew Jude was all too aware of that.

"I can't believe fate gave me a second chance to connect with you," Clancy said.

"Funny, you don't strike me as a woman who'd believe in fate or destiny."

"I do believe that some mystical force has put people in my life to either help me or teach me something."

"So, am I here to help you or teach you?"

"Oh, I'm sure you could teach me a great many things," Clancy drawled, pushing her leg between Jude's and pressing closer still. "Look at that. We fit together like a charm."

Jude was so close Clancy could feel her hard nipples pressing through the thin cotton of her uniform shirt. They brushed against Clancy's chest with every breath Jude took. She feared she'd combust from the teasing touches. Clancy's black denim shirt mercifully hid her own responses to being stimulated by the sexiest butch in the room.

She knew Jude was feeling something too. The hitch in her breath in Clancy's ear told her so as Clancy deliberately shifted her leg further to press Jude's thighs a little more apart.

Clancy wanted to kiss her so badly, but she knew it wouldn't be wise to start something that could quickly turn hot and heated on the dance floor. She didn't know if she could stop once she'd tasted Jude's lips.

"Christ, the clientele in this bar has gone to hell since I ran it. Now it reeks of filthy queers, practicing their perversions for all to witness. I'd set the whole place ablaze if I could. Clear them right out and their disgusting habits. Send them straight to a welcoming hell."

The vile vitriol spewed over into Clancy's ear from a male voice, dark and angry.

"You gonna let that poor excuse for a woman rub your cunt, girlie? Look at you, trying so hard to look like a man yourself. You ain't got no dick, girl. But I could show you how a real man..."

Clancy slammed down her defenses and shut him out as best she could. She tried to focus just on Jude, but the number of people in the room she could hear, plus the voices of the ones no one but she could *see*, was becoming overwhelming. The bar was full of long-dead people attached to the area, all congregating where the energy was at its highest.

Clancy was woefully outnumbered.

"Are you okay?" Jude stopped moving and raised her hands to cradle Clancy's face.

Clancy relished Jude's gentle touch. She could feel another touch, neither kind nor caring, of the darker presence surrounding her. She cursed under her breath as they congregated en masse and started to leech the light out of the room...at least to Clancy's sensitive eyes. She cursed herself quietly because any time she allowed herself a moment of vulnerability and let her walls down to *feel*, the dead rushed to her, like moths to a burning flame. And their voices echoed through her head like a desperate dirge.

"Help us! Help me! Where am I? Release me! Why did no one come for me? Where's the goddamn light? Don't leave me here for eternity, rotting in this place. Why can't anyone hear me? Am I dead? Listen to me! Get me out of here!"

"WE'RE ALL DEAD!"

"Hey, baby, are you okay?" Jude shook Clancy a little from her stupor.

"Make the voices stop," Clancy muttered, trying to get her bearings.

Jude lowered her ear to Clancy's lips. "What?"

"Get me out of here, please."

Jude immediately pulled Clancy off the dance floor. She kept her close as they headed back in the direction of the bar. Jude exchanged a few whispered words with the bartender who'd taken her place serving. Clancy didn't hear what she said, but the woman passed Jude a bottle of water and nodded at whatever Jude had asked. Jude guided Clancy through a *Staff Only* door and didn't stop until they were far away from the noise of the music. They were in a hallway that led to the main office, staff rooms, and staff-only bathrooms. Jude hesitated for a second then steered Clancy into the bathrooms, shut the door, paused again, then locked it behind her. She handed Clancy the water.

"Drink."

Clancy twisted the top off and did as she was bid. The water was cold and it cooled Clancy down a little.

"What happened out there?" Jude asked, edging closer.

"It suddenly got overwhelming," Clancy admitted. "I get that sometimes, if there's too much stimulation and noise." *With the ghosts of barkeepers past dissing my sex life while the rest of the dead realized they were finally being heard.*

"And was *I* too much of that stimulation?" Jude stepped closer still and tenderly brushed Clancy's hair back from her face. She left her hand cupping the side of Clancy's head, rubbing a little.

The gentle friction calmed Clancy down. The voices hadn't followed her. Her mind was clearing and all she could see and hear was Jude. Then all Clancy could feel was the strength of her own desire rising inside her like a tidal wave ready to strike. She set the bottle aside and reached for Jude's face.

"You'll never be too much," Clancy said, pressing her lips to Jude's and kissing her.

Chapter Seven

Jude loved a dominant woman. One who knew what she wanted and took it. Clancy's kiss made Jude's knees buckle. It wasn't tentative or gentle. Clancy's kiss was passionate and heated and Jude couldn't get enough. She pulled Clancy to her and felt the gasp escape from Clancy's lips as she held Clancy close. She squeezed Clancy tighter and registered her moan.

Intriguing, Jude thought. She didn't often get to show off her strength. Most women liked to be held gently and chastised her if she held them too tight. Clancy clung harder around Jude's neck and seemed to relish the tight hold.

Jude loosened her grip to run her hands down Clancy's back, delighting in the feel of her, loving the width of her shoulders encased in black denim. She tugged at the shirt roughly, removing it from Clancy's jeans. She wanted to feel her, needed to touch naked skin. Clancy's back was damp from all the dancing, and her skin hot to the touch.

Jude's fingers clenched when Clancy used her teeth to nip along her jaw line. Jude angled her head so Clancy could reach more with her tongue and teeth. For a moment, Clancy bit gently into Jude's neck and Jude stilled, waiting. Clancy replaced teeth with her tongue and soothed the sting.

"Marking me as your own already?" Jude asked, pulling Clancy's shirt completely free and starting to pop the studs one by one.

"Your arms around me have already ruined me for another."
Clancy gripped Jude's forearms and squeezed the muscles. "God, I
love a butch woman who's built fit as fuck."

"No skinny butches in their undershirts trying to look edgy like
James Dean?" Jude spread her fingers across Clancy's stomach, tracing
circles around her belly button. Clancy squirmed under her touch.

"No, they're just wannabes. I want a strong butch." She kissed
down Jude's neck, nudging her shirt's collar aside. "Someone who
can flip me like a pancake."

Jude pulled back a little to stare at her. Clancy started to laugh.
Her hazel eyes twinkled with amusement and Jude fell even further
for her.

"Too much levity?"

"Not if you mean it, because I'd like very much to get you on
your back and spread myself all over you." Jude savored the wanton
groan that Clancy let out before she grabbed Jude's head and tugged
her down for another kiss.

Jude couldn't stop touching her. She couldn't get enough of
the feel of Clancy's skin, of her warmth, of how her muscles were
solid under Jude's pressing fingertips. She traced the clear line down
Clancy's chest. "What exercise do you do to look like this?"

"I swim a lot. Sometimes I lift weights." Clancy started to tug
Jude's shirt open impatiently.

"I'd pay good money to see you in your swimsuit."

Clancy chuckled. "Darlin', for you I'd skinny dip."

Jude growled and tugged Clancy close for a bruising kiss. Clancy
looked a little dazed when she finally came up for air. Jude loved that
look on her. She turned Clancy around to face the large mirror that
hung in the bathroom.

"Look at you." Jude nuzzled into Clancy's hair and kissed
down her exposed neck. Jude spread open Clancy's shirt and ran her
hand across the sports bra's name band. "Calvin Klein?" She slowly
dragged her spread hand down Clancy's stomach and to the waistband
of her jeans. Jude flicked open the buttons one-handed and exposed a
matching band. Jude dipped her fingers lower to stroke over Clancy's
belly. "These are suddenly my favorite brand."

Clancy's breath was coming out in short pants, her skin flushed, and her body pressing up for more wherever Jude touched. They looked at each other in the mirror, both breathing heavy.

"I really want to fuck you," Jude said, watching Clancy's face.

"I really want to be fucked."

Jude didn't need to be told twice. She spun Clancy around and pushed her toward the largest toilet stall in the room. She shut the door behind them. "Just making sure that if someone unlocks that door, I'm not tongue deep in your pussy for all to see."

Clancy began pushing Jude's shirt off. In the heat of their need to remove clothes, Jude made sure that their shirts were hung on the back of the door. She could hear Clancy's soft laughter at her being so careful.

"Hey, I have to go back out there to work. My buddy can only cover me for so long, and if I go out with a shirt that looks wrinkled as hell, I'm going to be in trouble." Satisfied the clothing was safe, Jude turned back to push Clancy roughly against the wall. She rested her arms on either side of Clancy's head and leaned in so their breasts were crushed between them. Jude ran her tongue over Clancy's smiling lips, pressing further in to taste her, teasing Clancy's tongue with her own.

"There are so many things I want to do to you, to this body of yours." Jude ran her tongue down Clancy's chin, then down her vulnerable throat that vibrated with stifled moans. She nuzzled into the fabric of Clancy's bra. Clancy's nipples pebbled through the thin fabric. Jude pressed a kiss to each one then sucked hard, leaving a wet patch behind. Clancy's hands were in Jude's hair, pressing her on, urging her to do more. Jude lifted the bra over Clancy's breasts and freed them.

"Fuck, your hands are huge," Clancy said when Jude palmed her breasts and squeezed.

Clancy writhed under Jude's handling of her breasts. She wasn't brutal but she wasn't gentle either, recognizing Clancy obviously liked her sex a little rough. She rubbed her thumbs over Clancy's nipples, making them harder still, then sucked and licked them until Clancy's fingers were almost hurting in Jude's hair.

Jude loved it though. She marveled at the fact that she'd finally encountered a woman who could handle what Jude liked to give. She sucked on Clancy's nipples until they were red and shiny with her saliva. She pulled back to examine her handiwork. Satisfied, Jude deliberately wiped her wet mouth off on Clancy's bra and kissed her again, hard.

"I want to do all this to you too," Clancy said, pawing at Jude's shoulders, trying to touch her. Jude stopped her with one hand trapping both of hers.

"I know, and I want you to. You don't know how much I want you to. But for now, this is all for you. So, be a good boi." Jude undid the thin belt around her waist. She saw Clancy grow still. "I can't have you touch me so I'm going to tie your hands behind your back." Jude touched her nose to Clancy's and rubbed it gently. "Do you trust me?"

Clancy nodded.

"Do you want this?" Jude spun Clancy around, her face and naked breasts pressed against the metal of the stall. Jude began to slip the leather belt around Clancy's wrists. She paused before she pulled it tight.

"Safe word," Clancy said, visibly shaking with need.

"Give me yours, baby." Jude licked a path down Clancy's back.

"Exorcist."

Jude chuckled at the absurd word that fell from Clancy's lips. "I've never known anyone like you before."

"I'm kind of a one off," Clancy muttered.

"You're unique. I like that." Jude tightened the belt, watching Clancy wince. "Too tight?"

"Just tight enough," Clancy said.

Jude turned her around again, and pressed Clancy back against the stall. She kissed her gently for the first time, learning every curve of Clancy's mouth, the tip of her tongue, and the edge of her teeth. She licked down her neck, found Clancy's pulse point and sucked hard. Clancy shuddered against her, straining her neck for more, whimpering so beautifully while Jude marked her.

"Tonight, you're mine," Jude whispered in Clancy's ear, catching the fleshy lobe between her teeth and biting down carefully.

"Fuck," Clancy gasped. "You're going to have me come in my Kleins."

"Not yet," Jude warned her. "You'll come when I say so." She ran her blunt fingernails slowly down Clancy's chest, stomach, and under the band of her boxers. She guided her hand lower, brushing over hair that Jude deliberately tugged on, making Clancy gasp and squirm. Jude loved that they were almost the same height. She stared straight into Clancy's heated gaze and slid her hand lower, pushing her fingers between Clancy's lips, delighting in how much wetness soaked her hand.

"Oh. You're more than ready to take me, baby," Jude said, drawing circles around Clancy's clit with a firm finger.

Clancy fought to stay upright. Jude could feel her legs trembling the more Jude worked on that tight bundle of nerves. A litany of *fuck*s fell from Clancy's lips. Jude kissed her, loving how Clancy's eyes were fighting to stay open. Jude moved lower but stopped at Clancy's entrance.

"Do you like penetration?" Jude never took her eyes from Clancy's face, waiting for permission.

Clancy nodded vigorously.

"Use your words, Clancy."

Clancy shuddered out a "Yes" and Jude wasted no time sliding a finger inside her. Clancy's head clanged off the stall wall as she bowed under Jude's touch.

Jude quickly cradled Clancy's head in her hand to make sure she didn't hurt herself or draw anyone's attention to the bathroom with any more bangs. Jude nudged Clancy's feet apart a fraction more to get a better angle to slide her finger deep. Clancy was shaking. Jude could see her arms flexing, trying to break free of the belt trapping her hands.

"Don't struggle. You'll hurt yourself. I'll untie you just as soon as I make you scream my name."

"Jude." Clancy's voice was shaky as she tried to speak.

"Nope, not loud enough yet." Jude smiled at her, enjoying watching this proud butch fall to pieces while Jude's finger pressed inside her. "Can you take two?" Jude didn't wait for an answer, she pressed two fingers inside Clancy and picked up the speed. Clancy pitched forward and rested her head in Jude's neck. Her breath was hot and heavy against Jude's skin.

"One more, Clancy? Can you take me all in?" Jude curled three fingers together and pushed deeper into Clancy's tightening walls. "You going to come for me? Come all over my hand so I can lick it all off? It will do until I can get my face between your legs, spread you wide, and fuck you on my tongue." Jude didn't let up on her strokes, brushing against the hidden spot that was starting to make Clancy shudder and quake under her touch. "You can come, Clancy. Come for me." Jude fucked her faster, rejoicing at the keening wail that escaped Clancy's lips that were pressed firmly into Jude's neck. Whatever Clancy shouted as she climaxed was burrowed deep in Jude's flesh along with Clancy's teeth.

Jude felt her sex clench in unison with Clancy's explosive climax. She knew she didn't have time, but she couldn't stop herself from mounting Clancy's leg and rubbing herself off hard against her jeans. Clancy urged her on in breathy pants and encouraging sounds. Jude came quickly, staring blindly at the ceiling while her clit pounded in tune to her racing heart.

"Fuck, that was sexy as hell!" Clancy said, finally coming back to reality. "Pity we were both still wearing jeans. I'd have loved to feel you come all over my leg."

Jude groaned and stood upright. "That wasn't supposed to happen. I usually have more restraint than that." She gingerly spread her legs. "Fuck! I'm going to need to change my underwear." She caught Clancy looking at her with a happy face. "Look at you, all blissed out." She gestured for Clancy to turn around and she swiftly freed her hands. Clancy shook her hands out then reached to touch Jude's shoulder.

"Sorry, Jude, but you're going to have a monster bruise here tomorrow." She leaned forward to brush a kiss on the tender skin. "I had no choice; I had to muffle myself. You nearly blew my head off!"

Jude forced herself not to look as smug as she felt. She reached for their shirts and put hers back on while she watched Clancy tuck herself back into her bra. She mourned the loss.

"As sexy as it was watching you hump my leg, I'd like to return the favor at some point. You know, be more hands on this time." Clancy fastened her shirt and tucked it back in her jeans.

Jude was staring at her hand.

"Jude?"

"I don't want to wash it. I want to be able to smell you on me for the rest of the night." She quickly jammed her three fingers into her mouth and licked them clean. She groaned, unhappy she had to abide by health and safety rules. She unlocked the stall door so she could quickly wash her hands. "Think you can go back to the bar while I raid my locker for clean underwear?"

"Sure."

"I get off at midnight," Jude said.

"I'd say you've already gotten off," Clancy said, grinning.

"Does Inez expect you home tonight?" Jude pressed on, ignoring her.

"I don't have a curfew if that's what you mean."

"Come home with me then." She hesitated. "If you want to, that is."

Clancy wrapped her arms around her and squeezed. "I want to, very much."

"Then go before I drag you back in there for round two." Jude couldn't help herself. She brushed Clancy's hair back to tidy it up and almost couldn't let go.

Clancy hesitated. Jude groaned at the pure desire shining in Clancy's eyes, all directed at *her*.

"No, you've already had me go against character and fuck you in my place of work. I'm taking you home. Round two is in my bed."

"We could start on the settee," Clancy said, a smile on her lips and temptation in her eyes.

"No, I have a cat. If he finds us buck naked on the settee, he's going to carve his initials on your ass cheek. I'd like to keep your ass to myself."

"Can I sit at the bar with you again?"

"Can I trust you to behave?"

"I'll be the model of decorum and no one will ever suspect you've just fucked me raw in the staff bathroom."

"Okay."

"And I didn't call for an exorcist once." Clancy swaggered past Jude looking immensely proud of herself.

"You're a weird one, Clancy."

"You have no idea." Clancy unlocked the door and peeked out into the hallway. She looked back over her shoulder. "Don't bother putting any new underwear on. I'll only rip it off later."

Jude shook her head at her as she left then spared a quick look at herself in the mirror. She hastened to fix her clothes. Hopefully no one would be able to tell what she'd just been doing and she prayed the lighting in the bar would hide her flushed face. Now all she had to do was act normal around Clancy and try not to drag her back in here before her shift ended.

❖

Clancy wished Jude hadn't driven to work. They were going back to Jude's apartment; Jude was in her car with Clancy following behind on her motorcycle. Clancy would have given anything to have Jude's strong arms wrapped around her as she rode through the streets.

Outside the apartment, Clancy chained her motorcycle while Jude watched in silence. When it was secure, Jude reached out a hand for Clancy to take. She locked their fingers together, a solid hand hold, strong just like Jude. Clancy followed her up the steps to the second floor and waited for her to open the door. Though Clancy was desperate to immediately get Jude naked and writhing on her tongue, she remembered Jude telling her she had a cat. She could hear him the second Jude put her key in the lock.

"Hey, Smokey Joe," Jude called, loosening her grip on Clancy to greet the cat who jumped off the top of the settee and into her arms.

"Holy smokes, that's a big cat," Clancy exclaimed. Jude gave her a strange look. "What? He's definitely not kitten-sized."

"My nickname for him is Holy Smokes," Jude said, petting the purring cat.

Clancy hoped that had been a coincidence and not someone whispering in her ear. "Well, he's a fine figure of a feline."

"Do you have much to do with cats?" Jude carried him into the kitchen. His meows got louder and more insistent. "I'm feeding you. Give me a minute."

"Back in Chicago I was brought up surrounded by them. Every neighbor has a familiar." Clancy cursed herself for not minding her words. Her home was part of Rainbow's Wiccan commune when she wasn't on the road. Male or female practitioners in the coven always had a cat or two. She was constantly refusing kittens.

"Sorry, I didn't catch that over the sounds of this one claiming he's starving," Jude said, putting Smokey Joe's supper down for him.

"I said where I grew up I was surrounded by familiar cats." Clancy leaned against a wall to watch Jude care for hers. "How long have you had him?"

"Over a month. I got him by default but I wouldn't be without him now." Jude looked over at her. "It's a long story. One I won't regale you with tonight." Jude washed up and watched Smokey Joe eat. "He's been a good companion. If he'd just quit leaving hairballs in the hallway, he'd be the perfect roommate." Jude walked back over to her. "He's fed, then he'll sleep in his bed. He's a creature of habit. You and I, however, have unfinished business." She kissed Clancy, long and slow.

Clancy only let her take the lead for so long before pushing out of Jude's arms. "Switch time, Romeo. You deserve more than a dry hump to get off."

Jude reached for her again. "Believe me, I wasn't dry." She guided Clancy down the hall to her bedroom and began to strip without preamble.

Clancy leaned against the doorframe and took her fill of Jude's body being revealed. Clancy's mouth watered when Jude tugged off her sports bra. When Jude unzipped her pants, Clancy was surprised to see no underwear, just a flash of blond hair. She pushed away from the door and closed it behind her.

"You were going commando this whole time?"

"I didn't have time to change." Jude pulled her underwear from her pocket.

"I hope those aren't a favorite pair because I aim on taking those home with me."

"You in need of a new pair of briefs?" Jude swung them around her finger as she toe-heeled her shoes off.

"Yes, especially ones scented by you." Clancy made a grab for them but Jude tossed them over on a chair. In retaliation, Clancy pushed Jude's jeans down off her hips. Jude stepped out of them, naked except for her socks.

Clancy pushed her back toward the bed making Jude sit down with a bounce. Clancy immediately fell to her knees. "I promise to worship every inch of you until you can't catch your breath, but if I don't taste you first, I'm going to go insane." She crowded between Jude's sturdy legs and ran a string of kisses up the taut flesh. "You could probably crush me between your thighs. We'll revisit that particular fantasy later too." Clancy spread Jude wider and ran her tongue the full length of her sex, spreading Jude's lips, tonguing her opening, then circling her tongue around Jude's thick clit.

Jude shuddered, a deep groan escaping her. "Fuck," she said, her voice cracking. She fell back, braced on her elbows, keeping herself upright to watch as Clancy tasted every inch of her.

Clancy couldn't stop. Jude tasted divine and Clancy was desperate to worship at the source. Her fingers ran through the trimmed curls that framed Jude's sex. Jude was already bucking beneath her, but Clancy wasn't going to make this quick. She lifted one of Jude's legs over her shoulder and felt Jude collapse back on the bed. She traced fast circles around Jude's firm clit, licking around the hood, sucking her clit hard. She chastised herself for not having been prepared enough to have packed her favorite toy. But she hadn't expected to meet Jude. Jude, the gorgeous butch who was letting Clancy bury her face between her legs. Jude, whose blond pubes were tickling at Clancy's nose as she speared her tongue into Jude's entrance. Jude, who was writhing so much Clancy had to push a hand down on her stomach to stop her from bucking Clancy loose.

Clancy knew she only had a limited time to fuck this woman. Clancy couldn't offer anyone her undivided attention. How could she? She was constantly surrounded by spirits of the dead, wanting answers, wanting their release. The talent she possessed, once revealed, had cost Clancy her family, friends, and lovers.

So, she lived in the moment. In the feel of Jude clenching around her, in the rush of her desire that covered Clancy's tongue, in the hoarse shout that Clancy ripped from Jude's chest as her climax hit. In the aftermath, she closed her eyes and rested her head on Jude's stomach. She felt Jude's shaking hand run through her hair. Clancy pressed small kisses to Jude's belly, loving the aftershocks that made Jude's stomach clench and release beneath Clancy's spread palm.

She committed every moment to memory. Jude was a rare find but Clancy knew she couldn't keep her.

"Get up here and sit on my face," Jude said, tugging at her to get up.

Clancy smiled and kissed Jude's stomach again. Time to make more memories.

CHAPTER EIGHT

Clancy lay boneless across Jude's broad chest. Jude's arms were wrapped around her and Clancy was in heaven.

"You want to sleep over?" Jude's voice was quiet as if she wasn't sure she should ask.

"Considering I can't feel my legs, I'd be grateful," Clancy said, idly tracing her finger around Jude's nipple and watching her areola pebble.

Jude pressed a hand down to stop Clancy's teasing. "Don't you start that again. You've already had me inform the neighbors I can come hard and fast from nipple play alone." Jude nuzzled at Clancy's forehead, kissing along her hairline.

Clancy smiled, smug that her talents had left Jude in a full body flush. The red was only just starting to fade.

"Tell me something not everyone knows about you," Jude said, lifting Clancy's hand off her breast and kissing her palm before placing it somewhere less incendiary.

Clancy felt safe and warm enough in Jude's care to let a secret out. "I nearly drowned as a kid."

Jude's arm tightened around her a fraction more. "Geez, that's terrifying. How old were you?"

"Fourteen. It's not that big a deal really. My grandma got me out."

"I'm glad she was there to save you. I'm glad you're here with me now, safe and sound."

Clancy's heart ached at the sweet sentiment. "Yeah, me too." She lifted her head to see Jude lit only by the moonlight shining through the blinds. "Your turn. What's something not many know about you?"

Jude looked lost in thought for a moment then answered, "I lost my virginity to two butch lesbians before I enlisted in the navy."

Clancy shifted to look down at Jude's smiling face. "Usually, I'd be all over the navy thing but, for some reason, my brain can't seem to get past the *threesome*."

Jude brought her arms up to put her hands under her head. Clancy was instantly distracted by how broad her shoulders were, how muscled her arms were, and how damn pleased with herself Jude looked. The pose also raised Jude's breasts and Clancy would freely admit those were distracting enough on their own. She forced herself to concentrate.

"*Two?*" Clancy pushed for more details.

"I graduated high school with my eyes firmly fixed on being a navy diver. I'd already spoken to a recruiter about what I needed to do, and by my eighteenth birthday I was ready to enlist. I drove myself to Kansas City and walked into the first lesbian bar I could find. I was a baby butch on a mission, with no idea how to start. I'd been too busy busting my balls to get good grades to even think about dating. Besides, the girls in school weren't the kind I'd trust to get naked with without getting my bare ass photographed and pinned to the school notice board."

"So, you just walked into a bar looking to get your cherry busted?"

"I did. I ended up talking to these two friends. Both were extremely butch, tattooed, pierced, totally women for me to aspire to be. They got my story out of me over a soda. They helped me check out everyone in the room as a possible candidate, but I only had eyes for them. I knew then, femmes weren't going to be where my desires lay."

"I'm grateful for that," Clancy said, leaning down to press a kiss on Jude's chest.

"So, I asked, what about them. They asked which one of them I wanted."

Clancy grinned at the look on Jude's face. For someone who could be stoic, her eyes were twinkling with mischief at the story she was telling. It was cute but Clancy wasn't about to tell her that.

"I said how about both? They looked at each other, got off their barstools, and took me home with them."

"And...?"

"I graduated with honors from their teaching too!"

"Damn, I'm so jealous." Clancy flopped back down by Jude's side. "But as a beneficiary of their tutelage, I salute them." Clancy looked over at Jude. "Dare I ask how old they were?"

"How old are you?"

"Thirty-four."

"They were older than you," Jude said.

Clancy gave her a considering look. "How old are you?"

"Forty. The age they were when we met."

Clancy hooted with delight. "You fucked two forty-year-old BILFs when you were just eighteen. Respect!"

Jude looked puzzled. "BILFs?"

"Butches I'd Love To Fuck!" Clancy laughed. "Man, that's an awesome story. My virginity was lost to a teenage swimming instructor when I was sixteen. She was lean and muscular and I thought I was so damn special, but she was working her way through her pupils like a shark through water. At least I learned to be more selective and not as trusting as I grew up."

"Yet, here we are." Jude shifted on her side to face her. She brushed her hand through Clancy's hair.

Clancy would have happily succumbed to that gentle touch all night. She knew she was touch-starved. She craved it. But no one had touched her and made her truly *feel* like Jude did. It would have been disconcerting if Clancy hadn't been too busy soaking it up like a sponge.

"You're special. I knew it from that first look at the restaurant. I felt it from the first moment our eyes met at the bar. I can't explain it," Clancy said.

"Do you think it's one of those fate things you believe in?" Jude traced her hand down Clancy's face and along the edge of her jaw.

"Do *you*?"

"I've never had much reason to believe in such things." Jude stared at her. "Until now." She ran her finger across Clancy's bottom lip. "Are we going to be more than a one-night stand?" She put her lips close to Clancy's. "I'd really like more of this." She followed through with a kiss.

Clancy opened her mouth willingly to accept Jude's tongue that teased hers then retreated, leaving her empty. "I'm rubbish at relationships," she admitted.

"Maybe that's why you met me. You said fate gives you people who are sent to help you or teach you. Maybe we're meant to help each other. Or maybe you're here to teach *me* something, help *me* with something."

Clancy froze for a moment, remembering what else she'd seen at the restaurant with Jude that day. "Do you need help?"

"What I need is for you to think about it. But not right now. Right now, I need to *help* you." Jude's lips latched on to Clancy's nipple and began to suck it into a firm peak. She licked and flicked it rapidly with her tongue, driving Clancy to distraction.

But not so distracted that she missed the wall behind the bed bulge and stretch as arms threatened to push through, frantic hands grabbing at air. The wall snapped back to normal as if whatever it was had been snatched back by force. All that remained were silent shadows. Clancy forced herself to ignore it and concentrate on Jude's hands as they anchored her to the world.

Inez was sitting at the table eating toast when Clancy let herself into the RV. Inez looked her over with a keen eye.

"So, how's *Jude*?" she said, leaning behind her to grab a coffee cup but choosing to switch it to a much bigger mug. "You look like you need the extra caffeine. Did you sleep at all last night?" She poured steaming coffee into the mug and slid it across the table.

"Enough," Clancy said, reaching gratefully for the black coffee and savoring every drop.

"Was she nice? Or did you forego pleasantries and just skip to the chase?"

Clancy glared at her. She was not telling Inez she had inadvertently followed her advice to the letter. She'd never hear the last of it. "You're asking a lot of questions."

"You texted me saying you wouldn't be back last night and that you'd met the woman from the restaurant. The one I saw eye-fucking you for the whole time we were there. You bet I have questions. Spill!"

"She's a bartender at the bar you sent me to."

Inez's toast was left dangling in midair. "Whoa, that's oddly serendipitous."

"Crazy, eh?"

"Do you know her birthday? Aunt Sage could read her cards for you, to see if you're compatible."

"Believe me, we were *plenty* compatible last night...and this morning." Clancy smiled at the memories.

"Are you going to see her again?"

Clancy nodded. "Yeah, I think I might. She was good company, a great dancer, and so fucking gorgeous. We're going to be here for a while. I'd be an idiot not to see her again."

"And my mother didn't raise you to be an idiot." Inez reached across the table to touch Clancy's arm. "Do you *like* her?"

Clancy nodded. "I like her a lot. And before you ask, she's single, has her own place, and she has a cat."

Inez's eyes lit up. "A cat!"

"A big black hole of a cat, immensely fluffy, big yellow eyes, and long white whiskers. I woke up this morning to find him curled up in my armpit."

"You've always been a cat magnet. We should get—"

Clancy interrupted before Inez could go further. "No. No cats in the RV. We have everything just how we want it in here."

"Cory's cat had kittens," Inez said, looking hopeful.

"Cory's cat needs to get fixed. No cats. When we get back to the commune and hunker down for winter maybe you can have one of your own then. In *your* own home. But I don't need a pet." Clancy eyed Inez over the rim of her mug. "I have enough with you shedding hair."

Inez made a face at her. "Did your butch Adonis fix you breakfast?"

"She offered but I didn't want to impose on her day off. I needed to get back too. I want to take my motorcycle and ride to the starting point of the river we're going to cover next week. Just to get a feel for it all. I figure I can complete it in a few days and that will bring us closer to our present location. I know we'll attract some attention here, but the local law is ready to keep people out of our way if it gets too much." Clancy took Inez's half-eaten piece of toast out of her hand and tossed it back on its plate. "Want to come with me? I'll treat us to breakfast."

"You don't have to ask me twice. I'll go fire up Betsy."

Clancy shook her head at the pet name Inez had given her scooter. "You'll never be able to keep up with me on that thing."

"Then you'll have to slow down and not be so hell-bent on breaking both the speed limit and the sound barrier. You have a gal to see again, I'm sure she'd rather you be in one piece." Inez got up and gently nudged Clancy's head to the side. "Though it looks like she almost took a piece of you for herself."

Clancy self-consciously touched the spot where Jude had left a very prominent hickey in retaliation for Clancy biting her shoulder. The bruise would fade eventually. Clancy was more in fear of Jude taking something more permanent. Something like her heart. It had nearly killed Clancy getting out of the bed they'd shared and leaving when all she wanted to do was stay. That was a first for her. Just as wanting to see Jude for more than one night was. The feelings she was experiencing left her with a lot to think about.

But not today.

She'd played hooky long enough. The river wasn't going to reveal all its secrets by itself.

CHAPTER NINE

Jude left her apartment and was locking the door when a neighbor called out her name. She looked up to see Mrs. Baker hurry down the hallway to catch up with her. Jude dutifully waited. Mrs. Baker was an eighty-year-old fount of knowledge and a gatherer of gossip. She looked as sweet as Betty White but was a regular Miss Marple. Jude wondered how long it took her to know Jude had a guest over last night. She thought she'd seen the curtains twitching when Clancy's motorcycle roared in behind her.

"Good morning, Jude. How's Smokey Joe settling in?"

"He's doing fine, I think. He seems happy enough."

"Still no word on Mia?"

Jude shook her head. "I keep checking with the police, but I get the same answers every time. There was no sign of foul play in her apartment. Her license plate hasn't registered on any cameras around town. She's probably moved out to live with the boyfriend all of us heard about but no one got his name and none of us saw him." Jude was beyond frustrated with their lack of help and excuses for her disappearance.

"She wouldn't just walk away from Smokey Joe," Mrs. Baker said. "And she wouldn't have left her job without telling them first. She loved that job. She was in line for a promotion. She'd been so excited when she told me." Mrs. Baker waved Jude closer and lowered her voice. "The landlord contacted Mia's sister. She's paying the rent for a while until Mia returns." She looked up at Jude. "You don't think she's coming back though, do you?"

Jude shook her head. "I don't think so."

"I don't think so either." Mrs. Baker bit her lip, fighting to hold back tears. She rummaged in her handbag and pulled out a bag of cat treats. "Here, you give that poor boy these."

Clancy took them and smiled at the brand. "Oh, he loves these."

"Of course he does, I'm the one who got him hooked on them." Mrs. Baker gripped Jude's arm and shook it. "You keep pestering those police. I want my Mia back."

Jude nodded. She wanted Mia back too.

"You off?" Mrs. Baker gave Jude a small smile. "Going to meet that motorcycling gal of yours again?"

"You don't miss a thing, do you?" Jude wasn't surprised. She'd been more surprised Mrs. Baker hadn't been out on her doorstep, wrapped in her dressing gown, checking on who Jude was bringing home.

Mrs. Baker gave her a toothy grin. "I'll tell you something else I haven't missed. There's a huge fancy RV parked in the lot at the police station. They don't give parking spaces out to just anyone. So, I asked around."

"You and your sources." Jude chuckled, knowing full well Mrs. Baker had multiple friends throughout Kansas City and they networked their information. Everything from the lowest price of produce to who had been seen stepping out with whom.

"Rumor has it the RV is owned by one of those people like they have on that YouTube. You know, the ones who post videos as they dredge up old cars and junk from the rivers to keep them clean. Salvage hunters."

Jude's ears pricked at the word salvage. "Really?" Now she was genuinely interested. She had no idea where Clancy was staying. They'd exchanged phone numbers but Jude didn't want to seem too pushy, or desperate, even though she'd love to know where Clancy was. She wondered if Clancy felt as unmoored as Jude did now, cast adrift, feeling lost without her.

"I hear this woman and her team are going to be boating up and down the Missouri River."

Jude wondered if this was indeed Clancy. They hadn't really talked much about her job. They'd chatted at the bar while Jude served, but it had been mostly about the bar itself, what Jude thought about the area, and Clancy's first impressions. Jude was too busy wanting less talk and more action. She knew, by the look in Clancy's eyes, that she too had little patience for meaningless chitchat.

Last night was not spent wasted on idle conversation either. Lust, desire, and their bodies had been doing all the talking.

"Are you going to get your groceries?"

Mrs. Baker's voice startled Jude back to the present. She gave Mrs. Baker a knowing look. "Yes, I am, like I do every Saturday."

Mrs. Baker gave her a hopeful look. An old lady's version of Puss in Boots's huge pleading eyes. Jude had received that look quite often since she'd moved in and had met this feisty woman.

"Do you want to come with me and get your groceries too?" Jude asked, knowing the answer already.

"How kind of you to ask." Mrs. Baker slipped her arm through Jude's. "I'd be delighted to accompany you."

Jude escorted her down to the parking lot to her car. "When we get back, how about you come visit with Smokey Joe and give him some of these treats yourself?"

Mrs. Baker squeezed Jude's arm in gratitude. "That would make my day."

Jude lasted all day without texting Clancy. By eleven o'clock, she lay on her bed, replaying the previous night in her head. It only served to make her feel lonely and uncomfortably aroused. Jude groaned at herself and buried her nose in the pillow that Clancy had slept on. She could smell the cologne Clancy wore. Jude breathed it in, missing her even more. Sandalwood, citrus, a hint of cloves, a clean scent that reminded Jude of being on the beach. Clancy had told her it was called Inis—The Energy of the Sea. Jude had searched out all the places Clancy had dabbed the cologne, loving how it smelled mixed with Clancy's natural scent.

Jude flopped over on her back and stared at the ceiling. What if Clancy didn't get in contact again with her? What if that one night of wild and passionate sex had been all Jude would have to remember her by?

"God, you're pathetic." Jude berated herself. She normally handled one-night stands a lot better than this. Still, they were few and far between occurrences. Clancy hadn't felt like a random pickup. She'd felt *known*. It was like somewhere, deep inside, Jude had known Clancy from the minute their eyes met in the bar. Her body had reacted to Clancy's presence. Her heart had felt revitalized. Touching Clancy intimately, hearing her sighs and groans, felt familiar. It was as if Jude had been making love to Clancy for years instead of mere hours.

Jude missed holding her tight. She loved how strong Clancy was, but the minute Jude tightened her hold and held Clancy *still*, Clancy melted into her. It was a heady feeling of power, control, and trust.

"And now I'm lying here, too nervous to text her."

A meow drew Jude's attention elsewhere. Big yellow eyes stared at her from over the side of the bed. She switched the pillows around quickly so Smokey Joe could lie on hers while Jude rested her head where Clancy's had lain. He promptly lay on his back, paws akimbo, and just stared at her.

"You're such a furry weirdo." Jude grabbed up her phone and took a photo of him. She typed a text quickly before she changed her mind.

He's in your spot.

She sent the message off, not expecting a reply. Jude lay listening to his purring and they both jumped at the sound of a text arriving.

Wish I was there. I spent the day on my motorcycle. I much prefer it when I'm straddling you for hours instead.

Jude thought that was the most romantic thing anyone had ever sent her. Another text arrived shortly after.

Tell Smokey Joe not to get too comfortable. I intend to take up all that space again very soon.

Jude let out a relieved breath and messaged back.

I look forward to that. I miss you in my arms.

An answer dinged back almost immediately.

Are you working Friday? Will you dance with me again?

Jude's mind went back to their first meeting, the dancing that wasn't close enough, and then their wild time in the bathroom that was.

Yes, but I don't know if I can get away with another raunchy bathroom break.

Jude waited for Clancy's reply.

We can always just reenact it at yours.

Jude knew she was screwed. Clancy had ruined her for any other woman after just one intimate close encounter.

Another text came. A photo attached. Clancy was baring her neck in it, showing a large angry hickey. The message read *I think you left something behind.*

Jude stared at the picture. She could just catch the sharp edge of Clancy's jawline. She couldn't miss the purpling mark. She knew she should feel regret for marring Clancy's skin. She also knew she'd happily do it again given the chance.

I'll kiss it better. Jude promised.

I'll hold you to that. See you Friday. Bring extra underwear just in case.

Jude laughed at Clancy's parting remark. She put her phone away, smiling to herself in the dark and wishing the week away.

"Don't get too comfy there, Smokey Joe. That spot is reserved for someone way more sexy and less likely to shed."

CHAPTER TEN

Monday morning usually meant Jude could stay in bed an hour longer. Instead, she'd woken to a knock at the door and Mrs. Baker standing there, looking contrite. Her usual ride out of the city had canceled on her and a trip to the nursing home to see her sister was in jeopardy. Jude ushered her in and hastened to get dressed.

"You're such a sweetheart to do this for me," Mrs. Baker said, fussing over Smokey Joe.

"It's no problem." Jude snatched up her car keys. "I've taken you before. You sure her son is going to drive you home?"

"Yes, you're off the hook for the return trip."

The hour-long drive had been pleasant. Mrs. Baker always kept the conversation flowing. Smokey Joe was along for the ride, fastened safely in his car seat where he was able to look out the window and watch the world go by.

Jude escorted Mrs. Baker into the home. She was thankful that Mrs. Baker didn't need that kind of assistance herself yet. The feisty old woman would likely outlive them all.

"I'm hungry. Holy Smokes, how'd you fancy a trip to that riverside restaurant I took you to last time we were playing taxi service? You can go in your carrier and watch the river flow by." Jude took the meow he gave her as a yes.

The restaurant wasn't very far from the nursing home. Jude parked with no problem and transferred Smokey Joe to his carrier with equal ease. She wore it like a backpack. She couldn't help but wonder what her navy buddies would have said about her being such a cat mom.

She walked through the parking lot, past a huge RV parked to the side. She stopped for a moment and just stared at it. "Fuck, that thing is huge," she muttered under her breath. "You could fit half my apartment block in it!"

The view of the Missouri River was one of the best features from the restaurant's rooftop terrace. Jude made sure to have a table where she could see the long stretch of river.

"I miss the sea, Smokey Joe. I spent so much time under water." She perused the menu. "Maybe I should find a scuba diving group to keep my skills sharp. Who knows, it might come in handy one day."

Her breakfast was served quickly, and Jude tucked in. The sun was out, the sky bright and clear. The water below was sparkling like a million little diamonds where the sunlight caught it. It was early enough that the restaurant was still reasonably quiet and Jude enjoyed the moment of peaceful tranquility. She unzipped the front of Smokey Joe's carrier and let him watch their surroundings. A bird flew by and Smokey Joe chattered after it.

"Yeah, that isn't on the menu today, boy." She fed him a small piece of sausage. "Here, just don't tell your other mother I feed you people food on occasion."

Jude watched the water flow. It soothed her. Her ears soon picked up the sound of a motorboat putt-putting along. She looked up the river and could see a blue boat cutting through the water. She watched it cruise along at a steady rate then turn and go back the way it had come. After a while Jude noticed a pattern emerging in the boat's meandering.

"What are you searching for, little boat?" Jude watched a while longer. The boat slowly made its way closer toward the restaurant. Jude's brain finally clicked. There was an RV in the parking lot, and a little boat trawling the river. Was this the one Mrs. Baker had told her about? The salvage hunters? She strained her eyes to try to see who was manning the boat. Clancy had said she worked in salvage. She'd never mentioned living in an RV though. Jude paused for a moment and tried to think if during their time together they had touched on anything connected to where Clancy was living. Jude didn't think so. They'd been too busy getting naked. Even when they'd exchanged numbers Clancy hadn't mentioned where she was staying. Jude hadn't thought anything of it. She'd brought Clancy home. Clancy didn't need to inform her of her own address in exchange.

Was Clancy the salvage hunter being gossiped about by Mrs. Baker's cronies?

The little boat cruised closer and Jude could see a person manning it. She could also make out monitor screens on the front of the boat. They were using sonar to scan the river. Jude wanted desperately to be in that boat to decipher the scans and see what lay beneath the Missouri River.

The boat headed toward a dock. Jude grabbed Smokey Joe and zipped him back up. He peered at her through the mesh.

"Let's go see who that is down there," Jude said, gathering up her bill to pay.

The person in the boat had been dark-haired but the life jacket masked their gender. Jude wished the dock had been closer so she could have seen their face. She mused it wouldn't hurt anything to just take a little walk to the river. Just a woman and her cat, taking in the scenery.

If nothing else, maybe Jude could get some information before Mrs. Baker for once.

Clancy moored her boat and clambered out of it. Once on the dock, she unfastened her life jacket and shucked it off. She stretched to pop out all the kinks and creases sitting for two hours had given her. She'd stopped for a bathroom break, to grab a snack or two, and to stretch her legs before getting back to her task. She'd had a very early start. She'd left Inez still in her pajamas getting all the tech switched on. Clancy had woken up agitated. She didn't know if that meant she was going to find something, or if something else was going to happen, but she couldn't sleep so had started her charting.

Evan was parked at the dock, fast asleep in his car. The RV would have blocked the whole road to the water's edge so she'd parked in the restaurant's parking lot. Clancy was not leaving her boat and all its equipment alone while she went back to the RV. She walked over to Evan's car and rapped on the window. He jerked awake with a start.

"Earn your keep, sailor boy. Guard the boat. I'll be back in five."

She watched him rub at his eyes and hasten to sit up. He opened his mouth but Clancy held up a hand to silence him. "Yes, I'll grab you a coffee. Yes, Inez made you muffins. Yes, I will kick your ass all the way to Alaska if you try anything with her she does not want. Capiche?"

He nodded mutely.

"Go sit on the boat. Don't touch anything. I will be back." Clancy left him scrambling out of the car to do as he was told.

She walked up the path, disappointed that so far there'd been nothing to find in this stretch of the river but, at the same time, grateful there hadn't been. She caught sight of someone coming from the parking lot through the path between some bushes and stopped dead in her tracks.

"*Jude?*" Clancy wasn't sure if she was hallucinating after staring at the monitors for so long.

Jude halted mid step at Clancy's voice then strode toward her. Clancy couldn't help but be turned on by that powerful gait. Jude wore blue jeans and a V-necked T-shirt. They only enhanced her strength. Desire, hot and yearning, shot through Clancy's veins. She hastened her step to go meet her.

"Hey you," Jude said, reaching out to tenderly brush Clancy's hair back from her face. "Fancy meeting you here."

Clancy pulled Jude into her arms and kissed her like a starving woman. She rejoiced when Jude's arms wrapped around her. Clancy never felt safer than in her hold. She finally drew back, loving how Jude's eyes sparkled at her.

"What are you doing here?" Clancy couldn't stop touching Jude's shoulders, reassuring herself she was real.

"I've just had breakfast at the restaurant. I had to drive a friend out here so was treating myself before I drove home." She kissed

Clancy again, pulling back with a sly brush of her tongue along Clancy's bottom lip. "Who knew the real treat was out here?"

"Fuck, I want to just keep kissing you, but Evan is in the boat behind me probably watching us like some stalker." She looked over her shoulder at Evan who visibly jumped and turned his head away quickly. "Also, I need to pee so bad, so I need to get to the RV as quick as I can." She pulled Jude after her as she hurried to the parking lot.

"That big thing is yours?" Jude nudged Clancy's shoulder. "I know you're not compensating for something."

Clancy laughed. "It was a gift from a client. It's our home and office while we travel."

"Ours?"

"Inez lives in it with me."

"And Evan?"

"Fuck no. That guy is a loaner, he comes with the KC territory. When we leave, he stays here, thank God." She made a face. "Unless Inez decides his particular brand of courting ritual is to her liking. He's trying his hardest to capture her attention, but she's got taste and is ignoring him."

Clancy knocked a peculiar rhythm out on the RV door and opened it. She gestured for Jude to walk in ahead of her.

"Well, hello there, Smokey Joe!" Clancy spotted the cat in the carrier. He meowed loudly at her.

"Do I hear a cat in here?" Inez came out from the kitchen, dressed now in shorts and a T-shirt. She immediately held out a hand to Jude to shake. "Hi, I'm Inez and you're obviously Jude. I'd just like to inform you that Clancy's my honorary aunt and part-time other mother so that there's no mistaking our relationship."

Clancy groaned.

"You're also the first woman Clancy has invited in here."

Clancy wondered if it would be impolite to push Jude out of the way to slap a hand over Inez's mouth. Jude just shook Inez's hand and smiled at her.

"Thank you for the clarification and the information." She looked behind her at Clancy. "I bet she keeps you on your toes."

"Too damn smart for her own good," Clancy grumbled. "And I'm going to regret leaving you two alone for a minute while I go to the bathroom." She brushed past Jude, then roughly grabbed her shoulders to turn her around. She directed Inez's attention to the carrier on her back, said "Look! A kitty!" and left them both to it. She could hear Inez's excited cooing at the cat all down the length of the RV.

Locked inside the bathroom, Clancy cleaned up as best she could. She ran wet hands through her hair to try to tame it and then splashed her face to get rid of the river spray. She tugged at her T-shirt, cursing the visible sweat stains on it from being wrapped in a bulky life jacket under a hot sun. She grabbed a clean one from out of the laundry pile and sprayed fresh deodorant on just in case. Her heart was beating double-time in her chest because Jude was in her RV. Jude was *here* and Clancy had invited her into her home. She never did that. She never brought a woman home to her sanctuary. She had no idea what she was doing but she knew she had to go back out there before Inez learned Jude's life story before Clancy had a chance to tell her. Or Inez told tales on *her*.

She needn't have worried. Inez was too captivated by Smokey Joe. He was out of his carrier and in her lap, purring up a storm.

"Clancy, isn't he just the most handsome cat you've ever seen?" Inez petted him reverently.

Clancy shared a look with Jude. "I didn't expect him to be portable," she teased her.

"I don't always like leaving him during the day, not when I'm out all night, working. So, he's got his carrier and a seat for the car. Luckily, he doesn't get carsick and, best of all, he doesn't criticize my driving."

Clancy leaned against the kitchen cabinets and tried not to stare too much at how beautiful Jude looked sun-kissed and in casual clothes.

"Are you two aware there's a whole gossip thread for you and your RV gathering momentum around Kansas City?" Jude said, leaning back in her seat and looking like she was right at home.

"What's the gossip this time? That we're lovers or mother and daughter? Or *father* and daughter? We've had that more times than I can count." Inez rolled her eyes and cupped Smokey Joe's face in her hands, talking to him in a baby voice. "People are stupid, yes they are."

Clancy huffed with annoyance. They were there to do a job. Who they were was of no importance to anyone else.

Jude shook her head. "The general consensus amid the eighty-year-old gossip mongers is that you're either salvage hunters or eco-warriors, cleaning the river of old rubbish or buried treasure." Jude looked up at Clancy. "You did say you worked in salvage."

Clancy nodded. "We've cleared a lot of cars and old junk from rivers we've worked on. Found a few guns too."

"One was from a robbery. That was an awesome find. The police were very grateful," Inez added.

Jude looked up and down the RV's length with an appreciative gaze. "This is a beautiful vehicle. I can't get over how large it is and how many different rooms you appear to have."

"We drive from city to city. It was easier and worked out cheaper to have a portable base than to pay for endless hotels and work out of a pickup, especially when I have so much equipment to carry," Clancy said.

Jude looked toward the front of the vehicle that was their office. "That's a ton of tech you're hauling."

"Those are my babies. From that control room I can watch everything Clancy does on and under the water." Inez's face turned serious. "She's always safe on my watch."

Clancy suddenly remembered something. "Damn, I left Evan watching over my boat. He'll think I've forgotten him."

"You had," Inez said with a grin. "Wouldn't be the first time, either."

Clancy hurried to get the drinks ready.

"I'll head off so you can get back to work." Jude stood and Inez reluctantly let Smokey Joe go so he could be put back in his carrier. Once he was settled, Jude caught Clancy's attention. "Maybe one day I could join you? I used to be a diver so I'm more than used to being on the water or under it. I've got all my own equipment and I know proper boating etiquette."

"No dangling your feet in the water," Inez said, mimicking Clancy's tone. "My least favorite boating rule."

Clancy never took anyone along with her, but the thought of having Jude by her side had her uncharacteristically agreeing. "We'll sort something out."

"I'm still seeing you on Friday, right?"

Jude sounded unsure and Clancy hastened to assure her she'd be there. "Wild horses couldn't keep me away."

Inez took the travel cup out of Clancy's hand and grabbed a plate of muffins. "Jude, it was lovely to meet you. I'm going to relieve Evan while leaving you two alone to say goodbye without me in the way." She winked at Clancy and left, shutting the door behind her.

"I like her," Jude said, her gaze not wavering from Clancy's face.

"She's a great kid and helps me more than she'll ever know." Clancy took a step forward. "I really want to give you a whole tour of this vehicle, but that would mean we'd eventually reach my bedroom and once you'd stepped foot in there, I wouldn't let you leave."

"We'll save that for another day then. One where Inez is busy elsewhere and not liable to walk in on us." Jude reached out to run her hand around the neck of Clancy's T-shirt. She trailed it lower and spread her fingers out over Clancy's breast, claiming it. "I like this shirt on you, but I prefer what lies underneath." She squeezed gently, trapping Clancy's nipple between her fingers and tightening her hold.

Clancy didn't move. Her breath stilled in her chest as she waited to see what Jude would do next. Jude was watching Clancy closely.

"Friday, I serve, we dance, then we leave. I'm owed a favor to get to leave early. I want you under me, over me, in me, and riding me."

Clancy shuddered at the promise in Jude's voice. "I can pack if you're into that?"

Jude squeezed her hand harder. "I'm very into that. With you, I'm into everything." She released Clancy's breast and brushed her hand down along Clancy's side, resting on her hip. Jude leaned forward to speak in Clancy's ear. "Pack long and hard."

Clancy's control broke. She kissed Jude with a hunger she couldn't control. Her enthusiasm propelled Jude, already off balance with the cat carrier, backward along the narrow hall. The carrier hit something and a stack of files scattered their contents across the floor.

Clancy reluctantly pulled back from Jude. She groaned at the escaped paperwork. "Sorry, I was supposed to file these." Clancy quickly knelt to sort them out.

Jude knelt to help her. She tidied some papers together but stopped and picked up a loose photograph. "Why do you have a picture of Kelly Hu?" She held the photo out to Clancy.

Clancy took it from her. "How do you know her?"

"She was friends with my neighbor, Mia. They worked at the hospital together. Kelly moved to another job and Mia never heard from her again. She thought Kelly ghosted her."

Clancy tried not to react to Jude's all too accurate choice of words. "Are you sure this is her?"

"I think so. Mia had a photo on her message board of a staff party from a few years ago. She'd pointed Kelly out to me." Jude stood up and stared down at Clancy. "Why do you have a file with her picture in it?"

Clancy hesitated a moment then stood up to face Jude.

"Because not all the cars I find in the water are empty." She waved the photo gently. "I found Kelly Hu's remains in her car in Iowa." Clancy stuck the photograph back in its file. "Do you think Mia would be agreeable to talk to me about her?" The sudden flash of pain visible in Jude's eyes made Clancy reach out for her. "Hey, what's wrong?"

"Mia's been missing for over a month."

The apparition Clancy had seen with Jude at the restaurant and the hands coming through the shared wall in Jude's apartment made sense now.

"I've been to the police multiple times but they've found nothing. They think she just ran away to start a new life." Jude's frustration was blatantly evident.

"But you don't believe that."

"No, she'd never leave her cat behind."

Clancy understood more now. "I need to pack my boat up. Will you follow us back to the police station where we're staying? You

and I need to talk more. I'll finish this stretch of the river tomorrow."
Clancy wasn't going to start asking questions now and leave Jude
with the hour's drive back alone. Not when what was revealed could
be devastating to her.

"You're not salvage hunters. You're specifically looking for
missing people," Jude said as realization struck.

Clancy nodded. "And that information is not for the gossip mill.
I need to know I can trust you to keep this operation quiet so I can do
my job without reporters or people wanting to watch."

"You have my word."

Clancy nodded. She knew wholeheartedly she could trust Jude
to keep her secret. At least, *this* one.

"And you have my help now. If Mia is out there, I'll help you
find her." *One way or another.*

CHAPTER ELEVEN

After the long drive back to downtown, Clancy parked her RV in its allotted space at the police station. Jude had to get gas so Clancy sat out on the RV steps waiting for her. She welcomed the small reprieve before she had to somehow tell Jude that Mia was trying desperately to reach out through the veil to her.

"You really like her, don't you?" Inez asked from behind her. "I've never seen you like this with someone before."

"I barely know her but I feel like I've always known her," Clancy admitted. "Your mother would have a field day with this."

"She won't hear it from me. This is your story to tell. But I know she'll be thrilled you've found someone who lasted beyond one night." Inez rested her hands on Clancy's shoulders and squeezed. "Jude's really attractive. You make a striking couple."

"You and I are just here to chart the river. I'm not here to settle down and play house. It's not in my soul contract to play Mary Homemaker." Clancy tipped her head back to look at her. "Besides, you've forgotten the fucking great elephant in the room. She doesn't know I'm psychic and I aim on keeping it that way for as long as we spend time together."

"She might not be bothered by that."

"Inez, when I'm not diving, I get paid to go to people's houses and give them messages from their dead relatives. I'm the butch version of Tyler Henry. She's ex-navy, an honorable profession. Me? I'm a sideshow attraction."

"You are a gifted psychic medium with an incredible accuracy rate. You find the lost. The DDU came to *you* for this assignment, you didn't seek them out."

"Yeah, well, I'd like to know who ratted me out to a place called the Deviant Data Unit." Clancy swiveled around on the step and lowered her voice. "They know angels, Inez. Real, white-winged *angels*! And I can see one of them!"

Inez patted her lightly on the head. "That's because you're special. And the way Jude looks at you, she thinks you're mighty special too."

Clancy liked hearing that just a little too much. But she knew, once the psychic cat was out of the bag, nothing ever remained the same with a lover. It was easier to hide it, to stifle that part of her down so deep that it didn't show, then lie and leave. That was how she'd dealt with all her past liaisons. That was why she was alone.

"Has Evan stayed with us?" Clancy asked, looking around the lot for his car.

"He's here. He's chatting up one of the policewomen inside."

"Can you ask him to go pick up whatever a cat needs? Like some treats, kibble stuff, and maybe a toy?" She pulled out her wallet and counted out some bills. "We can't keep Jude here while we interview her and not make sure Smokey Joe is comfortable." She got out an extra ten dollars. "Get a bed of some sort too. He can't sleep in that carrier thing. He's a big cat. He needs to stretch out."

"You're an old softy, do you know that?" Inez leaned down to hug her from behind.

"You take that back," Clancy threatened her, trying to shrug her off with little success.

"You do know that Evan isn't your personal gopher, don't you?" Inez leaned over Clancy's shoulder to pluck another ten-dollar bill from her wallet to add to the pile.

Clancy shook her head. "It's business. We need Jude to be comfortable and I'm sure she'd be happier with Smokey Joe content. I can't leave the RV and neither can you, so that leaves him. He slept all morning. It won't kill him to do something productive."

"Strictly business. Yeah, yeah, keep telling yourself that." Inez plucked the money out of Clancy's hand and carefully climbed over her to get down from the RV. "I'll go give him his to-do list." Inez shot Clancy a considering look. "Are you going to contact Detective Chandler?"

"I wasn't planning on it. I'm merely going to ask Jude some questions. We'll record it just in case. If anything needs to be reported to the unit, then I'll do it. But we don't even know if Jude's missing friend has anything to do with what we're searching for here."

"You don't believe that though. I mean, what are the odds of you working these cases and a woman you meet out of the blue just happens to have a friend who's missing too. That's a serious coincidence," Inez said, then added, "One might even say *fate*."

"Either that or I need to change my name to Jessica Fletcher." Clancy knew she was a magnet for death, just like the character Angela Lansbury had made so popular.

Inez laughed at her and left to go find Evan. Clancy spaced out watching the traffic go by.

Fate, coincidence, whatever had brought Jude into Clancy's world, Clancy was grateful for it. She just hoped that Mia wasn't involved in the case she was working on. She didn't want her added to the steadily growing number of bodies piling up in the Missouri River. She also hoped, whatever the outcome for Jude's friend, that Jude wouldn't want to shoot the messenger. Clancy very rarely got to be the bearer of good news. She shouldered other people's grief like adding patches onto an already worn-out jacket. Everyone's pain was another scar she bore.

For once, she'd like to tell someone their loved one was alive and well and coming home. The deepening dread she was beginning to feel for Mia Murray was not the ending she wanted for Jude.

"It's a dirty job, but someone's got to do it, right?" She looked to the sky, hoping for an answer.

None came.

Clancy stood as soon as she saw Jude's car enter the lot. Keeping this strictly business was going to be harder than she cared to confess.

❖

Jude had to admit, watching Clancy be professional was quite the turn-on. She found she liked all the sides to Clancy she'd seen so far. The charismatic flirt, the passionate lover who reveled in the moment whether she was the one being taken or the one taking. The woman whose eyes flared with joy when she saw Jude, a flare that switched to flames the minute she was within touching distance.

Investigative Clancy was intriguing. She was serious and though Jude thought Clancy could see right through to her soul, in this role she *felt* it.

Jude had a seat in their office area. She had been watching Inez bring up a series of files on her laptop screen. Inez was also different once her tech-savvy persona kicked in.

"Before we start, this is not an interrogation." Clancy pulled up a seat opposite Jude. "I'm not a cop, I'm not a private investigator. I search waterways for missing people and I get employed *by* law enforcement to assist them."

"Because her record of finding people is phenomenal," Inez interjected with pride.

"I wasn't going to blow my own trumpet." The twinkle in Clancy's eyes mocked the self-deprecation she feigned.

"That's okay," Inez said. "I'll toot a whole orchestra for you." She spun in her seat to face Jude. "She's the best in her field. We've been all over the country working cases she's been asked to look into. She could be working for some of the biggest missing person bureaus."

"But I prefer doing things my own way, not following someone else's rule book," Clancy explained. "I'm not much for letting someone else take charge."

Jude fought back a smirk. She remembered Clancy being *more* than willing to follow Jude's lead.

Clancy easily read her mind and smirked back.

There was a knock on the door. Inez jumped up to answer it. "Thank God. I was worried I was going to be stuck between whatever mind-reading sex thing you two are indulging in right now."

Jude enjoyed the faint blush of color in Clancy's cheeks as they both remembered their first encounter.

"You let me take charge of you quite spectacularly." Jude kept her voice deliberately low for Clancy's ears alone.

"You're the exception to my every rule it seems." Clancy spoke with a sincerity that warmed Jude's heart.

"You're a charmer, Clancy Madsen."

"Only with ones who matter." Clancy was about to say more but Inez bustled back in with her arms full of bags.

"Here you go. Evan cleared out the entire pet department for you it seems." Inez placed all the bags at Clancy's feet.

Jude was surprised to see how much deeper the color could go in Clancy's cheeks. Clancy quickly checked through the bags then pushed them toward Jude.

"These are for you, well, for Smokey Joe."

Jude peered inside the bags. "You brought my cat a bed?" She was confused. "He has one at home."

"This is for here, for now," Clancy said, starting to unpack the bags and lay it all out. "I don't know how long we'll be and it seems cruel to leave him without a few necessary things like treats." Clancy held up a bag and shook them. Smokey Joe, spread out in the living room on the settee like he owned the place, immediately came to see what was available. Clancy handed the bag to Jude. "You know what he's allowed to have."

Jude shook her head at her. "You brought my cat all this stuff so he can feel at home here?"

"People are easy. I can order us in a pizza or Mexican when we're finished, but this furball has other requirements. Don't question it, just put out what you think he needs for now. It's no big deal." Clancy wasn't looking at Jude. Instead, she was glaring at the look Inez was giving her.

"It's a very big deal, *Aunty* Clancy," Inez whispered at her before spinning around in her chair to peruse the monitors once more.

Jude found the most unobtrusive areas to put the items down. She raised her eyebrows at the expensive cat kibble that had been chosen. Smokey Joe had better not develop a taste for it. "I always carry a litter box for him when we travel. I warn you, if he uses it, you won't think kindly of him."

"He can use it. I'm just glad I'm not the one cleaning up after him," Clancy said.

"We'll make you a cat mom yet."

Jude heard Inez's sassy comment, followed by a squeal where Clancy obviously retaliated.

Smokey Joe took a drink from his new water bowl that was included in the goodies. He then clambered up onto the settee where his new bed had been placed, trod a few circles in it to get it just right, then settled in for a nap.

Jude returned to her seat. Before she sat down, she cupped Clancy's face gently in her hands and kissed her. "Thank you."

"You're welcome." Clancy's shy smile did curious things to Jude's simmering desire. It made her imagine things they could be doing together, away from all this.

"We're so getting a cat," Inez muttered and squealed when Clancy poked her in her side again.

"Time to get serious." Clancy reached for a notepad. "Are you okay if we record this too? We'll stop anytime you feel uncomfortable. Or, if you'd rather talk to the detective in charge of this investigation, I can get her involved."

"I'd rather just talk to you," Jude said, trusting Clancy more than some unknown detective.

Clancy nodded for Inez to start the recording.

Clancy dutifully logged the interview with the date and time. "This is my interview with Jude Patterson. Jude, what can you tell us about Mia Murray?"

Chapter Twelve

It was weird talking to someone who wanted to hear what Jude had to say. She told Clancy how long she'd known Mia, what a friend she'd become. She hoped she built a true picture of the woman who had been a delight to be around. Jude missed her desperately.

"You say she was active on a dating app. Did she ever introduce you to any of the men she met?" Clancy asked.

"No. Some barely lasted beyond the first date. She'd been burned so bad from her divorce but she still chased that white picket fence dream of hers. I asked her one time why she kept looking for princes when the app seemed to be full of nothing but frogs."

"What did she say?"

Jude remembered the conversation as if it had been yesterday. They'd sat in Mia's apartment and Mia had been rattling on about the date she was going on. She was giddy with excitement over the evening they had planned. Jude had been less than enthusiastic.

"What do you know about this guy? You've only conversed over text. Wouldn't it be better if you drove yourself to the restaurant? That way you can always bail if he's not the thirty-five-year-old blond athletic type in his profile and instead is a balding sixty-year-old using his son's picture."

"Jude, chill out. You can't expect to find love if you don't put yourself out there."

"But 'out there' isn't safe, Mia. We've all heard the horror stories of dates gone wrong."

"Isn't life all about taking risks? You dove under the sea every day in your job. What if your equipment had failed? What if you'd gotten stuck under a girder and no one could help get you free? What if you simply ran out of air? We all take risks. Some can end in catastrophe. Some disappoint you and you chalk it up as a bad experience. You learn from it. You move on and try again. *You* know from experience that you can't tread water indefinitely."

Jude came back to the present and shook her head. "She excused every damn one of them. The one who ordered a huge meal for himself then bailed when the bill arrived. The one who brought his three kids along because his ex-wife hated him dating, and she sabotaged his trying. She found every loser out there but kept on swiping right. But this last one, he was one she strangely kept quiet about."

"Did you get a name?"

"I don't remember her ever saying it. I have to be honest, the guys all started to blur one into another and I've never been one with much interest in talking about boys." She shared a look of understanding with Clancy. "But he lasted longer than the others."

"Was she usually this secretive about the men?"

"No, but she didn't give me a blow-by-blow breakdown on each date either so I never paid attention to it...until she went missing. I spoke to a woman Mia had worked with. The consensus of the women in the office was they all figured he was a married man. They thought that's why Mia was more cautious, not revealing so much."

"What do you think?"

"I don't think she'd date a married man. She'd been cheated on repeatedly by the scumbag she'd been married to. She wouldn't do that to another woman."

"Could she have met him *at* the hospital instead?" Clancy checked her notes. "She worked in administration, right?"

Jude shrugged. "I guess she could have met him there. Working in administration meant she was a port of call for nearly everyone employed there." Jude sighed. "She loved that job. She was a people person."

"Could she have just up and left? Would meeting her Mr. Right have been enough of an excuse for her to leave?"

Jude shook her head. "She would never have left Smokey Joe. If she had come home, packed everything into her car, and fled into the night she still would have taken her cat." Jude looked through to where he was fast asleep. "He was, *is*, the most important man in her life."

"That last night, Mia drove her own car to work and to the date, right?"

Jude nodded. "The police can't find her car anywhere. That vanished too."

Clancy looked at the screen Inez was typing on. Jude watched her intently. Clancy's face didn't give anything away but Jude knew something was wrong.

"What is it?" Jude had to know.

"I need to remind you that the cases I'm working on are not to be discussed outside of this room. The public and the press are unaware of what has been found so far. Not even the families have the full details as it's an ongoing investigation."

"I've told you; I won't betray your confidence." Jude pressed her palms down onto her thighs to stop her legs from shaking at the seriousness in Clancy's tone.

Inez moved so that Jude could see a screen. She counted the photos displayed on it. Eight women who had all posed for the camera in happier times were now lined up in two somber rows.

Jude had a horrible feeling Mia was going to join that list. And, judging by the look on Clancy's face, she knew it too.

"Are these the women you're looking for in the Missouri River?" Jude looked at each photo. None of them resembled Mia or each other.

"These are the women I have *found* so far." Clancy pointed to each picture. "These two in North Dakota. These two, South Dakota." She pointed to two more women and then included Kelly Hu. "All in Iowa."

Jude stared at Kelly's picture. "Kelly had a new job in Iowa. She and Mia kept in touch throughout the move, but then Kelly just stopped all contact."

"She wasn't in Iowa long," Clancy said. The ominous double meaning came through loud and clear. "There were still boxes in her apartment that hadn't been unpacked."

Before Jude could begin to process that, Clancy pointed to the last picture.

"I found Joanna in Kansas just a few weeks ago."

"And now you're in Missouri and you think that Mia might be like these women?" Jude could feel an intense pain building up with increasing pressure behind her eyes. She rubbed at her forehead briskly; she didn't have time for a stress migraine.

"I'm just following the river until its end. We have no idea how many more there are. The state police forces never linked these cases together. Why would they? But Detective Chandler's unit picked up on it because they have folks who specifically look for patterns, however random. They realized there was a number of women missing under the same type of circumstances. From what you've told us, and what Inez managed to look into, she fits the profile," Clancy said.

"Do you have any idea who's doing it? Who's killing them and dumping them?" Jude couldn't wrap her head around the fact one of Mia's dating app guys could be a serial killer. That was the stuff of horror stories on the nightly news, not in Kansas City. And it certainly couldn't happen to Mia who was the kindest woman Jude had ever met.

"We don't have a firm fix on the guy yet. We have numerous descriptions being investigated so it's either a group or he's some sort of chameleon. No one description is ever the same. But all these women worked in hospitals, they all used a dating app, they all drove their own cars that last day, and all of them disappeared into thin air."

"Until *you* found them," Jude said.

"Until I found them in their cars, sunk in the Missouri River, all along its run."

"Did you really just start at the Rocky Mountains and work your way down to Missouri? Searching *all* that water?" Jude couldn't believe it. It seemed such a huge undertaking for a two-woman, one-man team.

"It's what we do. It's been weeks of intense searching. It's paid off. We have eight women found so far," Clancy said.

"How did you know they'd be there?" Jude was curious and wanted to know everything but her eyes were starting to blur. An all too familiar black dot appeared in one eye, followed by a colorful shimmer that spun like a crystal sun catcher. Her eyesight was immediately affected; her right eye saw nothing but flashing rainbows. A migraine was imminent. Jude couldn't believe her stupid luck.

"Initially, we had no idea they'd be there. Searches led by the North Dakota police found nothing. When a pattern started to emerge as more women started to disappear, some higher-ups in a special unit in Chicago asked me to do *my* search of the river. They already had an intensive search going on land. They were hedging their bets." Clancy leaned forward a little in her chair. "Hey, are you okay? Do you need us to stop?"

Jude rubbed at her temples but shook her head. "No, I'm fine. It's just a lot to take in. I mean, Mia has been missing for over a month, the police have constantly brushed me off because there's nothing to prove foul play, and yet you're here thinking she's the next victim to add to your photo lineup."

"She fits all the criteria of the profile that has been generated for the case," Inez said, opening a tiny fridge by her feet, and passing Jude a cold bottle of water. "Drink this. You've gone really pale."

Jude twisted the top off and sipped at the water carefully. She was starting to feel nauseous as the migraine started to sink its claws into her brain.

"How long have you suffered with migraines?" Inez asked knowledgably as she got up and headed into the kitchen.

"I get them when I'm stressed, which thankfully, isn't often. I think all this," Jude gestured to the screens, "might have been a trigger."

"It came on fast," Clancy said, getting up to guide Jude into the living room to sit on the settee. "Mine do the same. Zero to sixty and I'm down for the count." She carefully lifted a napping Smokey Joe off the seat first, while still in his bed, to make Jude more comfortable. She placed him on the floor without him stirring once.

Inez handed Jude a white pill. Jude squinted at it, noticing it wasn't a store-bought brand. "What is it?"

"We have a herbalist back home. This remedy always helps Clancy when she gets migraines. I'm hoping it works its magic with you." Inez urged Jude to take it.

Clancy sat down beside Jude, watching while she took the pill and washed it down with some more water.

"I can't believe this is happening right now. God, my timing sucks. I still have questions." Jude leaned her head gingerly against the back of the settee and closed her eyes.

"It can't be easy, hearing your neighbor might be part of a serial killer's spree. I really hope we're wrong on that." Clancy touched Jude's cheek. "Do you want to go lie down on my bed?"

Jude smiled, despite herself. "Not now, sweetheart, I have a headache." She heard Clancy chuckle and Inez stifling a giggle.

"Do you want to just spread out on the settee instead and try to rest? You can put your head on my lap, if you want." Clancy put her lips close to Jude's ear and whispered," I know you're not adverse to a bit of snuggling."

Jude cracked open an eye to see Clancy staring at her intensely. She was totally serious. Jude really wanted to sleep the migraine away but she didn't want to be alone. Not after what she'd just learned from Clancy. "That sounds nice," Jude said, "but don't you have better things to do today? You've already halted the search because of me."

"I'm more than happy to spend quality time with you, helping you crush your migraine. Let me just go grab my iPad and we'll get you comfy." Clancy disappeared back into the office area. Inez knelt on the floor beside Jude.

"I wish we were back home. Uncle Julius is a Reiki healer. He'd be able to ease some of your stress."

Jude looked at her. "I think finding Mia would alleviate my stress more."

Inez nodded. "That's Clancy's area of expertise. We can't always promise a happy ending, but we do provide closure. It's not perfect but it's a place to start over from."

Clancy came back with her iPad and a can of Coke. She settled on the settee and patted her lap for Jude. "I had the settee sized so that I could stretch out and fall asleep in front of the TV. It's long enough for you too, Big Bird."

Jude frowned at her as much as she could with her aching head. "That name is not sticking." She kicked off her Nikes and lay down facing Clancy's stomach. She laid her forehead against the soft warmth. "I'll be okay in a while. That tablet is already working." She closed her eyes and breathed in Clancy's distinctive scent. She nuzzled her face into Clancy's belly, willing the warmth to soothe her and for her racing thoughts to dissipate. She gave no thought to Inez watching her. All she focused on was the grounding presence of Clancy.

The photos of the dead women lingered in her mind, ruining any chance she had of trying to relax. Unbidden, a tear leaked from Jude's eye.

Clancy's hand rested on Jude's hair. "It's okay. I'm here." She gently ran her fingers through it. "You're safe. Find your peace." The repetitive touch eventually lulled Jude into a dreamless sleep.

The dark waters of the Missouri River carried Clancy along in its watery embrace. She was untethered, adrift, and directed by the water as it took her deeper and deeper. She couldn't see very clearly and cried out in pain as she slammed a hip off something solid in her way. She grabbed onto it, feeling her way along it. It was a car. She instinctively pulled herself along to reach the driver's side window. It was miraculously clear. Compelled, she peered inside.

Maddie Cooke, the first of the missing women found, stared back at Clancy with sightless eyes. Her skin was crumbling away in slow motion, looking like ashes blown on a breeze. It revealed her skull, smashed into pieces, exposing what was left of her battered and bloody brain. Glass fragments lay embedded deep in her head. Only the broken brandy bottle's neck was left intact. It lay discarded on the seat beside her.

Maddie's eyes came alive and she looked straight at Clancy.

"Help me."

Clancy lifted a hand to reach out to her, but she was ripped from the car and flung farther down the river. She struggled against its pull and smacked her back off another car. She scrambled to get a hold on the car's frame, her gloveless fingers were cut open on its sharp edges and bled into the water. She was turned upside down to look through the window of the car that had flipped in the water and was resting on its roof.

Savannah Rankin sat inside. Handcuffs dug into her wrists while her hands were cuffed to the steering wheel. A plastic bag covered her head. Black duct tape was messily wrapped around both it and her neck, sealing the bag tight. Clancy watched her panic, frantically struggling to breathe, sucking the plastic into her mouth with every breath. Water filled the interior of the car as it had sunk. Savannah was fighting against no air in the bag, and drowning at the same time. She fought to free her hands, rubbing her wrists raw on the metal cuffs. There was no escape. The white bag turned translucent and Clancy watched Savannah's chest hitch and stall as her oxygen ran out and she suffocated. Her face purple, her mouth wide open. She was frozen in that moment of catching her last breath.

She looked at Clancy.

"Find him."

Clancy let the water yank her away again. She welcomed the slam of another car into her legs and she quickly searched for the window. Bethany Needham sat inside, smoldering from the immolation she'd suffered. Any skin she had left was charred to a crisp. The fire had burned half her face away, right down to the bone. What remained was a terrible mask, a Harvey Dent visage, a cruel end to such a pretty woman. The inside of the car was partially burned out. Clancy could see where Bethany had been tied to the driver's seat by a chain that resembled a motorcycle lock. Chained, set on fire, and pushed into the river.

Bethany looked at Clancy with her one remaining eye.

"Help us."

The river pulled Clancy in another direction. She knew who was next. She grabbed onto the small car and plunged deeper to find Jennifer Slate in her watery resting place. Jennifer, the youngest victim, had been stabbed to death. She lay across the car seats, looking like she was just sleeping. Her flowery dress, once white with yellow blooms, was blood soaked and rigid. The actual count of the knife wounds was inconclusive. The killer had stabbed her so many times he had obliterated the initial stab wounds. A death by a thousand cuts. The knives he had used were left embedded in her, stabbed right through to her bones. He'd used an entire knife block and left his butchery for all to see. She'd been found within days with enough flesh still intact that the coroner had no doubt what she'd suffered through.

Jennifer lifted her head. One side of her face was marred by a cruel game of tic-tac-toe carved into her cheek.

"He's still out there."

Clancy knew Jennifer had gone into the light, but seeing her again twisted Clancy's insides into painful knots. She was always too late. Too late to save them.

Clancy struggled against the river's hold. She was aware now that she was asleep and dreaming. She was being forced to relive the nightmare of each find. She pushed herself off the car, trying to swim up and away. If she could just reach the surface, then maybe she would wake.

The river refused to let her go. It roughly pulled her back down and pushed her forward. She had to surrender to the river's hold as it dragged her defeated body along.

The slam of a truck's grill into her chest made Clancy cry out in pain. She clutched at her ribs as the agony rolled through her. She pulled herself up the hood of the vehicle and peered through the windshield. Inside sat Roseanne Evans. She was the oldest of the women found so far. She looked so serene sitting in the truck. Her clothing was untouched, she had no visible bruising. She stared out at Clancy and smiled. Clancy moved closer until she could see fully inside. Roseanne beckoned her closer, with hands stained with blood. Her skirt had been raised and an ugly, ragged wound was clearly visible. Roseanne's legs were glued to the leather seat. She'd had no way to escape once the killer had stabbed her in her femoral artery with a screwdriver. Clancy knew he had sat in the truck with Roseanne, watching her try desperately to stop the flow of blood. Roseanne had told her how he'd studied her as she sat there, dying, immobile as a bug pinned to a board. He'd watched the blood pool down at her feet while ignoring her begging and pleading for her life. He'd waited until she was starting to fall unconscious from the blood loss then he pushed the vehicle into the water.

Roseanne's blood washed away as the river poured through the truck's windows and drowned her in her seat.

Clancy could still hear her prayers for her loved ones as she expired.

"Stop him."

Clancy swam with the current. Eager to get to the next car, desperate for the dream to end. She wanted to wake up, to be out of the water. She didn't want to see any more. She remembered all too well seeing each death in their vivid, ghoulish, reconstructions. She didn't need to keep seeing it playing out in her dreams.

Kelly Hu's car roof was crushed and battered. The car was near a busy pier and every large boat that docked there had scratched the roof and caved it in as their hulls rested on top of the car. The driver's side window had been shattered by the pressure from above. Kelly's body had been ejected out of the car window but was stuck, half in, half out. Her body was pulled by the ebb and flow of the river. She looked like she was waving, calling for help that would be too late to save her. Clancy swam up to where Kelly's body swayed in the river's embrace. Clancy's presence frightened the fish away from their feasting on dead flesh. Kelly's head rolled to one side, exposing the length of cord wrapped around her neck that had strangled her to death. She stared at Clancy with bloodshot eyes.

"Avenge us."

Clancy nodded at her and repeated the promise she made to all those she found. *"You are going home, you are free now, and justice will be served upon the evildoer."* Clancy knew, whether in this life, or the afterlife, the one who had killed these women would receive judgment. He was eight women down. Clancy didn't want to have to find more bearing his particular brand of evil.

Clancy couldn't miss the next car she was drawn to. The scant few feet of water above it let the sunlight shine upon its roof, glinting off the metal. She moved to the back of the car, remembering where Sally Ferrer had been found. The trunk popped open as Clancy drew near. Sally lay inside in a fetal position, bound, and gagged. She'd been deliberately left in a stretch of the river that wasn't very deep. The car was clearly visible if you knew where to look. Only Clancy had searched there. She wondered if the killer came back to visit the site often, to get his rocks off knowing that Sally was so close to the surface yet so far away from her family. The DDU believed this murder was a message. He was taunting them that he could bury his victims in the depths or leave them just a few feet under and he'd still never be caught. Sally was the only one whose car hadn't immediately been dumped. He'd kept her somewhere, waiting for her to be near death from starvation, before he got rid of her and her car. He never killed the same way twice. He had no pattern, except to dispose of them in the Missouri River.

Sally's dull eyes in her gaunt, skeletal face cried tears made from the river's water that had finally, mercifully, drowned her.

"Find her."

Joanna Drysdale was waiting beside her car when Clancy finally swam by. Clancy groaned. This was no run-of-the-mill nightmare like she usually suffered with. If Joanna was there, *outside* of her car, then this was a prophetic vision and Clancy hated it when she got those.

"You're about to be betrayed."

"By who?" Clancy swam in place beside Joanna. She couldn't help but notice how Joanna was in her radiance, while the others had been presented in their deaths or the aftermath.

Joanna shrugged. *"I'm only to give you the warning."*

"Next time, tell the Powers That Be to save me the nightmare of victims past and cut straight to the chase."

"You still tread these waters, Clancy. In many ways, you're as trapped in the deep as we were."

Clancy's patience snapped. "That's enough. I am not being head shrunk in my dreams. You've delivered your message wrapped in the bodies of women I know full well have seen the light. Now let me wake up." Clancy took off to reach the water's surface. She could see the sunlight and pushed herself harder to leave the dead and dying in the river. She needed to wake up, but she could hear their voices calling after her. As one voice, they repeated their message.

"Find her."

Their voices never stopped; the words rang in Clancy's head like a million bells tolling out a dire warning. She swam until her lungs began to burst in her exertion. Suddenly, she felt hands grasp at her legs, threatening to pull her back down. She looked but nothing was there. Clancy panicked. She kicked out wildly and tried to break loose. She could see the surface just out of her reach. The voices grew louder as she was dragged back down and Clancy wished she could put her hands to her ears to drown them out. She screamed into her mask as, for every stroke she swam up, she was pulled down three.

She remembered another warning she'd received recently.

"Be careful in those waters, Clancy. Not only the dead swim there."

She broke free and swam as hard as she could. "Not today, you fuckers, not today." Clancy screamed inside her mask as she exerted every ounce of energy she had left into getting away.

She finally surfaced right beside a pier. Gasping for air, she tried to gather her senses as she clung to a wooden post. Something dripped onto her face mask. Blood trickled down the front, right before her eyes. Clancy looked up and reared back in shock as a face appeared with a thud over the side of the wooden decking. The woman's sightless eyes looked straight at her. Blood continued to drip drip drip onto Clancy's facemask.

Clancy knew that face. Jude had given them a photo of her.

Mia Murray suddenly opened her mouth and a hundred voices poured out from behind her bloody lips.

"FIND HER. FIND HER. FIND HER!"

CHAPTER THIRTEEN

Jude was pulled out of a deep sleep by Clancy sitting bolt upright in the bed. She was struggling to breathe and looked like she was trying to push something away.

"Hey, hey, Clancy, wake up." Jude sat up and clutched at Clancy's shoulders. She didn't shake her, instead she held her firmly and kept talking to her. "Wake up, Clancy. Come on, babe, wake up." She watched as Clancy's face shifted from whatever nightmare she was experiencing to realizing she was awake.

"Fuck me," Clancy groaned, sticking her face in her hands. She shuddered with every breath she took in.

Jude stroked the back of her neck for comfort. "I've had better invitations, but I'd rather wait until you're more awake before I test out your RV bed springs."

Clancy rubbed at her face. Her question was muffled into her hands. "Did I scream?"

Jude shook her head. "No, but you sat up like Dracula rising from the crypt so it was a little freaky. Are you okay?"

Clancy nodded and looked at Jude with a wry expression. "I suffer sometimes with nightmares. Finding people dead in their cars doesn't always give me dreams filled with flower fields and pretty ponies."

Jude could see the lingering horror of whatever Clancy had dreamt still haunting her. She lay back down and drew Clancy down with her. Clancy spread herself across Jude's chest and under her chin. Jude recognized it as Clancy's favorite spot. They were roughly the same height, but when Jude held her, Clancy immediately cuddled in. Jude loved that. None of her previous lovers had loved to cuddle and be cuddled. She laid a kiss on Clancy's head.

"You like me holding you tight. Why is that?" Jude asked, her voice quiet in the still of the night.

"It makes me feel safe." Clancy rubbed her cheek against Jude's flesh. "I could give you a long rambling sob story about my parents never showing me enough affection, but who needs to hear that? I love that you're so fucking strong that you make me feel protected when I'm in your arms. That I can just relax and enjoy the closeness." She rubbed her nose into Jude's neck. "And your scent drives me crazy." Clancy pressed a kiss on Jude's pulse point. "*You* drive me crazy."

"In a good way, I hope." Jude loved how her body reacted to Clancy's. She was already thrumming with desire.

"In a way I've never felt before. I'm a fuck and go kind of gal, but you keep making me want to stay for more." Clancy shifted to look up at Jude. "And not just for sex, though that is a huge benefit because you're so fucking sexy."

Jude smiled and basked in her praise.

"But I really *like* you too. I like learning new things about you, like when I watch you eat. It's cute how you plan out what mouthful you're going to have next." Clancy snuggled back down. Jude could feel her smile against the thin T-shirt Clancy had loaned her to wear to bed.

"Where you like to have multiple plates so you can graze off every one of them."

Jude thought back to earlier that evening when she'd finally woken up from her nap. Clancy had ordered in takeout and Jude had been amazed by how many different boxes of Chinese food arrived. Clancy had worked her way through them all, finding which ones she liked best, which ones she could pass on, yet still making sure everyone else had plenty to eat too. Jude had even been promised leftovers to take home with her.

"My folks used withholding food as a punishment. I promised myself when I got older, I'd never go hungry again."

Jude noticed that both times Clancy had mentioned her parents it featured them depriving her of something. Jude hated them with a passion already.

"My mother will love you. I grew up on a farm where food was homegrown and plentiful. We didn't leave the table until we'd had to undo the top button of our pants."

Clancy ran a hand over Jude's shoulder and down her arm. "So that's how you got so big and strong." She traced a lazy pattern down Jude's skin. "You'd take me home to meet your mother?"

Jude nodded. "My dad too. They still run the farm, with my brother's help now. My mom does a cherry pie you'd die for." Jude reached down to brush Clancy's hair back from her face. "I know you have a wicked sweet tooth. No one else I know would make an ice cream run for Dairy Queen after eating their fill of Chinese." She looked Clancy up and down. "Where do you put it all?"

"It's burned off lifting that damn boat on and off its trailer." Clancy flexed her arm muscles. "And there's always room for ice cream." She shifted to lie at Jude's side. Clancy began trailing her fingers over her tattoo sleeve. "Tell me the story behind this gorgeous work of art."

Jude shifted so that Clancy could see it all. "As a kid I wanted off that damn farm so bad. I wanted to see the world and I wanted to dive in every ocean. So, I joined the navy and did both. On shore leave one time I found a tattoo shop and spent my week off in it. I wanted something that depicted my love for the sea. The guy there drew this up for me, saying a lighthouse is the staunch protector against anything the sea could throw at it, including sea monsters. I loved the symbolism. And it's such a badass tattoo."

"You're the lighthouse," Clancy said, her voice so soft Jude could barely hear her. "My lighthouse. In the midst of my storms, when I'm washed out to sea, you'll protect me." Clancy grimaced, realizing she'd spoken aloud. She grinned sheepishly and promptly kissed Jude to distract her. "And yes, it's totally a badass tattoo on a badass butch."

Jude wasn't sure what Clancy had been referring to about her protecting her, but she accepted the kiss with relish and pushed the words aside to ponder over later. She let her own curiosity run and traced her fingers over the Celtic knot around Clancy's wrist. As she paid more attention to it, Jude felt a distinct ridge in Clancy's skin. It was across her wrist, marking a line over her veins.

"What's the story with the rainbow knot?"

Clancy stared down at her wrist and, for a moment, Jude wasn't sure she was going to answer.

"It's the symbol of rebirth. I got it after I nearly drowned. You know, to celebrate my being spit out from the water, born again." Clancy's words were flippant and her attention fixed anywhere but on Jude.

"You said your grandmother saved you."

Clancy looked up at her in surprise. "You remembered that?"

"I do listen when you talk, Clancy. I want to know everything about you."

Clancy ducked her head again. "Yeah, well, not everything about me is worth knowing."

"Try me." Jude ran her finger across Clancy's wrist. The scar was unmistakable now. She deliberately let Clancy know she was aware of it hidden under the ink. "I felt this before, on our first night together. I had you flat on your back, your hands pinned in mine, as I tribbed you into submission." She deliberately rubbed her finger back and forth over the scar.

"I did not submit," Clancy grumbled.

"Yes, you did. All over me as I recall." Jude enjoyed seeing the fierce blush that colored Clancy's face as Jude teased her. She tapped Clancy's wrist gently. "Can you tell me about it?"

Clancy took a deep breath. "When I was fourteen, my parents kicked me out of their house because I was gay. There was other stuff too, but I was a good kid, and didn't deserve what they did. I had nowhere to go, I didn't exactly make friends easily so had no buddy whose doorstep I could turn up on. It had been a real crappy week. I'd been beaten for kissing a girl, thanks to some nosy neighbor ratting me out. I was kicked out with only the clothes on my back, and it was the middle of winter. I had no idea what to do so I just walked. I eventually found myself by a lake, sitting on a rock, listening to the voices of my parents playing on repeat in my head telling me to get out, that I was no daughter of theirs because I was a freak, and I would be better off dead."

Jude linked her fingers through Clancy's and squeezed. She felt Clancy squeeze back.

"So, I did what any kid would do in that stress-filled situation. I found a piece of glass." Clancy hesitated at the memory but continued. "I tentatively cut my wrist and watched it bleed, then cut it deeper but that really fucking hurt." She smiled self-depreciatingly. "Stupid kid. So, I decided to walk into the lake."

"Oh, Clancy." Jude's heart wept for the child she had been.

"It's okay, it gets better. Spoiler alert; I got a happy ending." Clancy ran her finger over the pattern of her tattoo. "The abridged version is, I went in the water, I nearly drowned, my grandmother got me out but couldn't stick around or take me with her." She looked at Jude briefly. "That's a whole other story. Anyway, I'm crawling out of the water, coughing up most of it and cursing my fate, when a young woman comes along, pregnant as heck, and helps me back to drier ground." Clancy finally smiled. "Wendy 'Rainbow' Wilson, my light and savior."

Jude smiled. "Inez's mother."

"Yes. She didn't know me from Adam, but she gathered me up, bundled me into her car, and drove me back to her home. I had no thought about Stranger Danger, I was past caring by that point. She shoved me in the shower, bundled me up in warm clothes, and tended my wounds. She fed me, got my story out of me, and then left me to sleep on the settee in front of a real fire. The next day the whole of the Wiccan commune adopted me as their own and I never went home again. My folks never listed me as missing. I was considered a runaway. I literally fell off the face of the planet and it felt so good."

"A Wiccan commune?"

"Yeah, a tight little community on a huge plot of land where everything was self-sufficient, unless someone wanted Cheetos, then I was usually the designated gopher to visit the local store."

"You lived there?" Jude was fascinated and was trying to picture what it would look like.

"I still do. They built me a house when I turned eighteen because I couldn't live with Rainbow forever. Inez was a super cute kid though and I'd helped Rainbow out as best as a baby butch could do with zero knowledge of babies. *That* was a learning experience."

"And the tattoo?"

"One of the girls offered to ink me to hide the ugly scar I'd defaced myself with when trying to slit my wrist. Rainbow and I pored over the different designs and she explained to me the meaning of the Celtic knot. The rainbow was done for her, but also for gay pride, which I was allowed to have there among my new family."

"You live on a Wiccan commune." Jude was amused by the thought.

"Yeah. I get alternative medication for all that ails me and can recommend a crystal should you need to align your chakras."

"I think you can align my chakras all by yourself." Jude tugged Clancy down on top of her. She deliberately kissed Clancy's wrist where the scar was. "I'm forever grateful you're here with me." She kissed Clancy's palm. "I'm forever in debt to Rainbow and Inez for giving you a true family." She kissed Clancy's forehead. "And I'd love to be your lighthouse." She pulled back and looked into Clancy's eyes. "And thank you for sharing your alternative medication because it cleared my headache. Thank you for feeding me, then inviting my cat and I to a sleepover. I know that's not really your thing."

Jude could hardly believe that they'd literally just met but were already fitting together in each other's lives so easily. It wasn't wise. Jude was falling for this handsome butch with the playful eyes, but Clancy wasn't staying and neither of them did forever.

But forever was starting to sound awfully nice.

"Well, I think Smokey Joe is sleeping with Inez," Clancy said.

"You need to get that girl a cat."

Clancy sighed. "Her mom already has asked for the pick of the latest litter for her when we go home. One of the ragdoll cats is knocked up. He or she will be a fluffy little furball."

Jude's heart sank a little at the thought of Clancy leaving. She couldn't afford to think about that yet. She also couldn't allow herself to think about what she'd learned today. About Mia's possible fate.

About all the others before her. About Clancy diving to find them and suffering nightmares at what she uncovered.

"How much can Inez hear when you're in here?" Jude began pressing kisses down Clancy's jawline while pushing aside the sheets to reveal them dressed modestly in boxer shorts and T-shirts.

"The bathroom is between us. It's enough of a sound barrier. But we can't be too loud or your dang cat will come to investigate."

"He looked so cute, asleep beside you that morning." Jude smiled at the memory of their last time together.

"I'd rather you be in my arms." Clancy pushed Jude back against the mattress and straddled her.

Jude couldn't get her fill of looking at Clancy. Her wild hair, her gorgeous smile. She was making Jude yearn for things she hadn't wanted in years. She wanted forever with Clancy. But if that wasn't how this would end, then she'd settle for every minute she could grab. "I need to forget everything for now. I need you to fuck me senseless so that all I touch, taste, feel, is *you*."

Clancy's smile was wicked and Jude's heart clenched at the promise in her eyes.

"Damn, and here I was preparing to do all that Friday night when I bury myself deep inside you. I don't dare to pack in the RV..."

"If the RV is rockin'..." Jude grinned at her.

"Then our boots are definitely knockin'!" Clancy laughed and whipped her T-shirt over her head.

Jude's mouth began to water.

"Oh no, baby," Clancy tossed the shirt aside. "You're not touching any of this." She leaned forward, her breasts barely touching Jude's. "How about I edge you to within an inch of your life? But you need to be *my* good boi and not make a sound." Clancy ran her tongue over Jude's lips and teased a little inside. "Do you think you can do that? Because, if not, I might have to *make* you."

Jude was torn between knowing they needed to be quiet but wanting to know what Clancy would do if she *wasn't*.

Clancy read it on her face. "Oh, I can see I'm going to have my work cut out for me with you tonight." She caught Jude's bottom lip between her teeth and bit down gently.

Jude let out a whine, needing more. Clancy kissed her, roughly swallowing any noises Jude made.

"Remember, no touching," Clancy admonished her. "Or I'll leave you hanging." She pulled her shorts off and climbed back on the bed, deliberately straddling Jude's head.

Jude groaned as Clancy began to touch herself above her. Jude forced herself not to move a muscle, even though she wanted desperately to stick her face between Clancy's legs and lick her out. Instead, she settled back to see just how much fun could be had in an RV.

Jude had no idea how long Clancy had been teasing her. She'd lost track of time, languishing in the attention Clancy was lavishing on her. Jude was used to taking charge, most of her lovers expected it. But receiving Clancy's deliberate touch was something Jude would gladly give up her need for control for.

Her stomach was tight, the muscles aching from how many times Clancy had teased her clit to the point of coming, only to pull back and calm her back down again. Clancy centered all her attention on Jude's clit, licking it, sucking it, the softest of bites to ramp Jude's need up to a fever pitch, only to stop before Jude could climax. Jude could feel her legs shaking uncontrollably, spread wide for Clancy's broad shoulders to press between. Her head was buried between Jude's thighs and Jude had already been admonished for daring to put her hands in Clancy's hair to try to guide her where she was needed the most. Jude now had her hands trapped under her butt. It pulled on her shoulders but she welcomed that extra agony. She was at Clancy's mercy, willingly.

"I forgot," Clancy said, pulling back just enough that Jude could still feel her breath on her nether lips. "I should have asked if you had a safe word."

Jude snorted then groaned as Clancy ran her tongue around her entrance, catching her desire and transferring it back up to coat Jude's clit. Jude shuddered as the pleasure/pain of being edged to the point of insanity ramped up again.

"Kraken," Jude said, gasping for air. She felt Clancy chuckle against her flesh.

"Be sure to use it if you want me to stop."

Jude glared down at her. "You'd better *not* stop."

"You about ready to come?" Clancy teased Jude's aching clit with the tip of her nose, rubbing the already raw and tender nub.

"I would like to but I'm afraid I'll shatter into a million pieces," Jude admitted, her breath shaking as everything concentrated on the energy Clancy was building up on her sensitive clit.

"Don't worry, baby, I'll put you back together again." Clancy raised her head and looked up at Jude. "You're so beautiful like this, do you know that?" She ran her fingers over Jude's hot flesh. "You're so wet, you're shaking, your clit is straining from under its hood and I want to shatter you. But you're going to have to be quiet."

Jude had no idea if she could be now. Every touch, taste, and tease Clancy had bestowed on her had worked her to a fever pitch and she had no idea what was going to happen when Clancy finished her. No one else had ever gotten her this turned on.

"I'm not sure if I can," Jude said.

Clancy moved and Jude groaned at the loss.

"It's okay, I'm just repositioning." Clancy's voice soothed her.

Jude looked down to find Clancy on her knees, one hand now working Jude feverishly between her legs and the other she ran up Jude's chest, roughly rubbing over her nipples and then resting for a moment on her throat.

Clancy obviously felt Jude's breath hitch. "Sorry, lover, but I'm not into autoerotic asphyxiation."

Jude nodded roughly in relief. "Me neither."

Clancy gently covered Jude's mouth with her hand. "But I am going to stifle your screams."

Jude tried desperately to keep her eyes open, to watch Clancy's face as she rubbed Jude's clit hard between her fingers and, this time, had no intention of stopping. Jude's whimpers were muffled by Clancy's wet hand. Jude could taste herself on her fingers. The pressure was building inside her, Jude bucked and writhed while Clancy watched her with such bright eyes. She saw Clancy's excitement, loved that she was enjoying every minute as much as Jude. She also loved the look of determination that Clancy wore to bring Jude to an earth-shattering climax.

Jude's muscles clenched tight in her stomach, her back bowing under the pressure as she climaxed. Her yell was barely contained by the pressure of Clancy's hand. Jude jerked and squeezed her eyes shut at every thumping pulse from the contractions inside her. It hurt, but it was such a delicious agony. She felt Clancy's fingers capturing Jude's wetness from her swollen flesh. Jude groaned some more, watching Clancy licking it off her fingertips like a delicacy. She jolted with another moan when Clancy ran a finger inside her sensitive, pulsing opening, gathering more of her spilling juices. Clancy moved up the bed to prop herself up at Jude's side. She wiped her sticky fingers all over Jude's breasts and began to lick it all off again, teasing Jude's nipples as she feasted.

Jude didn't have the energy to moan anymore. She was blissed out, wrecked, fucked raw.

"You okay there, Jude?" Clancy asked, squeezing Jude's nipple between two fingers before sucking it back between her lips.

Jude barely managed to give her a thumbs up. Clancy laughed at her and shifted again on the bed. This time she lay back and pulled Jude's boneless body over her own to cuddle. Jude snuggled in close, enjoying the shift in their usual positions. Clancy stroked her hair and Jude relaxed completely. She became aware a few tears had escaped only when Clancy gently wiped at her cheek.

"Did I hurt you?" Clancy asked in a whisper.

"In all the best ways," Jude said.

"Happy tears then?"

"Yes." Jude paused a moment then admitted quietly, "And maybe a release." She buried her face into Clancy's neck. "I don't want my friend to be another face on your photo board, Clancy."

Clancy pulled Jude closer. "Have you cried for your friend since she disappeared?"

Jude shook her head. "Big girls don't cry. You know that."

"You can cry with me. I'll hold you close and no one need ever know. I've got you. I'll keep you safe. You can cry for her, Jude."

For a moment, Jude fought over the embarrassment of giving in to her emotions. It was stupid, she knew that. But for Mia the tears began to come. Clancy just held her without a word, without making banal promises she couldn't keep of how everything would be okay. Jude knew it wasn't going to be. But maybe, with Clancy beside her, she could face whatever outcome she was going to have to deal with. For now, she just wanted to lie in her lover's arms, breathe in her scent, and let Clancy love her.

The outside world would intrude soon enough. Jude just wanted this moment of peace to tuck away and keep safe for herself and her sanity.

CHAPTER FOURTEEN

Clancy was trying not to wish away the week until Friday. She hadn't seen Jude in a couple of days, though they'd still texted and FaceTimed. Clancy knew what she was doing was way out of her character, but Jude was different. Clancy was different *with* Jude.

She steered the boat farther along the river. The sonar wasn't showing anything worth inspecting and Clancy was about to call it a day. It was hot, she was tired, and the waters were clear. She turned the boat around to head back to the jetty.

"Uhm, Clancy? We appear to have a problem here." Inez sounded frustrated over the radio.

"What's up, kid?" Clancy picked up speed to get back to the dock.

"There appears to be a crowd congregating here. I've had a news crew knock on the RV's door. I spoke to them through the intercom. They want to know who we're looking for. I recited our salvage line, but they've heard your boat engine and are now heading to the river. Just giving you a heads up that you have an audience."

"What the fuck?" Clancy saw red. "Get the police down here immediately to disperse the looky-loos and then contact Chandler. We're not supposed to be interrupted here." Clancy turned off her mic and lost her temper. "Goddamn fuck it all to hell!" She switched the mic back on so as not to worry Inez. "I'm heading back."

❖

Clancy was met by a crowd of people and a few news cameras with reporters very eager to get a few words with her. Clancy deliberately tied her boat on the other side of the pier out of their sight. It didn't pay to have them see all the equipment she employed.

"Wow, I didn't expect this amount of excitement for someone who is just trawling the river for garbage." She gave the cameras her most disarming smile.

A male reporter pushed closer. "Sources say you're here to dredge the river for a body. Is there any truth to that rumor?"

Clancy steeled her reaction to look surprised. "I don't know who your sources are, but they're totally off base. I'm a conservationist, making the water a cleaner place for all the fish and fauna." She stared the reporter right in the eye. "The police are the ones who'd be doing the job you're talking about. You need to ask them." She looked over the man's shoulder. "You're in luck, here's some now."

Clancy pushed past the onlookers and walked straight to the group of police. "Hi, Officers. I think the city's rumor mill has been working overtime. I'm going to grab my lunch while you tell these nice people there's nothing to see here except me dredging up a few stolen shopping carts and an old cooler, minus its fisherman's beer."

Clancy walked away. She was the picture of calm and nonchalance to the people watching her. Inside, she was Mount Vesuvius ready to erupt and burn the whole city down. She deliberately didn't go near the RV and draw any more attention to it. She purposefully walked down the road and found the first open convenience store. She gathered chips, soda, some ready-made sandwiches, and a box of doughnuts for her and Inez. She deliberately took a slow walk back and was relieved to see the crowd had been disbursed and the reporter vans were driving away to their next scoop.

Clancy found the guy in charge, one of the few who knew why she was there. "Any clues as to how they came to the conclusion they did?"

He pulled Clancy aside. "They heard it from someone who knew enough to spark their interest. Someone alluded as to why you're *really* on the river."

"Thanks, and thanks for getting here so fast to move the people off."

"We've been told if you call, we jump." He didn't look all that pleased about it but was kind enough not to take it out on Clancy.

Clancy just smiled at him. "Wish the same could be said for my takeout deliveries." She bid him goodbye and wandered back to the RV. She knocked their special coded rap. "Little pig, little pig, let me in your house of curious metals. Or I'll huff, or maybe I'll puff…"

Inez opened the door. "Ooh, you have doughnuts! Come right on in, Mr. Wolf." She shut the door behind them. "Did the police tell you who ratted us out?"

"Someone who knew enough to think it was KCTV newsworthy." Clancy dumped her bag on the kitchen table and took out her phone. "I'll call in some friends, see what we can find out ourselves."

Inez peered over her shoulder to see who she was texting. "Please tell me you don't think…"

"I'm going to have to ask." Clancy put her phone down and started to unload her bag. "I got you that chocolate bar you like."

"You're being awfully calm about this." Inez sat at the table to watch her.

"I'll wait until my suspicions are confirmed. Then I'll Wolverine their ass." Clancy popped open a can and started to drink. "Damn, I'd better go get my boat racked first. I really need to hire someone to do that for me. It's such a chore."

"Evan was coming in later."

"Yeah, well, he's coming sooner than he hoped."

"And Jude too."

Yes, and Jude too, Clancy thought. She was desperate to see her, but not for this reason.

There was nothing like accusing the woman you were sleeping with of speaking to the press to totally ruin your top-secret ongoing serial killer investigation. As breakup excuses went, this was going to be a first.

Jude was surprised by the sudden invitation to visit Clancy, but she was looking forward to seeing her before their Friday date.

"Is it a date when she's hitting my bar to drink, dance, then come home with me so we can be as loud as we want while she fucks me?" Jude asked Smokey Joe, who was too busy getting his fur on her clean shirt that she had to wear. "Hey, quit fuzzing that, I've just pressed it." She shooed him away and folded it up neatly into her bag to take into work. They had an anniversary party to cater, and Jude needed to look presentable. She had to go in a little earlier to help set up the bar so had roped in Mrs. Baker to look in on Smokey Joe throughout the evening. Clancy's strange text was going to make her cut it a bit fine getting into work, but she didn't plan on staying long. She was curious why she'd been asked to drop by. She wondered if it had anything to do with Mia. That thought had her grabbing her keys and racing out to her car.

It didn't take her long to arrive at the lot. She couldn't help but think how weird it was driving to a police department to park beside the very conspicuous RV. Jude knocked on the door and Inez opened it immediately.

"Hi, Jude." Inez gestured for her to go through to the living room. Clancy sat waiting there.

"Hey," Jude said, leaning down to kiss her and smiling when her kiss was returned with as much need. "What's all this about?" She took a seat beside Clancy.

"We're just waiting on Evan and then we can start."

Jude rubbed her hands together nervously. "God, I hate surprises," she muttered.

"I'll remember that," Clancy said, her tone somber.

A knock sounded out and Inez went to let him in. Evan looked at them all for a moment then sat in the last free spot.

"Is this about Mia?" He directed his query to Clancy but was looking Jude over. She bristled at his impudent gaze.

Clancy stood up as Inez sat down. The room had a strange feeling to it, the amicable mood turned suddenly, alarmingly, chilly. There was a coldness to Clancy's eyes that gave Jude pause. That hadn't been there when they had just kissed. Jude felt like they were chess pieces, waiting to start moving across a board. She wondered who was the piece about to be sacrificed.

"This morning when I was searching, I came back to find TV reporters and a crowd had gathered." Clancy leaned back against a cupboard. "Rumor has it someone leaked the reason, the *real* reason, for us being here."

Jude was shocked. "Who the hell would do that?"

Evan agreed. "Yes, who would do that? You've got this all tied down tight so that no one knows anything. Who could leak it?" He looked at Jude. "Who would gain anything from it being leaked?"

Jude didn't answer his veiled accusation. She looked at Clancy. "*You* think I spoke to the press?"

Clancy didn't answer. Evan sounded out again.

"Well, I've been working on this assignment for weeks now. *You've* just come in, *your* friend is missing, and the police haven't done anything to find her. You'd totally force their hand if this became public knowledge. Then they'd have to investigate more or risk being condemned by the public."

Jude wanted to reach across the table so bad and grab him by the throat. "I did not reveal any confidences. Yes, I want Mia found, but I am not jeopardizing whatever Clancy and Inez are doing to find her or the others." She looked up at Clancy. "You have to believe that."

"What about you, Evan?" Clancy turned her attention to him. "Who could *you* have been talking to that you might have let slip that what we do here is more than what we advertise?"

Evan spluttered. "I'm a highly valued member of the dive team. I don't have time to sell secrets. It's more than my job is worth."

"Where have you parked your Mercedes today?" Inez asked. Evan froze like a deer in the headlights and stared at her.

"My what?"

"Your Mercedes that you got from your high-powered job in Covert Investigations that's so hush-hush even your boss isn't aware of it."

"My boss?" His face paled dramatically.

Clancy leaned forward on the table and looked at him. "I get it. You're new to an area, you need a release, so you pad the truth a little to find someone to scratch that itch with."

Evan narrowed his eyes at her. "Isn't that what you're doing with *her*?" He nodded toward Jude.

Jude shifted her chair back so fast Evan cowered away in fear. Clancy held out a hand to stop Jude from vaulting over the table at him.

"I was more discerning where Jude was concerned. And I don't lie."

"*Omission* is as bad as a lie," Evan said, his eyes darting everywhere as he started to panic.

Clancy stared him down. "Trust me, you really don't want to continue that line of conversation, Evan. See, a friend of a friend tells us you've been seeing a new recruit in the police department here. A pretty girl, apparently not too bright because she fell for your lines. She hasn't realized that your Mercedes is only parked in your *mind*." Clancy leaned closer to him. "So, what else did you embellish for her, Evan? Your IQ? How fat your wallet is? Maybe, the size of your dick? Or did you just whisper in her ear how cool it was being a part of a serial killer investigation that no one else knows about? Was that how you got her, Evan? Did you compromise the entire investigation so you could fuck a trainee?"

"It just slipped out," Evan yelled. "I didn't think. How was I to know she was going to blab it around and somehow the TV channels were tipped off? What can you do?"

Clancy stuck her face right in his. "If your stupidity means that we lose this investigation, I won't have to do anything. The people above me are coming for you as we speak. You're done. But if, because of your loose lips, this killer changes his MO and stops leaving his victims in the river, then I will make sure you regret every word that came from your damned stupid fucking mouth."

There was a loud knock at the door. Clancy smiled. "That's the head of Chicago's DDU. How lucky we were she was in Kansas when we called. She'd like to speak with you."

Jude watched Inez usher in a dark-haired woman who looked fire-spitting furious.

"Clancy, this is Detective Rafe Douglas, head of the DDU." Inez announced her with a professional air.

Rafe nodded at everyone except Evan. "So, are you the stupid fucking asshole who jeopardized the whole case just so you could fuck a bitch?"

Jude's eyebrows rose a little at her vitriol.

"Guys, come and drag this dickweed out of here. We'll deal with this back at home." Rafe called in two very large men who all but picked Evan up out of his seat and carried him out. His cries for help were ignored. "Guess we've got to comb through the applicants again to make sure we don't get another blabbermouth like him screwing things up for us." Rafe rubbed at her forehead. "Do you know if he has family who'll miss him?"

Jude gasped. "Are you going to *kill* him?"

Rafe smiled wickedly. "Oh, I wish I had the power to sign off on that. No, we'll just be detaining him for quite some time. Does he have a pet? No? Smart move. I have a great sitter for mine. Sometimes you just want to get away from all that stray hair." She plucked at her jacket and dropped a hair to the floor. "Clancy, you're doing a great job. Inez, it's always a pleasure to see you."

Jude was surprised by how fast Rafe switched from furious to appreciative. She was surprised when Rafe turned her attention on her.

"Jude, we've got our people looking for your friend. She hasn't been forgotten."

"Thank you." Jude was surprised but grateful.

Clancy put a hand on her shoulder. "Please, stay here a moment while I see the detective out."

Jude strained to hear them as they left. She heard Clancy exclaim something that sounded like "Why is he here? He's with *you*?" and Rafe's reply of "He's my wife's. I gained a plus-one with her." Jude sat back and gave up trying to eavesdrop. None of it made a bit of sense. Her whole afternoon hadn't. Had Clancy really thought she'd betrayed her confidence? Jude didn't know whether to be furious or just plain hurt.

Clancy soon came bounding back in. She pulled Jude out of her chair and hugged her tightly. Jude couldn't resist the feel of Clancy's arms and melted into her.

"Just for the record, I knew you hadn't told anyone anything." Clancy took Jude's face in her hands and held her still so she could see the sincerity in Clancy's eyes.

"I would never," Jude said, meaning every word.

"I know, and I also knew if I confronted Evan alone, he'd try to pin the blame on you, so to kill two birds with one stone I got you both here." Clancy gave her a big smile. "Fuck, you were hot when you shot up out of your chair and made him almost shit himself!"

"I wanted to hit him so bad," Jude said.

"And he'd have deserved it."

"Has he wrecked the investigation?" Jude couldn't imagine the amount of damage that could have been done to the investigation being kept under wraps.

"We're lucky to have people who can sow the seeds of disinformation. For the next few days, I'll be pulling soda cans from the water and making a big deal out of recycling them in case anyone is watching me. Then it's back to business."

"That detective reminded me of some of my 'take no nonsense, don't give a shit' senior officers."

"Yeah, she was all guns blazing awesome, wasn't she? She had a pretty little blond wife waiting in the car for her. I think we intruded on a honeymoon of sorts for them." Clancy grimaced.

"So, how are you going to make it up to me for making me feel like you didn't trust me?" Jude tightened her grip around Clancy. "I feel like you'd enjoy my punishment too much."

Clancy eyes sparkled at her. "I'm sure you'll think of something, but remember, Friday night is *my* night."

"Listen to you, giving me orders." Jude deliberately dropped her voice and was delighted to see Clancy react.

"You obey orders because you were a good little sailor," Clancy said, trying to keep the upper hand.

Jude narrowed her eyes at Clancy's innocent tone. "Friday night is going to be a long night. I'm sure I can think of something for payback." Clancy shivered in her arms. Jude laughed at her. "I love that you're so easy."

"I love that I can switch with you. It gets tiring being in charge all the time," Clancy said, resting her head on Jude's shoulder with a huge sigh. "I can't believe I've got to break in another fucking diver. How am I supposed to trust them now after the shit Evan just pulled?"

Jude commiserated then got a thought. Once it struck, she couldn't shake it. "I happen to know a diver you can trust."

Clancy pulled back. "Really?"

Jude gave her a look and waited for the penny to drop. It didn't take Clancy long to catch Jude's drift.

"You did say you had your own gear." Clancy considered her for a moment. "I'll get in touch with Detective Chandler. She'll have to run a check into your background, probably contact your superiors at your last job."

"I wouldn't expect anything less for a sensitive job such as this. I have nothing to hide."

"If you're accepted, you won't be able to sleep in when you're on call, but let me tell you, the money makes that inconvenience sting less."

"Smokey Joe isn't used to being alone during the day. Can I bring him with me?"

Inez shouted out from the office. "Yes!"

Jude startled. She laughed quietly and admitted in a whisper, "I'd forgotten she was in here."

"Yeah, you're gonna have to remember that if you're going to work with us." Clancy kissed her smiling lips. "Or if you stay, for a sleepover, perhaps."

"I'll be sure to have Smokey Joe pack a kitty case."

"And I'll keep the *packing* for your place."

Jude couldn't wish Friday to arrive any sooner.

Chapter Fifteen

Scuba diving suits had never been something Clancy considered sexy, but watching Jude slide the tight black suit over her gorgeously strong body was making it hard for Clancy to get into her own. Clancy wanted to peel Jude back out of it to enjoy the sight of her in the black sports bra and compression shorts she wore underneath.

"Do you need help getting into your suit, Clancy?" Jude reached behind her for the zip cord to fasten everything up.

"No, I'm just admiring the view."

Jude looked up and grinned at her. "You like seeing me in your underwear?"

"I'd like to see you out of it more." Clancy forced herself to pay attention to what they were gearing up for. "I've found they're the most comfortable thing to wear under a suit. But damn, you fill my shorts out better than I ever could."

Jude sauntered over and began to pull Clancy's suit up, deliberately brushing her knuckles against Clancy's nipples through her sports bra before zipping the suit shut.

"You can wrestle me out of them later," Jude promised. "For now, show me all the gadgets and gizmos we're wearing for this dive."

Clancy talked Jude through every piece of equipment professionally. She attached Jude's camera to her suit and switched both of theirs on, then she led Jude down to where they had the boat docked. Once they had climbed aboard, Clancy spent time going over the running of the boat and the sonar.

"I know you know all this stuff. The naval equipment you worked with probably makes this setup look like children's toys. But this sonar needs to be your eyes along every inch of this river because once you dive into the Big Mo you ain't gonna see shit."

Jude quirked her lips at Clancy's blunt choice of words.

"I'm going to take us out to where there's a nice drop-off. I've already placed a buoy there with a line for you to follow down. I need you to acclimatize to the poor vision this river affords us and I want to see if you can find what is hidden down there."

"You're sending me on a scavenger hunt?"

"That's pretty much my whole job out here. We search every inch of the water and we see what we can find. There are no vehicles in this stretch, I've already cleared it." Clancy looked out across the river then back at Jude, curious about her previous work. "Did you ever come across vehicles in your naval dives?"

"No, it was mostly boat wrecks or me patching up the hull of those still in service. I'm used to diving in water much deeper than this though and with better vision quality. But we both know any depth of water is dangerous, no matter how well you can see."

Clancy leaned over to turn on the radio. "Good morning, Inez. We're about to set sail and test this new recruit's ability and agility in the mighty Missouri River."

"Sound off, Sailor," Inez said.

"Good morning, Inez," Jude dutifully replied.

Smokey Joe's plaintive meow sounded out from the radio.

"Is he in the office with you already?" Clancy asked, not in the least surprised.

"I didn't bring him in. He found his own way here. I might not get much work done with him lying on my laptop's keyboard though."

Jude grimaced. "Yeah, sorry. He's a bugger for that. If you get up from your chair, be sure to check it before you sit back down. Smokey Joe gravitates to warm spots like a fuzzy magnet."

"Well, he and I are watching you live on stream to the RV and we can hear you. I repeat, *I can hear you*. Do I make myself clear?" Inez said.

"She means onay exsay alktay." Clancy intoned with mock seriousness to Jude.

"Clancy, you taught me the whole ixnay thing when I was five," Inez reminded her.

"Dammit," Clancy muttered. "I have no secrets from this kid."

"Message received loud and clear, Inez," Jude said, shaking her head at their antics. "How the fuck do you two get anything done? You're like kids."

"We're very professional when we need to be," Clancy promised her. "You're going to be diving on something Inez devised for you to find."

"Any last tips for someone who hasn't dived for a few months?" Jude trailed her hand in the water as they set off from the dock.

Clancy considered her question for a moment. "You'll be fine. Just take it slowly, we're not in any rush. Find your sea legs and just enjoy it. You've got my spare mask with the mic, which was way cooler than yours, so you'll be in constant contact with us once you're under the water. Then we'll switch so you can get used to following my lead."

Clancy and Jude shared a look between them and burst out laughing at Clancy's unintentional inuendo.

"Oh God, now I'm stuck with two of you. Smokey Joe and I are ignoring you."

Clancy laughed at Inez's playful teasing. She loved days like these. Easy laughter, great company, and there being nothing sinister lying on the bottom of the riverbed. A day to dive for pleasure and to enjoy the quiet of the water surrounding them.

Clancy took Jude's hand in her own and threaded their fingers together. Jude was framed against the bluest of skies. Her upturned face was bathed by the warm sun that brought out a hint of freckles on her cheeks.

Clancy knew she had never seen anyone more beautiful.

Jude smiled over at her. "Thanks for inviting me aboard, Captain."

"We're glad to have you sailing with us," Clancy said. "Me, especially."

Jude squeezed her hand tighter and Clancy filed away everything she was feeling in that moment in her memory.

It was a moment worth living for. Something she hadn't had in a very long time.

❖

Jude was totally in her element. The flashlight she shined on the riverbed helped cut through the cloying silt, but she still felt slightly claustrophobic. Especially with how dirty the water was and how little vision she was afforded by it.

"Missing the bright blue seas of the oceans?" Clancy asked as if reading her mind.

"Yes, but happier I'm not lugging down tools to have to weld a plate onto a ship's damaged hull."

"What made you quit?"

"It stopped being fun. I'd devoted a lot of my life to diving and fixing, following orders, playing by the rules. One day I realized that's all I had. An endless list of jobs to do and someone always telling me *what* to do."

"What made you choose bartending?"

"It was the first job Mia found for me when we met as neighbors. I think they hired me more for my size and no-nonsense face because they quickly glossed over the fact I couldn't mix a drink to save my life." Jude brushed her hand over a rock and watched the silt float off it. "But I learned real fast. Even know a few spins and flips for the total cocktail experience."

"You've been holding out on me. You haven't shown me any of your fancy tricks." Clancy sounded put out.

"I can't really get creative when all I'm doing is flipping the lid off a bottle of Coke for you." She brushed along a ridge and found a very distinct piece of wire. It was bright neon pink. "Who the hell ties pink wire around a rock and throws it in the river?" Jude muttered as she ran her fingers up the length of it. A bag was tied to the top. It fluttered like a flag as it caught in the current. Jude shone her flashlight on it. She found a photo, sealed inside the plastic. She inspected it and laughed. "You two are crazy, you know that, right?" The photo was Clancy and Inez making faces at the camera.

"Welcome to the team," Inez's voice sounded out in the mask. "I think you're going to fit right in."

"Be sure to gather all the wire so we leave the water as clean, and I use the term loosely, as we found it," Clancy said.

"I'm coming back up with my prize." Jude followed the line back up to the surface beside the boat. She handed Clancy the rock and wire first, then the plastic bag. "Don't lose that. That's my first find. I want to frame it."

Clancy helped her out of the water and back into the boat. Jude removed her mask and knew she was grinning like a little kid. "That was awesome, but you weren't joking. The visibility is really bad."

Clancy agreed. "Believe me, as someone who has ridden down the river from its starting point, it never gets any prettier. Which is why sonar is this diver's best friend."

"Do you think we'll find a car in this stretch?" Jude looked down the river's seemingly endless path.

"I hope not, but we still have Mia to find and, unfortunately, her story matches up too much with the previous finds." Clancy picked up her own mask. "I'm going to dive so you can watch me on the sonar. My rules are: I always dive on a vehicle first, with a watcher on the boat, and Inez observing all from the RV. I will identify the vehicle and, if possible, ascertain if there are remains inside. If it's not our vehicle, we'll get the local haulage company that Detective Chandler has assigned for us to come remove the vehicle and clear the area. If it *is* our vehicle, then we'll get the same haulage company but add in the DDU who will send their own coroner and investigators to the site. We will help with attaching the floats and chains to the car to get it out of the water and the haulage guys will do the rest. Then Chandler's folk will take it from there." Clancy made sure the full-face mask was clean and undamaged before putting it on. Jude was impressed by her attention to every detail. It made her feel safe under Clancy's watch.

"Inez, can you hear me?" Clancy asked.

"Loud and clear, Rubber Ducky."

Jude was amused by Inez's reply. Clancy spared her a glance.

"Don't think she won't come up with a call sign for you," she warned.

"I want the full story behind yours when you resurface," Jude said.

They shared a look that became serious really fast.

"Don't sail off without me," Clancy said.

"I wouldn't dream of it."

Clancy shifted to sit on the edge of the boat and, without preamble, tipped backward to enter the water.

Jude's eyes were glued to the sonar. Inez began walking her through everything she was seeing. Jude was an attentive student and Inez was a very informative teacher.

It was strange knowing that Clancy had nearly, deliberately, drowned herself. Yet, there she was, as comfortable in the water as she was on dry earth. A near victim who searched to find others who were less fortunate than she had been. Jude was humbled by her.

"Hey, Rubber Ducky?" she said, waiting for Clancy's voice to come over the radio.

"Yes, She-Hulk?"

Jude faltered. "Really? *That's* the name you'd pick for me? I was about to say you're a good person but I'm taking it back."

"No, no! You can't take it back. I love being praised."

"I know you do." Jude didn't care that Inez could hear. She deliberately employed the tone that made Clancy drop to her knees.

"Fuck! Don't do that!" Clancy sounded flustered. "Why were you going to say nice things about me anyway? I haven't done anything."

"I'm impressed by your professionalism and how much you care about your job and the people you search for. You bring the lost home. That's a beautiful kindness you bestow on people." Jude waited for Clancy to answer.

"Thank you. That means a lot coming from you." The shyness was evident in Clancy's quiet voice.

"You going to give me a better name than She-Hulk?"

"No. She-Hulk is a gorgeous figure of a woman, strong, powerful, one who uses her aggression to fight for what's right. She also has a wicked sex drive in the TV series. I mean, what's to hate there?"

"She has a TV series?" Jude only remembered comic books.

"Inez, be sure to coordinate with Ms. Patterson's calendar and find us a day to binge-watch *She-Hulk: Attorney at Law*. Jude, you're going to love Tatiana Maslany as Jennifer Walters."

"The chick from that clone show?"

"*Orphan Black*, yes!"

"Do we get popcorn at this binge-fest?"

"What do you think?"

"Every flavor and copious amounts?" Jude was beginning to know Clancy well.

"Rubber Ducky, she's got your number!" Inez said, sounding pleased.

"Yes, I think she has."

Jude watched the sonar screen and Clancy on it. She could even see the distortion of bubbles coming from the mask. She looked forward to learning more about this woman with every new day they would work together. That would soon show her if they were as compatible as Jude felt they were beginning to be.

Clancy made sure to move her arms in a more exaggerated way so that, back on the boat, Jude would be able to see her easily on the sonar screen. Inez had the camera feed. She recorded it every time in case they found something. They sent any vital footage to Detective Chandler so she could build their case against the serial killer that still eluded them.

The victims had all told Clancy about the man who had killed them. How he wined and dined them, love-bombed them so they were swept helplessly off their feet. All had thought they had found their perfect match in him. His description had been different for all. Brown hair, black hair, curls, straight, short, even a man bun. He had been cleanshaven, sported a moustache, or had been bearded. But all said he was white with blue eyes. Clancy sighed; they needed more. Was it just one man or could it possibly be a group? She recalled being pulled in on a case where there had been five school friends, who instead of teaming up to play video games, had taken turns to kidnap a woman each, to then kill and dump. Clancy had spoken to their last victim and she had identified them all. She'd been smart and scratched each of them. The DNA had condemned them. Her voice had led the police to each boy's door. But not every shark swam in packs.

Clancy suddenly stopped swimming. She could hear something. A tapping sound, faint but insistent. Clancy strained her ears to pinpoint its direction. It didn't sound like it came from off the land. It echoed like it was under water. Clancy knew she still had miles of river to search.

"Mia?" she whispered, desperate not to have Jude hear her as she tried to reach out to whatever or whoever was making the sound. She felt the water around her slow to a stop and she waited.

Nothing happened.

Clancy listened but the sound had stopped too. She was floating in place in a river that had stopped flowing and she couldn't call out. Clancy knew nothing was in this patch of water. But something had grabbed her attention. She needed to scan the next area alone and be able to call out.

Maybe someone would answer then.

"Clancy! Clancy, for fuck's sake, answer me!"

Jude's voice suddenly sounded loud in her ear and Clancy jolted back to reality. The water rushed past and pushed her back toward the boat's line. She caught it and her breath.

"I'm here, it's okay," she assured Jude and Inez. Inez would understand. But, fuck, how was she going to explain all this to Jude?

"What the fuck just happened?" Jude demanded. She sounded worried.

"Did you knock your com offline again?" Inez asked, giving her the excuse.

"Damn, I must have. Sorry, everyone. I didn't mean to freak you out. I'm coming back up." Clancy rose to the surface and came face to face with Jude who didn't just help her, she all but lifted Clancy out of the water.

"Fuck me, Jude, how freaking strong are you?" Clancy had to laugh as she was pulled into the boat with ease.

"You frightened the shit out of me," Jude said, helping Clancy remove her mask.

"How long were my coms out?" Clancy asked, noting how freaked Jude looked. For Clancy, it hadn't been long.

"Five minutes. I nearly came down there after you, but Inez said you were fine." Jude took a deep breath and blew it out to calm herself. "Fuck."

Clancy grabbed for her hand. "I'm sorry I scared you. I'll check my commlink and make sure it doesn't do that again."

"You were just down there, suspended and still. I didn't know what the fuck was happening and I couldn't get you to hear me." Jude drew Clancy close. "I thought you were dead. How crazy is that?" Jude absently stroked Clancy's tattooed wrist.

"I can assure you my death wish is under control."

Jude's gaze fixed Clancy in place. "But you have one still?"

Clancy considered lying but couldn't bring herself to treat Jude that way. "Sometimes, when I'm so close to all this death that it's all I can feel, breathe, see, and touch. But I fight it because who else is going to find these victims if I'm not here?"

Jude pulled Clancy into her arms and held her tight. "When you reach the end of the river and the job's done, we're going somewhere to get you away from it all. To decompress. Do you need peace and quiet or noise and distractions?"

Clancy hugged Jude back fiercely. "I've been promising Inez and Rainbow a trip to Disneyland after we're done here. Want to be Namaari to my Raya?"

"I have no idea what you're talking about." Jude looked honestly perplexed.

"They're our kind of Disney princesses. Believe me, you'll love them. They have swords, and dragons, and no male love interests."

Jude nodded against Clancy's head. "I'm not wearing mouse ears."

"Not even if I found you a pair of She-Hulk ones?"

"Don't make me throw you back into the water, boi." Jude growled in Clancy's ear, making her shiver.

"Let's go grab lunch then we can go mark out the next area to scan." Clancy reluctantly moved out of Jude's arms. "I'll sit back and watch you do it all while I take in the scenery and just chill."

Clancy steered the boat back to the jetty. She cast a look over her shoulder, back down the river. Maybe they'd be lucky, maybe they'd find Mia or someone else from the missings files that kept growing in number.

But she needed to do it alone, to get the boat out on the water and invite anyone who could hear her to answer back.

Chapter Sixteen

Jude couldn't get the key in her door quick enough. She heard Clancy groan as the key missed the lock for the second time. She was pressed up against Jude, her body radiating heat from all the dancing she'd been doing while Jude had served the bar's customers. The night air had done little to cool Clancy's temperature, nor her burning desire to get Jude into her apartment.

The key finally caught. Jude opened her door and Clancy all but pushed her inside.

"Finally!" Clancy shut the door behind them, locked it, then reached for Jude's shirt. She grabbed the collar and pulled Jude down for a passionate kiss. Clancy brushed her tongue against Jude's, then teased along Jude's lips. She roughly pushed Jude against the wall and crowded in, kissing her to distraction. Their kisses were wet and messy but Jude was just as ravenous.

Jude pulled Clancy in tighter. She only stopped her wandering hands when she felt something hard pressed between them.

"That's new," she said, removing her hand from Clancy's butt and brushing it over Clancy's stomach instead. She stilled over the front of Clancy's jeans. There was a very distinct bulge there. "That wasn't there earlier tonight when you had me dancing in your arms."

"Fuck, no. I learned early on that dancing and packing rubs me raw. I was able to kit up before we left the bar." Clancy pressed Jude's hand to the fly of her jeans. "We've got a long way to go before I'll let you see the present I have for you though."

Jude groaned. "I'm ready now."

Clancy shook her head. "You can be readier. Be a good boi and do as you're told. Start stripping."

Jude pulled at Clancy's T-shirt and got it half way up her chest. The black sports bra made Jude's hands itch to remove it so she could lay kisses all over Clancy's breasts.

"Not me! *You!*" Clancy tugged her shirt back down as Jude made a disgruntled noise. Clancy just laughed at her. "You can touch me later. Tonight, I want to fill you up and make you scream. There's no holding back this time. Inez is babysitting Smokey Joe so we have your apartment to ourselves."

Jude unbuttoned her shirt and tossed it aside. She wrestled her bra off and smiled at the look of appreciation on Clancy's face. "Like what you see?" Jude deliberately lifted her arms up and flexed a little. The look in Clancy's eyes darkened.

"I love it," she said, taking all of Jude in.

Jude held her breath for a moment. Love wasn't something they'd talked about. They were new, exciting, hot, and passionate. Yet Jude was already falling hard for Clancy. She'd been bowled over by her on first sight. Love was something for later. *If* they had a later. Jude didn't want to think about that now. She wanted to revel in the joy she experienced exploring Clancy's body. She wanted to feel the ecstasy of Clancy's hands on her. She just wanted to *feel*.

Jude took off her shoes and socks, then unzipped her jeans. She paused, then took Clancy's hand in her own and trailed it along the top of her briefs.

"Want to see how ready for you I have been all night?" She guided Clancy's hand inside her briefs until she felt Clancy's fingers brushing over her hair.

Clancy stopped Jude from going any further. She tightened her grip on the soft pubic hair and gently pulled. Her eyes bored into Jude's. "You are not topping me from the bottom." She tugged a little harder in reprimand.

Jude stared at her. "I wouldn't dream of it." Her eyes fluttered closed when Clancy slipped her hand lower and let her middle finger deliberately skim the hood of Jude's clit. A shiver of electricity ran through Jude's whole body. She waited to see what Clancy would do next but Clancy's fingers were still. She opened her eyes to find Clancy just looking at her. "What?" Jude was intrigued by the look in Clancy's eyes.

"I can't get over how fucking beautiful you are. You're so handsome, so strong, yet still every inch a woman. One I want to run my tongue all over and fuck until we're both breathless." Clancy rubbed across Jude's clit again. The gentle touch made Jude jerk in response. "Before we go any further, do you like being taken missionary, on your side, spread out on a table, or do you prefer on all fours, being fucked from behind?" Clancy ran her fingertip in little circles on Jude's clit as she asked.

Jude wasn't sure she could answer. Everything was concentrated on Clancy's hand in her briefs as she teased Jude to distraction with all those scenarios. Pleasure was building at Clancy's gentle ministrations. It was driving Jude insane. "Spread out on a table? You're giving me the story behind that position later. Which do you prefer?" She decided to ask, not sure she could choose how best to have Clancy take her when her attention was being distracted by Clancy's hand down her briefs.

Clancy withdrew her fingers and ran her wet fingertip in circles around Jude's belly button. "I'd like to lie on top of you and watch every expression on your face as I fuck deep inside you." She grabbed Jude's hand and pressed it tightly against her bulge. "You said to pack hard and long."

Jude nearly came then and there and Clancy *knew* it. A sensuous smile lit up her whole face and she dropped abruptly to her knees to lick around Jude's belly button to clean up the wetness she'd spread there. Clancy tugged down Jude's briefs and helped her step out of them. She pushed Jude back against the wall and pressed herself in between Jude's legs, forcing her to widen her stance, unbalancing Jude so that the only way she stayed upright was by keeping a hold on Clancy. Clancy spread Jude's lips, stuck her face between Jude's legs without any preamble, and feasted.

Jude held on to Clancy's head and fucked her face. It was rough, and raw, yet Jude had never felt so desired. She'd never heard the keening noises that escaped her throat, either. She was in her own home and not the RV. She could be as loud as she wanted to be. Clancy was going to make her scream if she kept flicking her tongue over her clit like that. Jude could feel her body tightening, readying, preparing to explode. She felt like she was suspended on a precipice and the next harsh suck on her clit would be the one to push her right over the edge.

"Come, baby," Clancy ordered.

Jude did so with a harsh cry torn from her lips. Her legs trapped Clancy between them as she rode out her pleasure on Clancy's mouth. Her hips bucked weakly when Clancy pulled back to watch her flesh pulse in release. She was still shaking when Clancy rose to her feet and gently cupped Jude's mons. She kissed Jude, letting her feel and taste Jude's sweet juices smeared on Clancy's face. Jude tried to catch her breath while Clancy grinned at her, evidently proud of herself for wrecking Jude's carefully erected composure.

"You've showed me yours." Clancy whipped her shirt up over her head and tossed it behind her. She nonchalantly slipped free the top button of her jeans. "Now, I get to show you *mine*."

Clancy knew she'd be sore in the morning, but she couldn't bring herself to care. She could feel the stinging trails left by Jude's blunt fingernails as she gripped tighter and tighter to Clancy's back. Sweat dripped from Clancy's face as she flexed her hips to bury herself deep inside Jude then withdraw the barest fraction, then push back in. She timed each thrust to the gasps and whispered words of *"more"* that fell from Jude's lips. Clancy couldn't tear her gaze from Jude's face. A deep red flush stained Jude's cheeks, neck, and chest as her arousal grew. Clancy was fascinated by it. She loved watching Jude's composure crack and disintegrate with every stroke of Clancy's strap-on inside her.

Jude had tried to distract Clancy when she'd seen how the black silicone dildo slotted into an O-ring as part of the black boxer harness she wore. Jude had cupped Clancy's butt, squeezing it through the tight spandex shorts until Clancy had pushed her back on the bed, lubed up, and sank into Jude's welcoming arms and body.

Now, Jude's legs were wrapped around Clancy's hips, her ankles drumming against Clancy's butt cheeks with every thrust.

"God, you're so tight," Clancy huffed against Jude's breast as she leaned to suck a hard nipple into her mouth.

"I don't do penetration often," Jude said.

Clancy's hips faltered and Jude tightened her hold.

"No, don't stop!" Jude begged.

Clancy picked up her rhythm again. "Is it okay we're doing this? I'd hate if you felt you were obligated to do it because I wanted to fuck you so bad."

"Believe me, I want it as much as you do." Jude clutched at Clancy's arms. "I guess I put off stone butch vibes and no one wants to mess with that. And I've never felt I could ask...until you."

Clancy smiled. "And yet, those stone butch vibes just make me want to do this more."

"You seek my pleasure as much as you seek your own. You're a rare boi, Clancy." Jude's shaking hand cupped Clancy's face.

Clancy rocked her hips a little faster at the praise. "I love it when you call me that," she admitted, hiding her face in Jude's chest.

Jude ruffled Clancy's hair. "You like being my best boi?"

Clancy lifted her head to look Jude straight in the eye. "I'd like to be your only boi."

Jude's smile was answer enough for Clancy to know what she was beginning to feel appeared to be mutual.

Jude's head crashed back down on the pillow, breaking their moment. "Fuck, you're hitting that sweet spot inside of me just right." Her voice strained and her body began to tighten further around Clancy's dick.

"You gonna come for me if I fuck you harder?" Clancy didn't wait for an answer, she sped up each thrust and watched Jude writhe beneath her. Jude was magnificent, her body a masterpiece of strength, and Clancy was making her come apart. She felt humbled watching Jude in her most vulnerable moments, her private self, the gorgeous woman that she was, exactly as she was.

Jude clutched Clancy to her as she climaxed. Clancy could barely move in her tight grip and she basked in it. Jude panted in her ear, murmuring nonsense as she fought to regain her breath.

"My best boi."

Clancy collapsed on top of her, burying her face in Jude's neck, seeking comfort for herself.

"Did you come?" Jude asked finally, her hand stroking Clancy's hair.

Clancy shook her head.

"Do you need to?" Jude shifted uncomfortably and Clancy reluctantly pulled out of her. They both tensed as Clancy withdrew. Clancy mourned the loss; she liked being that close to Jude. It was the ultimate intimacy.

"Soon," Clancy said, busying herself removing her boxers then climbing back onto the bed to sprawl on top of Jude. She had never craved closeness as much as she did with Jude. She couldn't get close enough, couldn't be held tight enough, couldn't love her enough.

Clancy froze in Jude's arms.

"You okay?" Jude instantly picked up on Clancy's mood.

Clancy snuggled back down and rubbed her sweaty body over Jude's, marking her territory, making Jude *hers*.

"You're like a damned cat," Jude muttered, laughing when Clancy finally settled down.

"I just like the feel of your skin against mine, it makes me want to rub all over you." Clancy lifted her head to press a kiss on Jude's smiling lips. "There aren't enough words for me to explain how you make me feel. You're breathtakingly handsome, you're built like a goddess, and you're sexy as fuck." Clancy punctuated each compliment with a kiss.

Jude ran her hands around Clancy's back and started to dig into her muscles. Clancy moaned appreciatively. "Are you going to be able to walk tomorrow?"

Clancy chuckled. "No more than you are." Jude dug in deeper and Clancy let out a grunt. She felt restless and moved under Jude's hands. "I need to get myself off on you. My clit feels like it's twice its size and ready to explode."

"Let me take care of that for you." Jude urged Clancy up to sit on her face. "Fuck me, you're soaked," she said when Clancy was in position.

"It's because I fucked you that I'm soaked." Clancy hissed at the first touch of Jude's tongue. "God, I'm so sensitive." She lifted herself up a fraction. "I just need..." Clancy pressed her hands on the wall above the bed and leaned her forehead to rest against it. "Okay, I'm ready. Just be warned I'm hyper-sensitive and liable to come in seconds and ruin my tough guy image."

"Nothing will ever ruin that. I like you all twitchy and desperate to come because you just rode me like a champ."

Clancy pressed her head against the wall for stability as Jude's talented tongue began to roam over her needy flesh. She closed her eyes and let herself go under Jude's skillful ministrations. Her arms shook as she felt her body strain for release. As she climbed toward her peak, the wall began to vibrate then shudder beneath her palms. Terrified, Clancy looked up to see ghostly hands reaching through the wall to grab her wrists, holding her firmly in place. She struggled but couldn't free herself from their grip. The wall bowed as if made of rubber. A body pressed forward and finally the head until it and Clancy were face to face. Clancy reared back, refusing to let it touch her but she couldn't move. She was pinned below by Jude's firm grip and held above by strong, unearthly, hands.

The second the ghostly head touched Clancy's she was blinded by a dazzling white light. In the blink of an eye, she found herself flying through the night air, miles above the ground. Streetlights were nothing more than streaks of color at the speed of Clancy's flight. She could feel the warm night air on her naked skin, feel it rush through her hair. She was jarred to an abrupt halt above a car. It was hidden in a small clearing, amid a dense growth of trees. She could hear a man's voice.

"I'll make sure you never tell anyone what you saw."

Clancy was whisked away again, her body flying in the darkness, speeding over the familiar twists and turns of the Missouri River lit by the moon's light. She was plunged down under the water before she could even gasp for a breath. She struggled against the hands holding her, fighting to break free. She couldn't speak. If she said one word aloud, Jude would hear her and her secret would be out. She wasn't prepared to lose her. Coming out to Jude as a psychic while Jude was eating her out was not how Clancy imagined having that conversation. She struggled against the hands pulling her down into the depths.

"Find me."

Clancy felt as if her chest was going to burst. She couldn't breathe. She was starting to see stars as her oxygen depleted.

She was drowning.

"You're killing me!" Clancy shouted.

Instantly, the hands let go of her and Clancy was shot out of the vision and back into Jude's bedroom, coming hard against Jude's face. Clancy shook and gulped in air, trying desperately to steady her rapidly pounding heart. Unaware of what Clancy had just been through, Jude pulled her down to cuddle against her chest.

"But what a way to go, eh?" Jude said smugly, pressing kisses on Clancy's damp forehead.

Clancy just clung to her. She was shaking and trying to catch her breath, while fighting so hard not to cry.

Chapter Seventeen

Jude savored the ache of a body well fucked. She felt invincible, confident, and smug as hell. She'd purposely dressed in a white muscle tee and tight black jeans just to watch Clancy stare at her over the kitchen table that morning. Jude loved that Clancy didn't hide her appreciation of Jude's build. She'd dated butches before but it had always ended up as a competition of who could out-butch who. Not with Clancy though. There was a mutual admiration and enjoyment over how they both looked and felt.

Jude knew she was smitten. Clancy was everything she'd ever wanted in a woman, and more than she'd ever dreamed of in a butch.

She was supposed to be going over to the RV later to pick up Smokey Joe from his sleep-over. Clancy had left after they'd shared a leisurely breakfast and a plethora of sweet kisses. They both complained that they couldn't just blow the day off and go straight back to bed. Clancy had things she needed to do and Jude had to get groceries so they'd reluctantly parted.

Jude gathered her weekly shop in record speed. She'd picked up a tray of twelve assorted doughnuts for Clancy and Inez to share later. The tray kept catching her eye as she wandered around the apartment trying to catch up on things she'd put off all week to do.

She stared at the laundry basket and instead grabbed for her car keys. She didn't want Smokey Joe to think she'd abandoned him and maybe Clancy would welcome seeing her sooner, rather than later. She picked up the doughnuts knowing Clancy would love them.

Sure, she was just going for her cat.

❖

The RV wasn't parked in the parking lot of the police station and for a moment Jude was at a loss. Clancy hadn't said anything about charting the river today. Jude knew all the spots they were due to sail on for the next week. She and Clancy had gone over the maps and found the best places to set off from and the biggest spots to park the RV at.

Jude drove to the area that was earmarked for Monday. The RV was there, unmissable and parked on the dirt road that led down to the dock. Jude felt a bit weird stalking them to this spot, but she *was* supposed to meet them. She looked at her watch. Admittedly, they had arranged to meet up four hours from now. Jude grimaced at how uncomfortable she felt just turning up on the RV's doorstep but not uncomfortable enough to turn around and go back home. She couldn't understand why they were here. Why was Clancy sailing without her?

Jude got out of her car and spared a look down at the dock. There was no sign of any boat and she couldn't hear the distinct sound of the boat's engine. She walked over to the RV and opened the door without thinking. She'd been walking in unannounced since she'd started working with Clancy. Inez wasn't in the office but Smokey Joe was sitting on her seat. He immediately started meowing when he saw Jude. He stood up on his hind legs, begging to be picked up. Jude cuddled him close.

"Holy Smokes. I missed you so much." Jude listened to his hearty purring as he headbutted her hello. "Have you been a good boy, hmm?"

"Okay, let's try this again."

Jude looked around at the sound of Clancy's voice. The monitor showed the view from Clancy's GoPro camera. She was out on the water. Jude reached down to trigger the mic so she could talk to her but was stopped by Clancy's next words.

"Mia Murray, are you out there? I'm here to take you home."

Jude dropped her hand away. She stared at the screen. Clancy wasn't moving. She was stopped in the middle of the river and she was *calling* to Mia.

"Hey, Smokey Joe, am I going to have to move you outta my seat…" Inez slapped a hand to her chest when she saw Jude. "For Goddess's sake, Jude! You nearly gave me a heart attack!"

"Mia Murray, are you here? I know you're close. Can you answer me? Make a noise? I know you're frightened. I'm here to help."

Jude stared at Inez. "What is she doing?"

Inez looked very uncomfortable and hurried over to the radio to turn it down. Jude stopped her.

"No, I need to hear this. *What* is she doing?"

Inez didn't look at her. Instead, she found something on her desk to move around until the silence grew too loud in the RV.

"A manifestation ritual?" Inez blurted out. "You know, 'if you speak it, she will come,' kinda thing?" Inez smiled disarmingly at her. "To butcher the *Field of Dreams* quote, which just happens to be my mom's favorite movie."

Jude didn't believe her and she didn't know why. "Clancy doesn't do any of that when we're on the water together."

Inez scoffed lightly. "Like she's going to do anything weird in front of you. Come on, you'd look at her exactly like you're looking at me now." Inez went to touch the radio, but Jude stopped her again as Clancy continued to talk.

"We found the clearing you showed me. A friend has her people scouring it now for clues. But he didn't dump you there, did he? So where are you, Mia? Show me. Let me find you. Your friends and family are waiting for you to come home. Help me to find you."

Jude stared at the screen. "What the fuck kind of crazy-ass game is this that you two are playing, Inez?"

Inez dodged around Jude and turned the microphone on. "Clancy, you need to get back to the RV right now."

The image on the screen shifted as Clancy moved on the boat. "Are you okay?"

"I'm fine." Inez spared Jude a look. "But Jude is here and she would probably like an explanation as to what she's just heard."

There was a moment of silence, then Clancy sighed. "Hey, Jude. You're a tad early for our arranged visit."

Jude watched the boat turn around on the screen. "I got you doughnuts. You weren't at the police station so I took a chance you'd be here."

"You're too smart for your own good, lover." Clancy sounded defeated.

"And you've got some explaining to do, boi," Jude said.

"Why couldn't you have just knocked for once?" Inez muttered under her breath.

"Because you've had me coming back and forth freely without tapping out the elaborate secret code Clancy uses." Jude watched the screen and could see the boat was running at speed.

"Inez, get Jude's apartment key off her and take Smokey Joe home. I'm sure he'll get a kick out of riding on your Vespa."

Jude could see that Inez wanted desperately to talk to Clancy alone, but Jude wasn't budging and Inez couldn't whisper quietly enough not to be overheard. "I'd rather stay with you in case—"

"I'm not arguing in front of the kids. Please, Inez, it'll be okay."

Jude wondered why Clancy expected an argument and why she wanted Inez out of the RV and at Jude's apartment instead.

Inez looked torn between stamping her feet in frustration and wanting to say something to Jude but couldn't.

"What the hell is going on, Inez?" Jude was exasperated by all the secrecy.

Inez stuck her hand out and waved it. "Just hand your key over and let me get Smokey Joe in his carrier."

"You don't have to leave," Jude said, not at all sure what was going on with Clancy wanting Inez out of the RV so fast.

"Clancy wants me out so I'm doing as I'm told." She stepped forward into Jude's personal space. "But I'm warning you. You hurt her and you'll feel the wrath of a seventh daughter of a seventh daughter."

Jude was confused. "I thought you were an only child."

"I am, but my mother isn't. And she's more protective of Clancy than I could ever be." Inez stood on her tiptoes. "You hurt her and I swear it will return to you threefold."

Jude felt oddly intimidated by Inez's no-nonsense tone. She handed over her key. "If an old woman two doors down questions you being there, just tell her you're Clancy's kid. Mrs. Baker thinks Clancy hung the moon."

Inez smiled softly to herself. "She did. She just doesn't realize how important her doing so *is*." She turned on her heel and set to gathering Smokey Joe and his stuff.

Jude could hear the familiar putt-putt sound of Clancy's boat returning. Inez passed Jude in the doorway, Smokey Joe looking out of his carrier on her back. Jude wondered what he made of all this.

"You might want to get those doughnuts," Inez said. She made a move to leave but stopped and eyed Jude carefully. "If you care for her as much as I think you do, you'll listen to her. You two are so good together. Don't fuck that up."

Inez stepped out of the RV and jogged down to the boat. Jude watched her give Clancy a huge hug then she jogged back to get her Vespa down off the trailer.

"You going to give me a hand with the boat?" Clancy yelled from where she was dismantling the equipment.

Jude went to help, and in silence they got the boat back on the trailer and the sonar screens stored away.

Clancy looked pensive as she gestured for Jude to precede her into the RV. "I guess the honeymoon is over. Now we talk."

CHAPTER EIGHTEEN

Clancy eyed the doughnuts mournfully. They looked delicious. Sprinkles, cream, and iced, all her favorites laid out so perfectly in their box that lay unopened on the kitchen table. Clancy's appetite had vanished as soon as she saw the look of distrust on Jude's face.

Clancy tugged at her T-shirt nervously. She'd showered and changed after her walk of shame back to the RV after last night's sleepover. She wished she'd dressed more appropriately than her favorite ripped jeans and a well-worn Harley-Davidson shirt. She hadn't expected Jude to turn up so early after she'd left the apartment. She hadn't expected Jude *at all* while she was out on the water, trying to strike up a conversation with Jude's missing neighbor.

Clancy sat at the kitchen table and gestured for Jude to do the same.

"How long have you been here?" Clancy asked.

"Long enough to hear you talking to Mia and something about searching a clearing Mia *showed* you? What the fuck, Clancy? What kind of bullshit crazy talk is this I've walked in on?"

Clancy took a deep calming breath that was of no use whatsoever and prayed her heart wouldn't break as she revealed her true self to Jude. Something flickering caught her eye and she started to see shadows emerging. This was *not* the time for more visitors. She turned her back on the apparitions.

"You know I search for the missing."

Jude gave her a withering look. Clancy continued, ripping the Band-Aid off to expose herself.

"Well, I have an advantage that the other guys who search the waters don't."

"They don't have the backing of whatever the hell it is Douglas and Chandler are a part of."

Clancy nodded. "True. They sought me out, wanting to employ my particular skill set in their unit. It was the offer of a lifetime. An opportunity too good to turn down."

"Inez said you were doing a manifestation ritual out there? Is that some kind of woo-woo Wiccan thing? You were calling for Mia. You believe Mia's dead, a victim of the serial killer you're hunting up and down the Missouri River. If she's dead, she isn't going to be talking to anyone."

"She can talk to me," Clancy said, calm in the knowledge that this truth was unshakable.

Jude stared at her, her stoic face in full force. "You think you're *psychic*?" Jude's tone held enough of an edge to it that Clancy bristled.

Just once could I fuck someone who isn't a skeptic?

"I don't think it, I *know* it." Clancy began wringing the hell out of her hands under the table. This line of conversation never went well unless it was someone paying for her services, desperately wanting to hear what Clancy had to say from a deceased loved one.

Jude's eyes bored into Clancy's. "*You're* psychic?"

Clancy nodded. The white noise that had started behind her began to grate on her nerves. She wished she could shush them, but she didn't want to alert Jude to what was manifesting inside the RV. They'd been with Clancy the last few days. Jude didn't need to know that either.

"I don't believe in any of that stuff." Jude folded her arms across her chest as if protecting herself.

"I understand. Not everyone does. That's okay, each to their own. But it doesn't change the fact that I have certain abilities."

"My grandma used to say that people who spoke to the dead were in line with the devil."

Clancy shifted in her chair enough to stare accusingly at one of the apparitions taking form behind her. "Did she now? Let me guess, she was a God-fearing woman who raised her family to be good little followers of faith and to shun the devil and all those who practiced his evil ways?" Clancy tried not to roll her eyes. "Yeah, I had parents like that."

Jude's eyes softened a fraction. "Did they kick you out because you said you could talk to the dead?"

"No, they kicked me out because I channeled my grandmother who told them, in no uncertain terms, that she thought they were the worst parents on the planet."

Jude frowned at her. "Wait, you said your grandmother *saved* you when you tried to drown yourself."

Clancy nodded. "She did. She'd been dead for three years when she pushed me back to shore for Rainbow to find."

Jude shook her head, her upbringing visibly warring with her belief in Clancy. Indecision was written all over her face. "Grandma said all psychics were charlatans, that they lied to get money from people who were mourning their lost. Besides, if it were real, why wouldn't we all have that power?"

"Because it's rare and apparently not meant for everyone to wield. I never asked for it. There are times when I can't cope with the responsibility it burdens me with. I believe we all do have it though, as children, when we're still open to the universe and the powers it can bestow on us. But a little kid with imaginary friends soon gets told that he's getting too old for all that nonsense. Adults easily erase what power children have, either by being dismissive of it, or by using faith as a scare tactic." Clancy sighed. "If you're told often enough that it's crazy talk, it makes you question yourself. You stifle your ability in order to fit in, to seem normal, to toe the line. We all know nothing sticks unless you work at it."

"And you worked at it?"

"I had no choice. I've been surrounded by the dead since birth. It took me years to realize that not everyone could see what I see. And no amount of beatings could knock the ability out of me or turn it off."

"My brother got a hold of a pack of tarot cards once when we were kids," Jude said. "We thought they were playing cards and were shuffling them for a game of Go Fish when Grandma walked in on us. She went batshit crazy and put the fear of God into us for handling something she said was pure evil. She said we'd bring down the wrath of God upon the family by dabbling in the occult and that we were never to touch anything like that again." Jude down looked at her hands. "She scrubbed our hands raw with a wire brush and disinfectant to cleanse our sin away."

Clancy suddenly understood Jude's reaction a whole lot better. "You were forced into an ungodly fear of the supernatural by a nonbeliever. It happens. I wish it didn't but it's common."

"Maybe as a grown up I could have researched it more, satisfied my own curiosity, but there's still that voice of my grandma condemning us all to hell ringing in my head." Jude looked abashed. "It sounds ridiculous now. I'm an adult, I don't even follow a particular religion anymore, yet I still have a healthy fear of things I was told were evil. Besides, there's enough YouTube psychics and card readers churning out easily fulfilled predictions and guesses for me to never take it seriously." Jude tapered off and gave Clancy a half-hearted shrug.

"No, please, continue telling me how I'm a charlatan and a con artist." Clancy teased her lightly, trying desperately to hide her hurt. She leaned back in her chair and gestured for Jude to bring it on.

"Why didn't you tell me before I had to find out for myself what you think you can do?"

Clancy laughed at her wording. "Again, with the denial. Because I feared this exact response. You know me, Jude. We've become very close, and I've shared things with you that no one else knows or has done with me. Do you really think I am that good at my job that I can just magically find missing people in the deepest of waters?"

"You've got the sonar to find the cars. That's not magic, that's technology," Jude said with a faint air of smugness.

"Yes, but it takes *me* talking to the missing to know which car they're actually *in*." Clancy inwardly cheered when she saw that comment make Jude pause. She cast her eyes to her side. She wasn't going to be able to hold *them* off indefinitely.

Time for the circus master to start the performance.

❖

Jude was intrigued by Clancy's wandering attention. She was talking to her with no problem, but Clancy's gaze kept drifting back toward the hallway. It was almost as if she was looking at someone there. Jude got goose bumps just thinking about it.

Clancy was supposedly psychic. Jude had to admit she was disappointed that her handsome, sexy as fuck butch was deluded enough to think she could talk to the dead. Jude didn't want anything to do with that. She dealt in facts and what she could see. She didn't want to mess with what she couldn't.

Clancy rubbed at her face. "Oh my God, there's always so many voices," she muttered.

Jude was reminded of the time, back at the bar, when Clancy had seemed overwhelmed on the dance floor. Jude remembered Clancy saying something similar.

"What's wrong?" she asked.

Clancy gave her a dismissive look. "You wouldn't believe me if I told you."

"Try me. This seems to be the day for revelations." Jude saw Clancy look down the hallway again. "What are you looking at?"

"I'm waiting for someone to step up and put things right," Clancy said cryptically. "And I'm worried if they do, you'll hightail it out of here and I'll never see you again."

Jude knew things had taken a weird turn in their fledgling relationship. She could see Clancy was hurting, no matter how hard she tried to put a brave face on it.

"Do you trust me enough to know that I have never lied to you?" Clancy reached across the table and laid her hand out for Jude to take.

A light bulb went off in Jude's head. "*Except by omission.* That's what Evan said." She looked at Clancy. "It makes sense now."

Clancy grimaced. "Yeah, that traitorous asshole had the nerve to call me out for not telling you I was psychic and he goes and blabs our secret mission here to score pussy points."

Jude took Clancy's hand in her own. She was surprised to feel a tremor running through it. "Why are you shaking?"

"Because I'm holding back about five generations of Pattersons who are all here wanting to talk to you." Clancy's eyes darkened.

"There's one who's really pushy and I'm going to have to let her speak because I am tired of her living in my head." Clancy let go of Jude's hand and sat up straighter. "Damn it. I usually have time to do my introduction speech and explain what my mission is. But no, she's not going to wait. Okay. Jude, I'm still here, I'm not leaving. You'll hear my voice but it won't be me talking. Don't be afraid. You'll come to no harm."

Jude frowned at her hurried speech. "What do you—"

"Jude! I can't believe how much you've grown. My goodness, you're the spitting image of your grandfather. I always knew you'd never be a pretty girl, but I suppose you're quite handsome in your own way."

Jude startled at the rapid-fire words that burst from Clancy's lips. The change in her was startling. Clancy was still in front of her, it was her voice speaking. But it wasn't her tone or her inflections. Jude recognized the damning praise all too well. Jude looked closer and realized Clancy's eyes had done more than darken. They had *changed*.

Jude knew exactly who those eyes belonged to.

The kitchen chair screeched across the floor as she shot up out of her seat and slammed herself back against the cupboards. "What the fuck?!"

"For shame, I didn't bring you up to use that kind of language! Sit down, child. This isn't the way I would have chosen to speak with you, but Clancy was agreeable and we need to talk."

Chastised and more than a little terrified, Jude slunk back onto her chair. She barely rested one butt cheek on it in case she needed to bolt like Clancy had feared.

"*Grandma?*" Jude couldn't believe what she was seeing and hearing.

"First things first. I know that you're…queer." The word was forced out of Clancy's mouth as if the speaker hadn't wanted to say it aloud. "I'm learning to understand that more from this side of things. It's not the life I would have chosen for you, but you have to make your own path. I *am* proud of who you are and all that you've accomplished."

Stunned, Jude leaned back in her chair as Clancy talked nonstop. Only it still wasn't Clancy. Jude recognized all the speech patterns and the uncanny facial mannerisms her grandma used to have. Clancy was *channeling* her grandma. Jude didn't have a clue how to react. Part of her wanted to run out the door. Another part was oddly angry.

"What kind of game is this? What are you doing to her?" Jude was concerned that Clancy wasn't moving. It was unnatural to see her so still. *All* of this was unnatural.

"She's letting me speak to you. She's been very patient. The minute I knew she was going to tell you what she could do I pestered her to let me speak with you."

"Grandma, if that *is* you, you never believed in any of this." Jude couldn't believe she was entertaining this charade.

"Tufty, I had to learn a great many things weren't what I believed them to be once I crossed over."

Jude rocked back in her chair in shock. She reeled at the use of a childhood nickname that no one outside of her closest family knew. Clancy had no way of knowing it. But her grandma would have.

"I learned none of it matters. Not what religion you are, what beliefs you have, if you worship one god or multiple gods, if you're high church or pagan. They all have their good and bad points and they all have a purpose in life to teach us something. Mostly, to see if you can respect other people's beliefs, even if they don't mix well with your own. Who knew, right?"

Jude couldn't believe what she was seeing *or* hearing; her grandma finally getting an ounce of understanding. Jude wondered if she was going crazy because this was about as bizarre as things could be.

"I'm aware, when I was alive, I would have condemned Clancy for communing with the dead. Yet, without her, I couldn't be talking to you now. She's genuine, Jude. She really does have these powers and she's using them for good in the world. You will too. You'll do great things together once you erase the damage I did in my ignorance and religious fervor. I could blame it on being raised in a different time. That we were brought up harsher and to be hard, and that punishment was always meant to frighten you into obedience and not be something you learned from. I can't say sorry enough. I was perpetuating the wrong visited on me. You know my father was a preacher who firmly believed in spare the rod, spoil the child."

Jude didn't know what to say. Her parents had raised her as best they could, but her grandma had been the punishing force in the household. She'd terrified Jude as a child.

"Where is Grandpa?" Jude's grandpa had been her saving grace. A kind man, whose life's work had been to keep the peace and hide his grandchildren as best he could from his abusive wife.

"He moved on. Some of us choose to stay behind in case our family needs us. I waited because I needed to reach out to you, Jude. I was wrong to force my fears onto you. You grew up so strong anyway and you served your country well. I'm so proud of you. And you did it all being a better person than I could ever have been."

Jude was dumfounded by the praise. It wasn't something her grandma ever did, no matter how high Jude's grades were. Jude had always studied fiercely, in fear of letting her down, and suffering the consequences.

"You always heeded my words when you were a child. Well, now I'm telling you that you *have* to believe in what Clancy can do and not be afraid of it."

Jude watched as Clancy's eyes started to flicker and she could see Clancy's blue start to emerge again. But her grandma wasn't finished.

"This thing you're doing now? Finding those women? You need to believe in your girl because it's the only way this is ever going to stop."

CHAPTER NINETEEN

Clancy slowly regained ownership of her body again. She felt Jude's grandma slip away, freeing her. Relieved, Clancy stretched to rid her body of the restrictive confines it had felt when she had been, for want of a better word, possessed.

"Well, that was weird," Clancy said when she came fully back to herself. "No goodbyes, just an abrupt ending. She never even said she loved you before she split. Those are usually the last words in every channeling I do."

"She never said it much when she was alive, I guess not everything changes when you get enlightened on the other side." Jude looked like she'd been put through an emotional wringer. She flipped open the box of doughnuts with shaky hands, took one out, and pushed the box toward Clancy. "I either take a sugar fix fast or I go buy a bottle of whiskey and drink it down in one."

"Your grandma's a piece of work." Clancy deliberated over the doughnuts then picked two out, one for each hand, and took a bite from each in turn. "To be honest, I like your aunt Dolly way more."

Jude choked on her doughnut. "You know my aunt Dolly?"

"She's been visiting on and off the last few days as well as your grandma. She told me she was the original big-breasted blond Dolly way before that Dolly Parton stole her title. She's a real card. Quite the sweetheart."

"My family has been *haunting* you?"

"*Visiting.* I should have known I was going to have to fess up by how many of them kept popping up to say hi and testing the waters, so to speak, as to whether I would let them speak to you." Clancy savored a mouthful of a perfectly glazed doughnut with a hum of bliss. "Apparently, your grandma won the coin toss and got to be the mouthpiece."

Jude's doughnut never reached her mouth. "If they've been *visiting*, did they watch us…you know?"

"*Now* you're suddenly shy?" Clancy was enchanted by the bloom of a blush on Jude's fear whitened cheeks. "No, they don't watch us having sex. They have some manners." Clancy finished off her doughnuts then picked out another two. "It's my own fault. I do this thing where I open up my channels and call out if there's anyone there. Your ancestors are aware we've been hanging out," Clancy waggled her eyebrows at Jude, "and decided I was inviting them in." She took a mouthful of a cream-filled doughnut and sighed. "These are great. Thank you for bringing them over."

Jude shook her head, clearly still shell-shocked. "How can you be so calm? My whole world has just been turned upside down. My grandma has just told me religion doesn't matter."

"Oh, lover, I could have told you that."

"And she apologized for being the absolute tyrant that she was." Jude was in utter disbelief.

"Yeah." Clancy smiled. "That was oddly sweet." She held up what was left of her doughnut. "What's this one?"

Jude checked it out. "Blueberry icing, chewy blueberry bubbles, and a lychee-flavored frosting."

Clancy shoved the remaining piece into her mouth. She spoke around it. "I like this one a lot."

"You've just let a dead person take control of your body and you're more interested in the doughnuts?" Jude gazed incredulously at her.

"You forget, I do this for a living. It's not a big deal for me. But new Krispy Kremes are very exciting."

"Is there anything else you haven't told me? Let's just get all of this out onto the table." Jude looked like she was bracing herself for an onslaught.

"I do occasional tours around town halls doing mediumship work. I'm also available for bachelorette parties and birthdays too. It pays the bills when it's too cold to dive. Birthday parties are awesome because I usually get cake."

"You know I'm freaking out inside but am too afraid to show it?" Jude's voice shook. Her eyes were still wide and wary.

"Yeah, I can tell but you're doing a great job trying not to run out, screaming into the road."

"You're a psychic and my dearly departed, flame- and brimstone-flinging grandma has just used you as her mouthpiece to tell me that's okay." Jude shook her head in disbelief. She started picking at a sprinkle on her doughnut. "Can I ask why you made Inez leave and take my cat with her?"

"Because I didn't know what kind of messages you were going to receive. Those should be private to you. I know from experience not all messages are what the receiver expects to hear. Also, I wasn't sure how Smokey Joe would react because animals can be incredibly sensitive to a visitation. I didn't want to freak both of you out. I kind of knew I was going to have to channel because your grandma is a pushy broad and wasn't going to take no for an answer." Clancy smiled at Jude. "I grew up in a household of abuse too. But Inez didn't. I was not prepared to subject her to you reacting poorly to my channeling or to whatever your grandma could have said."

"I'd never react with violence," Jude said, looking affronted.

"Disparaging words can be just as damaging too."

Mollified, Jude raised her doughnut as if she were raising a glass to Clancy. "No greater truth spoken." She took a bite from her doughnut. "I bet Inez never got as far as getting the key in the door before Mrs. Baker invited her over for a cup of tea."

Clancy laughed and agreed. "Yeah, you don't need to be psychic to know that's a fact."

The doughnuts were quickly polished off, mostly by Clancy who needed the sugar rush and carbs after the channeling. Clancy eyed Jude across the table. She hated the distance between them, but she was waiting for Jude to make the first move back into Clancy's arms. Jude had finally calmed down from her grandma's visit. Clancy wondered if now would be the best time to mention what else she'd been experiencing.

"You're making that face again," Jude said, her lips quirked just enough to warm Clancy's heart.

"What face when?"

"When you know I'm tired, but you either want to give me one more orgasm or you need me to get you off."

"I have a face for that?" Clancy was intrigued.

"It's like you want to ask me for something but you're not sure how I'll answer and you don't want to bother me…but you do."

"Wow, all that written on my face. No wonder you always know what I need."

"So, what else do you need to tell me that you're worried I'm going to freak out about?"

Clancy wished they had more doughnuts. "Sometimes, when I'm over at your place? ThewallsmoveandIseethings." Clancy figured the quicker she said it, the quicker they could move on.

"You're seeing things in *my* apartment?" Jude stared at her in barely disguised horror.

"Sometimes, like a shadow, or a movement out of the corner of my eye. And before you ask, no, it's not the cat." Clancy chewed on her lip, worried how to break the whole "hands coming through the walls" experience.

Jude reached over and ran her thumb over Clancy's lip. "Stop that. You'll hurt yourself."

Clancy loved how fast Jude could switch from being unnerved and then into protector mode. She licked at Jude's thumb, tasting a dash of frosting. "Do you believe me now?"

Jude nodded. "I have no choice. I think you proved it with Grandma."

Clancy was intrigued. "How so?"

"She called me a name that was only known by the family. A silly, childhood nickname that got lost as I grew up."

"*Tufty.*" Clancy smiled and reached over to touch Jude's hair. "Please tell me that's in honor of your *Herge's Adventures of TinTin* quiff bit going on at the front here." She playfully tugged at Jude's hair that stuck out.

Jude slapped her hand away. "That piece has always been unruly, even as a child."

"Tufty is a very cute name."

"Don't even think of introducing it into play," Jude warned her.

"It's quite the play on words though. It could mean this." Clancy risked another tug at Jude's hair. "Or tough. You grew up embodying that word."

"You are not calling me it, even as a tease." Jude's voice brooked no argument.

"What if you were sick and I was caring for you, and you're all feverish and snotty, and I'm holding you close, and soothing your brow, and I'm calling you my girl, and 'my sweet Tufty' slips out?"

Jude stared at her for a long moment, then asked stonily, "What the hell else is in my apartment that you are distracting me with that damned name instead of telling me?"

"Fuck, you're wicked smart," Clancy said, impressed with how quickly Jude saw through her shenanigans. "Every time I have slept with you there, I have had visions connected to Mia. Last night, while I was sitting on your face, I was taken by a faceless entity over the city, out to an area where Mia's car was parked and a guy was threatening her. Then I was flying over the river. I got pulled down into it, deep down into the water where I couldn't breathe and was close to drowning until I yelled out."

Jude's eyes went wide in realization. "I thought you were in the throes of passion screaming 'You're killing me!' I felt like a real stud pulling that out of you." She grimaced expressively. "Fuck, this is going to take some getting used to."

Clancy felt her heart tighten with hope. "You're going to stay?"

"With *you*? Yes, if you still want me to." Now Jude looked unsure.

"I think I'll always want you to, Tufty." Clancy gave Jude her most innocent smile.

Jude let out a heartfelt groan. "God, why couldn't you have just channeled Aunt Dolly instead?"

"By the way, did you notice your grandma called me 'your girl.'" Clancy had been shocked to hear that come out of her mouth, both hers *and* Grandma's.

Jude nodded. "I heard that too. In life, she'd have probably chased you off our property with her shotgun blazing if you'd come anywhere near me with your sinful ways."

Clancy started picking the icing off the box lid and licking it off her fingers. "I'm not sorry she's dead then," she stated.

Jude stifled her laughter.

"You can laugh," Clancy said. "Your grandma and her posse left ages ago. From now on I'll try to give you a heads up if we have *visitors*."

"Thank God." Jude pulled Clancy around the table to have her sit on her lap. She held Clancy tight. "I don't pretend to understand what you do. Truthfully, it frightens the shit out of me. But you *are* my girl and I'm not going anywhere. You'll have to be patient with me, though. I have a lifetime of fear and false teachings to cast aside to understand you more."

Relieved, Clancy snuggled in as close as she could get. Jude rubbed her chin gently over Clancy's hair.

"How about we go back to my place to assure Inez we're okay? We could grab a ton of tacos on the way?"

Clancy kissed Jude in gratitude. "See, you understand me perfectly already."

Chapter Twenty

Jude had never seen her apartment as a family home. It was where she kept her clothes, had food in the cupboards and slept before going to work. Even the inclusion of Smokey Joe hadn't elevated it to anything more than just an apartment…with a cat.

She watched as Clancy and Inez set out the food on the table. Inez was telling Clancy off for opening all the bags and boxes and trying to sample what was inside before they sat down properly to eat. Smokey Joe was rubbing himself against Jude's legs, meowing to make sure his voice was heard too.

"Hey, lover, you coming to join us?"

Clancy's voice called Jude out from her introspection. Jude took a seat beside her and helped herself to what was on offer.

"I'm really glad you know everything that we do now," Inez said, picking out a taco for herself, then adding one large over-stuffed taco, spilling out cheese and salsa, onto Clancy's plate. "I know you're still wary and a little uncertain about what this all means now, but it will be fine, I promise you."

Jude looked at her from over her taco. "What, is my face giving away that I'm still reeling a little after this morning?"

Clancy spoke with her mouth full. "Inez is an empath. She knows how you're feeling before you do."

Jude's eyebrows raised. "Is that because you're the daughter of a seventh daughter of a seventh daughter?"

Clancy snorted into her food. "Did you threaten Jude with that?" She wagged her finger at Inez. "Your mother said you can't keep using that line as fighting talk."

"I was just standing up for you." Inez was unrepentant.

"She was, and I'm very grateful to see you have her on your side. Empath, eh? So, what does that entail?" Jude was genuinely interested in learning more about Inez.

"I am highly attuned to what others are feeling. I can feel the emotions they are experiencing, and use it, if I need to, to help them get through trauma or pain."

"She's an excellent grief counselor," Clancy said. "When I was taken on for this job, I knew I needed someone who would be sympathetic to the families and what they were feeling. She also helps me get through what I see and do. She's invaluable in helping me face so much death and not go crazy with the grief connected to it."

"We've had a connection since before I was born." Inez said, smiling at Clancy with more than a little hero worship.

Jude looked at them both. "*Before* you were born?"

Clancy nodded. "When Rainbow was pregnant, I could *see* Inez. She was a little spirit, held in limbo, until she was due to be born. She was so damn cute, like a little Casper the Ghost, scampering around."

"You can see unborn babies?" Jude wondered why she was surprised.

"Sometimes, but not always. They're not completely tethered to the earth until they're born. I think I could see Inez because I was so close to her mother. Rainbow raised me from a teenager. She kept what she fished out of the river that day."

"She's still raising you," Inez muttered.

"Sad but true," Clancy agreed. "It's also true that it takes a village to raise a child and I had all the commune ready to teach me. I learned how to control my psychic ability and set boundaries. From birth I had always been overwhelmed by the spirits I could see in the living world. I had someone show me how to put up some walls to keep them at bay."

"You get overwhelmed by the voices," Jude said, realizing how hard it must be to have constant, otherworldly, distractions in your day-to-day life. "Wait. The night we met I remember you were struggling on the dance floor. What the fuck is at my workplace and do I not have anywhere to go free from ghostly presences?"

Clancy reached for more salsa and spooned it liberally on a taco. "There are some nasty patrons still in residence at the bar, including an owner with a distinct hatred for anything gay. You might want to get your friendly neighborhood smudgers to come in and cleanse the place. The atmosphere would lighten considerably once they are all crossed over."

Inez grinned at Jude. "We're really good at it and if all else fails, Clancy threatens them with sending in the reapers."

"And what are reapers?"

"Angels who reap the souls of the dead and dying? The ones who accompany you on your walk into the light?" Clancy said as if everyone should know that.

Jude's jaw dropped. "Angels? Like, *real* angels? White wings, left hand of God kind of angels?"

Clancy nodded and added cockily, "Now you know why your grandma thinks I'm kind of a catch. I've been known to consort with one or two."

"We have to revisit this conversation again sometime when my mind isn't so frazzled. My girlfriend can see the dead *and* angels." Jude blew out a breath as she took all that in. "I have a feeling I'm about to get a whole new perspective on life with you two." Jude startled when Smokey Joe jumped into her lap. "Make that three." She looked around her apartment apprehensively. "Are you sensing anything here now?"

Clancy shook her head. "No. I think I have to be..." She cut a glance at Inez who stopped eating once she realized Clancy was hesitating to finish.

"What?" Inez asked.

"In a heightened state of sexual euphoria which lets my walls down so whatever or whoever is making me see things can just walk right in and mess with my mind." Clancy smiled sheepishly at Jude.

"You're gonna need Aunty Joyce to strengthen those mental walls again," Inez said, continuing with her meal as if Clancy and

Jude's sexual practices hadn't just been bought up over the dinner table.

"Either that or we never have sex here in the apartment again." Jude added.

"Nooo!" Clancy complained. "I love coming here!"

Jude sniggered at Clancy's unintentional double entendre. Clancy groaned when she realized what she'd said and her cheeks reddened.

Inez just shook her head at them. "Many a true word is spoken in jest."

Clancy totally cracked up at Inez's calm and superior air. Her laughter set Jude off even more.

Inez just smiled at them both. "Welcome to the family, Jude. I think you're going to fit right in to the madness."

❖

Satisfied and slightly overstuffed, Clancy sprawled out on Jude's settee and gazed around the room. It was functional, sparce, and nothing really screamed out that this was Jude's home.

"You really need to stamp your personality on this place, Jude. It needs more stuff."

Jude was in a chair opposite, with Smokey Joe fast asleep in her lap. "To be honest, I never really considered the apartment was mine to stay in long. I guess I was so used to traveling in the navy that having a permanent place just seems wrong."

"Do you like it here though, in Kansas City?" Inez asked from her end of the settee, where she was curled up, clutching a pillow, and trying not to fall asleep in a food coma.

"It's been a change of scenery, that's for sure. And I've made a few friends." Jude stroked Smokey Joe's long fur. "I just didn't expect to lose one so quickly."

Clancy ached at Jude's loss. "I wish we could offer you a better ending to Mia's vanishing. At least now I can call for her while you're with me and not have to do extra trips in the boat."

"Did you map the areas while you went out on your own?"

"No, that would have made you suspicious. I just sailed out and called to her. But she hasn't called back yet."

"What if she never does?"

Jude sounded so despondent it broke Clancy's heart.

"I'll find her, Jude. I promise you, wherever she is, I will find her."

"But how can you be so sure?"

Clancy wondered if she should inform Jude of the first thing she'd noticed about her. Inez gave her a pointed look and Jude noticed their silent conversation.

"What is my world going to be rocked with now, with you two sharing *that* look between you?" Jude sat up straighter and Smokey Joe grumbled at being moved.

Clancy gave her a reassuring smile. "It's just that, when I first saw you? In the restaurant? You had someone with you."

Jude nodded. "Yes, I was with Amber."

"No, I saw someone *else* with you. An apparition, not well formed, not entirely present."

Jude stared at her. "You're saying I had a *ghost* with me?"

"I'm saying you had some kind of entity with you at that moment in time. I haven't seen it since."

Jude looked grateful for that. "So, who was it?"

Clancy shrugged. "I don't know. It was faceless and formless, but definitely with you and not with your friend."

"I never felt anything. Well, other than an instant attraction to the stunningly attractive, dark-haired butch who walked into the place and promptly ordered half the menu." Jude's eyes sparkled with humor.

"She's constantly hungry. Mom says it's like trying to keep a teenage boy fed," Inez said.

Clancy was enjoying Jude's admiring gaze on her. It warmed her like her touch did. "Can I go into your bedroom?" she asked before she could stop herself.

Jude smirked. "You don't normally ask."

Clancy laughed. "I want to try something."

"Do I need to go back to the RV?" Inez asked.

"No, not that kind of something," Clancy assured her. "You don't still have your spare key to Mia's apartment, do you. Jude?"

Jude shook her head. "I handed them over to her sister when she came to close the place up. Mrs. Baker said she saw a junk removal van here a while ago, taking stuff away, but I haven't been here enough to see anything myself. Why?"

"I was going to see if I could pick up anything from her apartment. That was her home, her energy would leave imprints there. And whatever is pushing at the walls is wanting me to notice them." She stood up and stretched, lazily scratching at her stomach. "I'll try something, then I'll go get us some ice cream."

"Oh my God," Inez groaned. "How can you possibly have room for anything else?"

"I always have room for ice cream." Clancy walked past Jude, brushing her fingers through Jude's hair just to touch her again.

"Can I come watch you?" Jude asked.

Clancy was surprised but happy that Jude was willing to embrace all that she was "Sure, but I'm told it's nothing spectacular. To the observer, I apparently go very still and am deaf to anyone talking to me."

Jude carried Smokey Joe over to Inez's welcoming arms. "Still and unresponsive like you did in the water that time?"

Clancy nodded, amazed at how sharp Jude was. "I'd thought I'd heard something so I reached out to it. I didn't mean to freak you out. I wasn't aware I had tuned out for as long as I did. I have no concept of time when I do it. The world literally grinds to a halt around me."

Jude reached out to link her fingers with Clancy's. "Show me. Let me recognize when your world stops while mine continues spinning."

Clancy led them into Jude's bedroom. It was as plain as the living room. But for Clancy it was the place she and Jude got to express their passion and she loved it.

Jude loosened her grip and sat on the bed. She waited for Clancy to start.

"I know it sounds silly, me calling for someone, but it's how this all works. How *I* work. Roll with me here."

Jude nodded and left Clancy to do her thing.

Clancy looked around the room. She was searching the walls for anything visible in the daylight. Nothing bowed out even a fraction for her to notice. "I am not sparking something off by having sex in here while Inez is in the other room," she said.

Inez's voice sounded out from the living room. "I appreciate that."

Clancy grinned at Jude and stole a kiss from her smiling lips. "Okay. Let's see if there's anyone here."

She closed her eyes and listened to the room. She could hear Jude's breathing, the odd creak of wood, the distant noise of a baby crying in another apartment. She tuned that out and felt for the psychic vibrations of the room. She opened her eyes and placed her hands against the wall. It was firm beneath her touch.

"Mia, are you here with us? You used to live here, on the other side of this wall. Are you still here? Can you come to me? Can you follow my voice and find me in Jude's room? She's worried about you, Mia. You've been gone a while now. I can help you. I can talk to you. I need you to tell me where you are so I can find you."

Clancy waited. She could hear only her heart beat and the faint buzz of electricity that ran through the walls.

"Mia, we're waiting for you."

Clancy felt something shift around her. She pressed her hands harder against the wall. She strained to hear. She could hear something, faint, muffled, coming closer.

"Mia, is that *you*?"

BANG! BANG! BANG!

Clancy startled as the wall vibrated beneath her with the deafening noise. She jumped back and braced herself for whatever was going to push through.

"Fucking hell!" Jude exclaimed, her hand on her chest.

"What the hell was that?" Inez rushed into the room, holding Smokey Joe close to her.

"Honey, I'm gonna need more nails!"

Everyone easily heard the muffled voice of a man shouting from next door.

Clancy rested her head against the wall and sighed. "I think that's your new neighbors hanging pictures on the adjoining wall, Jude."

Jude fell back on her bed with a groan. "Give a girl a heart attack."

Inez started to giggle.

Clancy patted the wall and shook her head. "Their energies will push Mia's aside. So, we keep looking elsewhere. The river still has miles to go." She clapped her hands as if dusting them off. "So, if no one here needs CPR, who wants ice cream?"

❖

Jude lay tucked under Clancy's chin, feeling safe and secure. It was an unusual shift in positions for them, but Jude needed the feel of Clancy's arms around her after the day she'd experienced.

They lay naked together in Clancy's bed in the RV. Jude had gone into work as usual that evening, but her mind hadn't been fully on her job and she'd sleepwalked through most of it. She'd been very surprised to see Clancy saunter in at closing time.

"After the day you've had, I didn't want you to be left alone."

She'd instructed Jude to follow her motorcycle on the short trip back to the police parking lot. She picked up an overnight bag from Jude's apartment, along with Smokey Joe who was already fast asleep in his second home's bed.

For Jude, it felt oddly like coming home too. Home to Clancy, happy to see Inez, and gratified to see Smokey Joe sprawled out, fed, watered, and snoring lightly.

Now Jude was running her fingertips along Clancy's collarbone, trying desperately to get her brain to shut down and let her rest. Sleep eluded her. Snippets of the day's revelations kept coming back to her in vivid colors. Her grandma, an unmistakable voice from beyond the grave. Clancy, calling out for Mia. Angels, according to her girlfriend, being *real*.

Jude didn't know if she'd ever sleep again.

"Did I ever tell you how I got this RV?" Clancy's voice was low in the darkness.

"You said it was a gift from a client. I have to admit, it's some gift."

"About three years ago, I was doing a town hall mediumship gig. I'd relayed messages for families, done my two hours, and was doing a meet and greet after…"

"You do meet and greets?"

"I'm quite well known in my field back home. I might even have groupies."

"You'd better not have groupies." Jude deliberately tweaked Clancy's nipple, making her squirm.

"They're all in their eighties, do they still count?" Clancy smoothed a hand over Jude's back to soothe her ire.

Jude grumbled a little and palmed Clancy's breast possessively.

"Anyway, I was meeting and greeting and ready to leave when a man came up to me. He looked very upset. I was hoping he wasn't expecting me to do a personal reading then and there seeing as I didn't really have time."

Clancy dug her fingers a little harder at a sore spot on Jude's shoulder she'd been favoring and Jude felt herself melt under her touch. "What did he want?" she asked, grunting softly as Clancy worked to loosen her tight muscles.

"He told me his son was missing. He and his wife were going through a very messy divorce and he'd been granted sole custody of the child. While he was at work, his wife had gone to the school and signed the boy out. He had no clue where they were. The police were involved, the FBI too for a missing child, but it had been three weeks and they'd found nothing."

"That's awful. So, he wanted you to try to find him?"

"Yeah, but I deal in the dead, not the living. I got the kid's name and called out to him but all I got was silence. I promised the guy I'd keep trying and took his number, but I didn't hold out much hope. If the kid was alive, I wouldn't be able to find him. And I really didn't want to find out he was dead."

"So, what happened?" Jude listened to Clancy's heartbeat under her ear. It was becoming her favorite sound.

"I called out to him, little Solomon Marshall, for two weeks."

Jude shifted in Clancy's arms. "I recognize that name."

"Yeah, he was all over the news. Mr. Marshall had the money to publicize the disappearance. He'd been contacted by a variety of psychics too, but nothing came of their visions. Every lead was a dead end."

"Did he ever say why he chose you?"

"He'd watched my show that night and saw I wasn't much for theatrics. I don't do the 'I have a man here who passed suddenly' that could be for anyone. I deal with the dead. They remember their earthly names and who they want to speak to. They don't have time to watch me play guessing games with an audience for dramatic effect." Clancy huffed in annoyance at the ones who employed that tactic. "But if someone genuine asks, I will do my damnedest to help them. So, I kept calling for Solomon. And one day, he replied."

Jude lifted herself up to look at Clancy. "You found him?"

"I *heard* him, it's not the same. I asked him where he was. He said he was locked in a room and that he felt funny and he was so cold. I asked if he could get up and go look out a window but he said he wasn't able to move his limbs anymore."

Jude's heart ached with realization. "You don't find the *living*."

Clancy nodded. "He was dying. Turns out his mother had been drugging him to keep him from running away from her. She'd overdosed him and I was able to hear him because he was slipping away. I told him he could get up if he tried hard enough and that I needed him to go downstairs and find anything with an address on it. I waited and heard him exclaim he was floating. He spirit-walked down the stairs and found an envelope with the address."

"Oh my God," Jude whispered, caught up in the story.

"I told him to go back upstairs, that I'd be there soon and I was bringing his father. But he had to go back into his body or we'd be too late." Clancy shook her head at the memory. "I called his father, raced over in my pickup to his house, all the while talking to Solomon and telling him to hang on. The wife hadn't gone far, she'd just been laying low under an assumed name and hidden by relatives. Mr. Marshall got us in one of his sport cars and we broke all speed limits getting to the house. You know, that man never flinched when I was next to him, talking into thin air, holding a conversation with his boy.

He had so much faith in me and I was fucking getting him to that kid if it was the last thing I ever did."

Jude kissed her chest. "I'm so proud of you."

"Mr. Marshall called the police. They didn't exactly believe him that a psychic said she'd found his son, but the department sent enough men for backup and called for an ambulance too."

"I seem to remember the kid being found alive?"

"Yeah, we got there in time. That dumb bitch opened the door when I said I was from a sweepstakes company. Mr. Marshall pushed her aside and we ran upstairs. The key was in the door and Solomon was inside, barely breathing but clinging on. I remember him saying 'You found me' before the medics rushed in and he was whisked away."

"Tell me the mother got time?"

"She's in prison for kidnapping and attempted murder. I should have decked her when I had the chance, but I was too busy trying to keep Solomon tethered to the earth. He came so close to passing over."

"I like happy endings." Jude settled back down in Clancy's arms.

"Me too. When Solomon was out of the hospital I was invited to visit and that kid was super cool. Mr. Marshall was asking me about my business. I was just starting to search waterways back then. I had a little boat, a small trailer hooked up to my pickup, and I slept in the truck while I traveled around. He asked if he and Solomon could sponsor me. I had no idea what that entailed, but he explained it all and what he wanted to do. He got me a better boat and all the equipment I use. Solomon picked me out a house on wheels so I didn't have to sleep in my truck anymore. To be honest, I was expecting a tent. You can imagine how dumbfounded I was when he gave me everything you see now. He had me pick out what I needed inside the RV so it was specifically designed for my needs. I tried to tell him it was way too much, that I didn't deserve it, but he wouldn't hear it. He said I'd found his son and he wanted me to help bring others home to their family. He knew how lucky he'd been. I don't save the living. Solomon is still the only one."

"If I remember right, Mr. Marshall was a self-made multi-millionaire?"

"Yes, he works in real estate. He's big on building homes for the homeless. I'm very proud to have that advertisement on my RV. He got some of his friends to sponsor me too and they kept me running and able to do the job I do until the DDU required my assistance and I was able to be more self-sufficient. I keep in touch regularly to let Mr. Marshall know how I'm doing." Clancy hugged Jude a little tighter. "Solomon visits us sometimes, at the commune. Seems his NDE gave him a gift to bring back with him."

"NDE?"

"Near-death experience. He gets visions now. He's got the makings of a seer."

Jude digested that. "Fuck, that's wild." Jude pressed her lips to Clancy's chest. "And you are amazing."

"I just listen and follow where I'm called."

"I wish all your cases were happy endings like Solomon's was." Jude knew how Clancy was affected by the sadness of it all. She felt Clancy's chest rise as she let out a sigh.

"Me too, lover, me too."

Chapter Twenty-one

Clancy was making the most of this being the last big stretch of quiet water before it headed into the city to flow amid the hustle and bustle of Kansas City's vibrant population. Here, no one was watching them. Further on, they would have less chance for anonymity and more boats to contend with.

Clancy kept her eyes fixed on the sonar screens while Jude expertly manned the boat. The prior search had been routine, all just part of the job she'd been hired to do. Scour the water, find something, tick a name off the list, move onto the next flow of water. Now it was personal. Clancy was searching for Mia Murray and Mia was Jude's friend. Jude was relying on her to be found, and Clancy felt dutybound to be that person.

Clancy shivered suddenly. She looked up, but the sun was still shining. What the fuck, she thought, running a hand over the hair that was standing up on her arm. "Stop the boat," she said.

Jude did so immediately and waited for further instructions.

"I've just gotten goose bumps," Clancy said, holding her arm up for Jude to see.

"If you're packing ice underneath your life jacket, hand some of it over, I'm sweating off pounds here." Jude reached out to run her fingers over Clancy's pebbled flesh. "What the hell, Clancy? You're freezing cold to the touch." She rubbed at Clancy's flesh to try to warm her up.

"Mia?" Clancy turned around in the boat and looked down the river to where they were due to sail next. "Is this you?" She listened intently but heard no sound. "Can anyone hear my voice? Come forward, call to me. I'll find you." She waited again.

Jude stopped touching her and stayed silent. Clancy appreciated how Jude didn't feel the need to question her every utterance. Evan had constantly asked what she heard, was anyone there, until she'd told him all she could hear was his damn voice. He'd been ejected from the boat, designated as backup-only within his first week.

"We need to sail farther along," Clancy said. Jude set the boat off while Clancy rubbed at her arms absentmindedly.

Jude brought them to a halt in the next quadrant. "What are you feeling?" she asked.

"I'm drawn farther down the river, but I'm mapping all this out first because I'm not missing something because I'm too eager to look somewhere else."

The river was clear. The sonar showed no anomalies as they sailed, keeping a steady pace. Clancy kept looking down river. The silence beckoned her on.

"I'm being drawn down that way." She gestured to Jude to stop the boat again. She closed her eyes and reached out. "Is there anyone here? If you can hear me, answer me, please. I'm here to find you. I'm here to take you home." She worried at her arms again, this time around her wrists. Clancy opened her eyes, half expecting them to be bleeding. "Whoever is making me feel this, I need you to stop. I'm here, let me find you and help you." She ran her finger over the welt masked beneath the tattoo's ink. "Inez, I think something's waiting for us here."

"Nobody is answering though, what's up with that?" Inez said over the radio.

"No idea. We'll keep mapping. I'm leaving no stone unscanned." She looked over at Jude whose face was deathly pale. She looked like she was going to throw up. "Are you okay?"

"I'm suddenly extremely nervous," Jude said, looking embarrassed at being so obvious.

"It's okay. Something is out here, messing with the ether. You might be picking up on it too."

"You're very kind. We both know I'm shit-scared that you're picking up on my friend, dead and buried in a car somewhere upstream." Jude shook her arms out and tilted her head back and forth to crack her neck as if readying herself for a fight. "I thought I was prepared for this, but being here, on the water, with you calling out her name? I just got really scared you're going to find her." Jude rubbed roughly at her face.

"You know if we find a car I am diving on it alone?"

Jude nodded. "I know. That makes me a little scared for you too. I know how much it affects you."

Clancy tugged Jude forward by her life jacket and kissed her soundly. "You can do this, sailor. I have every confidence in you. We're going to get through this together, okay? I'm here. I'm not leaving your side."

"You promise?" Jude's voice was quiet.

"I promise." Clancy whispered her words against Jude's lips. "Let's keep going."

Jude steered the boat farther along the river. They both spotted something at the same time.

"Is that a car?" Jude asked, pointing at the screen.

"Move us around a little, let's see it from a different angle." Clancy stared intently at the shape of something lying on the bottom of the river. As the boat moved and changed the angle of the sonar, the distinct shape of a vehicle made itself clear. "Inez, we have something."

"I see it. Drop a buoy then come get suited up," Inez said. "I'll move the RV down to the boat dock a quarter-mile back from where you are."

"We'll see you shortly." Clancy eyed Jude. "Care to take us above it so we can drop a line to mark its spot?"

Jude did so with a minimum of fuss. She looked over at the trees lining the bank, providing a shady canopy over the river. "Hey, is that space between the trees over there big enough to drive a car through?"

Clancy squinted at it as she tried to picture it. "I'd say yes. You can see where the foliage has been damaged. Something could have come through there. Inez is parking by the boat dock that has the ramp that runs straight into the water. This car wouldn't have entered the water from back there and floated all this way. The current isn't that fast here. So I'd say it's a very good chance that it was run through the foliage and pushed down the natural incline of the bank there. The killer doesn't stay long in the car once he's finished with the women. He pushes the cars into the water by ramming them with a heavy grill on the front of his truck."

Jude opened her mouth to ask something then stopped. "The women told you that, didn't they?"

"Yes. Their stories are all the same. They meet a guy, he's a gentleman, and they date. Then one night he changes, Mr. Hyde comes out and he kills them with no provocation. He then drives them to a pre-selected area and pushes them into the water with the truck he drives away in. No one sees him and no one is left alive to speak about him. Until I turn up."

"He's confident to leave a truck out in the open."

"A lot of the river has places to park alongside. No one is going to question a truck conveniently loaded with fishing gear by a riverside." Clancy studied the sonar screen. The car's shape was undeniable. "It was a Chevrolet she drove, right?"

"Yes, a black one. Totally not her color, but she got it cheap and it ran well."

Clancy gathered up the line with the magnet. "Let's tag it then get back to moor this thing so we can get our gear on. One way or another, we're diving on a car today." She nudged Jude. "Your first one."

"I've got a horrible feeling, Clancy." Jude nervously tugged at her jacket. "I was never this nervous in all the time I dove in the ocean."

"You were fixing things then. This is something you can't fix, no matter how hard you wish you could."

"Why aren't they talking to you?"

Clancy dropped the line into the water. "I don't honestly know."

But I guess I'll find out, she thought, watching the line sink deeper and deeper into the darkness below.

❖

Jude zipped up her wet suit. She was very aware that, this time, Clancy didn't make any sly comments about how sexy Jude looked in it. In fact, Clancy had barely spoken while she had gotten into her own suit.

"Do you believe something's in that car?" Jude asked, breaking the silence.

Clancy glanced over at her. "Yes."

"But whatever it is, it doesn't answer when you call?"

"Nope." Clancy pulled on her hood. "And that's not helping because my whole deal is, I call, they answer, we talk."

Inez sat on the RV steps watching them. "Please be careful. I have a really bad feeling about this."

"You and Jude both." Clancy started her regular routine of checks of her gear.

"Do *you*?" Inez asked her.

"You know me, kiddo. No matter how I feel, I just need to go dive on that car and hope we get our answers." Clancy leaned over and kissed Inez on her forehead. "Watch over us."

Inez nodded. "Always."

Clancy picked up her diving mask and handed Jude hers. "Let's go see what this car is doing at the bottom of the Mighty Missouri River."

They left Inez at the RV to monitor the dive. Jude couldn't help but feel something was off about Clancy, but then, this was the first time she'd been with her when there was a car to be dived on. Jude told herself to just trust Clancy's process. In this instance, she was the lead. Doing this was second nature to Clancy. This was still Jude's first time with a car involved. She'd watch and learn, like always.

"I wish they'd just answer me," Clancy said, trying to sound lighthearted and upbeat, but Jude could see it was weighing on her.

"Has this happened before?"

"No. I'm clairaudient, I hear the dead speak. And usually, when I speak, they answer back."

Jude slowed the boat as they reached where the buoy was marking its spot. Clancy looked into the water before speaking again.

"If there *is* someone in the car, you're going to hear me talking a lot. I wish I could split myself in two, because if this *is* Mia, then I want to be with her to release her. But I also want to be with you because I know how devastating it will be for you if we've found her."

"I'll take everything a step at a time. We have a job to do. I'll focus on that first." Jude wanted to assure Clancy that she wasn't going to let her down.

"I know you will, lover. That's why I'm glad to have you onboard." Clancy picked up her helmet then leaned in for a kiss. "Here's to helping someone find peace today."

Jude kissed her back. "You're a good person, Clancy Madsen. Go do your thing." She gave her one more kiss for good luck.

Clancy put her helmet on and made sure everything was set before signaling she was ready. She sat on the side of the boat then dove into the water.

Jude watched the ripples dissipate then quickly hunched over the screens to watch Clancy's descent from there.

"Inez?"

"Yes, She-Hulk?"

Jude could hear Clancy's muffled laughter in her ear.

"Just checking in." Jude couldn't explain how she felt. She was nervous. She was weirded out by Clancy not being on the boat with her where she could see her and touch her. Whatever it was in the ether that Clancy could sense, Jude was feeling apprehension settling over her like a thick, cloying, blanket.

"Thank you, sailor. I'm watching over you too. Keep our girl safe."

"Always," Jude said, respectfully repeating Inez's own promise. She kept her gaze firmly fixed on watching Clancy sink farther and farther down into the dark water.

CHAPTER TWENTY-TWO

Clancy cursed the silt that made visibility a nightmare. She shined her flashlight down past her flippers, but the riverbed could have been a million miles deeper for all she could see.

"Mia, I'm really feeling that it's you in this car. You've come to me in dreams. I've seen you push against the veil to reach out and grab my attention. Well, now I'm here. Can you answer me now? Can you speak to me, please?"

Clancy waited and strained her ears, but she heard nothing. The flashlight finally lit up the unmistakable length of the car beneath her.

"Roof's intact," Clancy said, noting how the river had already claimed the vehicle as its own by how much silt was trying to mask the car's identity. "I'm going to check for a license plate."

She swam around to the back of the car and felt below the bumper to get her bearings. She dug her gloves into the silt and revealed the place where the plate should have been. It was missing.

"Here's a first. The rear plate is missing." She heard Jude curse. "Let me go check the front." Clancy deliberately didn't look at the windows as she swam around the car. She wanted tangible evidence first. She dug into the silt pile that anchored the front of the car. "Front plate is missing too. Whoever dumped this car did not want it traced." Clancy tilted her flashlight away from the car to search the riverbed, but there were no remnants of a plate left anywhere that she could see.

"All the name badges and the logo have been stripped from the car too." Clancy felt around the car where there should have been a

Chevrolet symbol attached. The metal felt sharp as she ran her fingers over it. "They were ripped off. He damaged the car doing it too. Okay, I can't identify the car immediately so I'm going to do this my way now."

Clancy shifted the light to reflect off the windows. She sounded off on them being closed. "Front driver's seat window also closed." She took a breath to calm her jangling nerves and reached out.

"Mia Murray, are you in here?"

She wiped silt off the glass and peered in closer. There was the distinct shape of something in the driver's seat. Clancy worked harder to clear a bigger space so she could see better.

"Hello? Are you Mia? Whoever is in this car I'm here to help you. You're safe now. Can you talk to me, please? I need to know who you are."

Clancy shined the light inside and saw a body. "Confirming there is a something in the car," Clancy announced. "Mia, is this you?"

Clancy saw a movement that was deliberate. She was frozen in place as the head turned slowly toward her and transparent eyes stared through her. The body started swaying gently in the water trapped within the car.

"Why won't you talk to me? Do you not need my help? I'd like to identify you for your family. You need to go home."

A sound began to vibrate the car. Clancy touched the door and could feel it quaking even through her thick gloves. The sound intensified, muffled, but growing louder. The body in the car started to shift, shaken free of the confining seat belt, by the vibrations.

"Can you guys hear this noise?" Clancy asked urgently.

"I'm picking up no sound here," Inez told her.

"Nothing here," Jude said.

"Weird." Clancy's whole body began to vibrate with the sound's growing pitch. It sounded like an avalanche, starting at a rumble then growing in volume and speed. Clancy finally made out what it was she was hearing. Screams. The sound of unearthly screams, layered one upon the other, rising in tone, reaching a piercing frequency that made Clancy fear it would shatter the glass. She braced herself as the body inside twisted and flailed like something possessed. The decomposition that marred the skin faded and Clancy watched as death was erased and instead replaced by the last moments of this woman's life.

"Are you Mia?" Clancy shouted over the screaming. "Answer me!"

The woman's body spun around with force and her hands hit the windows with a jarring thud. Clancy recognized her from her photos. She stared into the terrified eyes of Mia Murray. An almost ear-piercing scream sounded above all the other noise, but it wasn't emanating from her. The sound rocked the car and shifted it on the riverbed. Silt rose like a curtain to cover them all.

"Mia, I'm here to help you."

Mia opened her mouth a fraction and blood began to pour out. Clancy realized why Mia had never answered.

"He cut her fucking tongue out."

Clancy was now yelling to hear herself over the deafening noise from the screams filling the car. Mia opened her mouth wider and Clancy recoiled at the damage that had been wrought. A large cloud of smoke erupted from Mia's mouth. It hung in the water like a stream blown out from a cigarette. It penetrated straight through the window's glass, and directly *into* Clancy's mask. Clancy thrashed at the intrusion but she had no escape. Clancy began coughing and struggling to breathe. She quickly became disorientated and dangerously sleepy.

"Oh shit," she gasped before her vision faded and she started to lose consciousness. She saw Mia watching her as she struggled. "Clor..a..clorafor…" she gasped, trying desperately to warn the ones above.

He chloroformed her, Clancy thought before she succumbed to the same fate.

Jude was reaching for her mask before Inez even had a chance to shout out.

"Jude, go get her! She's unconscious."

Jude didn't ask how. She didn't need to know at this moment. She secured her mask and wasted no time getting in the water. She pushed her descent as fast as she could without risking her own health, but it still wasn't fast enough.

"Is she okay?" she asked Inez.

"She's unresponsive but her vital signs are fine. Whatever hit her knocked her out clean."

"Was it something she got hit with from the car?" Jude had no clue what had happened, she'd just known intense fear at Clancy's sudden silence.

"It was a psychic attack, Jude."

Jude frowned as she processed this new information. "Are you telling me the ghost of Mia attacked Clancy?" She hadn't even had time to process that it was indeed her friend's body in the car. "How the fuck can that happen?"

"Clancy can be affected by the dead, Jude. She sees them as clearly as she sees you and me. But with the dead at crime scenes, she sees *more*. My guess is the killer incapacitated Mia and knocked her out. Clancy obviously couldn't block it in time and it knocked her out too."

"I need to know everything she can see and feel going forward with this." Jude was angry. Angry with Clancy for not telling her something as vital as this. Angry at herself for not being by Clancy's side because this dive was taking her forever and she didn't have time to waste. She was also angry with whatever the ghost of Mia had done, intentionally or not. And she was angry with Mia for a million reasons. She was angry her first true friend in the city had gone on a date and was now dead in the water. She was angry that Mia hadn't told her that this perfect guy she was seeing might have a dark side. She was angry that Mia hadn't called her when it looked like she was in trouble. And she was furious as hell that whatever was down here, the spirit, entity, soul of Mia, whatever it was, had psychically lashed out and hurt the one woman who could help her.

Diving on ships had been so much fucking simpler.

Her flashlight lit up Clancy's body and Jude let out a sigh of relief. She grabbed hold of Clancy's suit and pulled her up so she could secure a hold on her.

"Hey baby, what the hell kind of trouble have you gotten yourself into now?" Jude looked inside Clancy's facemask and was grateful to hear the sound of her breathing but Clancy was unresponsive and a dead weight in Jude's arms. "Inez, I've got her. I'm heading topside."

Jude started to follow the tether back up. For a split second, she spared a glance at the car window and thought she saw an arm, the skin mottled and dark.

"Oh, Mia, I'm sorry," she whispered then started to swim back up to the surface. She kept her eyes on Clancy's face. She looked peaceful, like she did when she was sleeping after they'd made love. "Geez, you are your own special brand of high maintenance, Clancy Madsen. But I wouldn't have you any other way. Just please don't do this kind of thing to me often."

"In her defense, she normally can get them to remove the 'time of death' projection so that she doesn't have to go through it with them. Mia definitely caught her off guard. Probably like the killer did with *her*." Inez was quiet for a moment then she said, "I'm so sorry for your loss, Jude."

Jude knew this was not the time for her to give way to the tidal wave of grief that was building inside her. The minute Clancy had confirmed Mia was the body in the car, Jude had battened down the hatches on any feelings she had. She was there to do a job. She had deliberately put herself in this work where the chances of her helping to find Mia were high. She'd seen part of the body. She'd seen part of the arm that had once hugged her, had danced with her, had been flung around her shoulder by the friend that Jude had been frantically searching for.

Mia was dead.

But Clancy needed to be on dry ground so that she could come to and explain what she had seen. Jude would have time to mourn later, once the car was out, once the investigation started, once Clancy channeled her and Jude could hear her friend's voice come through her lover's mouth.

"Thank you, Inez."

"We're here for you."

Jude stifled a sob at Inez's sweet voice. She'd grown to love this young woman. Clancy's sister by chance, her partner at work, a young woman loved enough to be considered a daughter, and someone Clancy plainly adored. Jude was beginning to cherish time spent with her too. Jude could find family here with them, if she was fortunate enough.

"I know you are."

"You'll find time to cry, Jude, maybe not now, but soon. You'll need to release the pain."

"Are you really empathing on me while I'm trying to rescue Clancy?" Jude tried to sound offended, but all she felt was cared for.

"I have time before you reach the surface. I'm multitasking."

"You're a good kid, Inez."

"That's what Clancy always says."

"Yeah, well she's right." Jude raised her eyes and could see the sunlight playing on the water. "We're about to surface."

"I'll be waiting at the dock."

Jude took one last look down into the water. "We'll be back, Mia."

You're finally found.

CHAPTER TWENTY-THREE

Warm air met Clancy's face as her mask was taken off and her breathing apparatus removed. She gasped for air, once, twice, then came to completely with a start and began gagging. She was rolled onto her side, but Clancy struggled to get up. She ended up on all fours, choking and retching, but nothing came out of her lungs. She dimly felt a hand rubbing soothingly on her back.

"You're okay, you're okay," Jude told her.

Clancy bowed her head against the warm wooden decking of the pier and groaned. "Smoke came out of her mouth. It came right through my mask and fucking knocked me out." She sank back down again and rolled over on her back. She spread out like a starfish. "Man, that sucked."

Inez sat cross-legged beside her, watching her closely. "You're normally quicker than that to stop them from affecting you."

"I remember thinking 'smoke?' then it was inside my mask and I was out. I think I tried to tell you?"

"I heard you try to say chloroform, then Jude was in the water after you."

Clancy squinted against the sunlight at Jude who knelt beside her. "My hero."

"I appreciated the practice rescue dive, but I'd rather not have to do it again." Jude ran her fingers through Clancy's hair. "That was beyond terrifying."

"I'm sorry. She took me by surprise too." Clancy put her hand on Jude's knee. "I saw her, Jude. I'm so sorry. It is Mia down there."

"I know. I've known it from the second you started to get feelings something was calling to you."

Jude looked resigned. Clancy knew Jude would be impenetrable as a rock until this was all sorted and then Jude could finally grieve.

"I have to go back down there." Clancy sat up and reached for her mask.

"Can you take five minutes first just to get your bearings back on track?" Jude stalled Clancy's hand. "I've just dragged you from the river and was ready to do CPR. Inez was the one who had to tell me it was a psychic thing."

"You stopped her from putting her mouth on me?" Clancy frowned at Inez. "Spoilsport."

"*Clancy.*"

Jude used her stern tone that made Clancy's insides quiver to attention. She capitulated without any more argument. "Okay, just five minutes *then* I'm going back to her. This time I can warn her not to share that with me."

"Do you really see how they die?" Jude looked fascinated by the idea but also disturbed.

Clancy nodded. "I get a film reel of them coming back to life. I get to see the damage done before they died."

"For fuck's sake, Clancy, how the hell do you cope with all that?" Jude brushed Clancy's hair back from her face. She was unashamed in her need to keep touching Clancy to reassure herself that Clancy was indeed okay.

"It's always been a part of me, seeing them, being able to talk to them. But when I started to be asked to help with murders, it took on something entirely different. My clairsentience kicked up a notch, meaning I can feel what they felt."

"Hence your need for protective psychic walls," Inez said.

"This is why your information about the women is so detailed. You've *seen* it." Jude looked impressed. "God, you're amazing."

Clancy soaked up the praise. "There's a part of me that would give it all up in a heartbeat, just to have a normal life without the yoke of death weighing on my shoulders." She turned her face into Jude's palm and relished the simple touch of support from her. "But if

I didn't do it, there'd still be eight women lying on the bottom of the river with no way to get peace." Clancy looked up at Jude. "I need to go bring Mia home. And I'm going to have to talk to her."

"I'd like to be there," Jude said. "I need to know what happened."

Clancy nodded. "I'm sure she'd appreciate a friendly face too. I'm just sorry I couldn't bring her back alive."

"You found her and I'm grateful for that. That's what your mission was." Jude helped Clancy to her feet and wrapped her arms around her, holding on tight. "Just promise me, this time, you'll remain removed from anything that can make you feel. We already have one empath in the family."

Clancy smiled at Jude referring to them as a family. She wanted to know if that was what Jude really felt, deep in her heart. But now wasn't the time. Reluctantly, Clancy pulled back from Jude's comforting hold. She looked over her shoulder at Inez.

"Shall we try this again?" Clancy pulled Inez to her and it became a group hug. "Go inform Chandler we have Mia. I'll bring Mia up..." Clancy felt Jude stiffen. "Spiritually, I'm not bringing her physical body up. Chandler's folk get to deal with all that."

"I know. I just..." Jude couldn't explain herself. She shook her head, lost at her reaction.

Clancy tightened her hold on her. "It's okay. I know this is going to be a nightmare for you. You're going to help me rig the car that has her inside. You're going to hear Mia talk through me which, I warn you now, is going to be incredibly hard for you to witness. More than your crazy grandmother was. But you chose to get in that boat and search for her with me. You made her more than just another victim. You gave her life to us. She's going to be mourned by *all* of us because she's your friend."

"*Was*," Jude said quietly.

"Believe me, she is and always will be, your friend. She's just got another path to take now without you. But you'll see her again. No one is ever really gone while you remember them."

A tear threatened to escape from Jude's eye and Clancy watched her furiously blink it back. "Big girls can cry, Jude. It shows we cared enough."

Jude sniffed and straightened her shoulders, pulling herself together and donning her most stoic face. "I can do this."

"Yes, you can because you never gave up hope of finding her. You found her, Jude. You completed your mission too."

Inez wiped at her own teary eyes. She pulled Clancy down to kiss her cheek and then gave Jude a look. Jude bent down and Inez gave her a kiss too. "No one leaves without an expression of love to carry with them," Inez informed her. "Get yourselves sorted. I'll go bring in the cavalry."

Clancy ran her fingers over her facemask, searching for imperfections. "I can't believe she knocked me out."

"I'm sure it wasn't intentional. To knock someone out with chloroform you'd have to hold it over their mouth for ages. Despite what Hollywood and writers would have you believe."

Clancy nodded. "I think it was more a metaphor for her being knocked out. I'm going to guess he incapacitated her in order to do what he did." Clancy couldn't rein in the shiver that shook her whole body. He'd mutilated Mia, removed her tongue. Clancy wondered if that had been a direct message to Mia. Did Mia tell someone about him? Was she going to and he stopped her?

"He cut out her tongue. Is that why she couldn't answer you?"

Clancy nodded. "It was still fresh for her in death. She'll be made whole again," Clancy assured her. "For now, let's get me back down there so I can get her safely back up on land. There'll be an angel who'll come and look after her until we can start the interview."

"You inhabit a truly bizarre world, Clancy." Jude still looked in awe of it all.

"I know. It can be isolating sometimes." Clancy rubbed at the ache of loneliness that still blossomed in her chest. Jude stilled her hand.

"I'm here. You're not alone."

Clancy stared into Jude's eyes and saw only truth in her words. "Are you really ready to embrace the bizarre, Jude?" She teased her because the air between them was quickly becoming intense.

"I've been embracing *her* for weeks now," Jude teased back.

Clancy smiled, delighted by Jude's quick retort. "So that's how it's going to be, eh?" She shook her head and started to walk back to the boat. "No respect."

"Oh, I have plenty of respect for you. I will gladly follow your lead."

Clancy paused. "But I like it when you're in charge best." She felt Jude come up behind her. Jude's breath warmed the back of Clancy's neck as she kissed her then grazed her teeth along Clancy's skin.

"I do too. But this is your territory, you're in charge here." Jude ghosted a kiss on the red mark she'd left. "That doesn't mean I'm not going to worry as you go back into the water after what's just happened."

"I'll be safe. I'm ready to observe, not participate." Clancy smiled wryly. "You know the old saying 'fool me once, shame on you, fool me twice…'"

"I wish I could see her like you will. I wish my most dominant thoughts won't be of her dead but instead be of her living." Jude's admission had been hard for her to voice. Clancy could see her struggling to keep her feelings under lock and key.

"I understand and what you're going to be a part of now won't make any of that easier. You can walk away. I would understand completely."

"No, I need to be here. I committed to this. I'm bringing her home with you."

"And that's what will make the pain a little easier to bear. No one believed you, Jude. You knew something had happened to her. You never stopped searching for her, and today, we've found her. Now I need to go get her free of that car. Then we can get it rigged up so Chandler's folk can haul it out of the river. Then there's an interview, an investigation, a funeral, and closure. *You* brought all that about. *You* set this in motion. *You're* bringing Mia home today."

Jude covered her mouth with an unsteady hand, emotion warring on her face.

Clancy climbed into her boat. "Let's get back on that river. I want to hear what Mia has to tell us that was so damning he cut her tongue out for it."

❖

Clancy followed the rope back down into the water. She was nervous, afraid to feel what Mia had gone through again.

"Don't forget to use your safe words, Clancy," Inez said in her ear.

Clancy could hear Jude snickering. "I'll remember," she assured Inez. She wished she could see Jude's face. "Jude, how you doing?"

"Watching over you like a hawk," Jude said.

"Glad to hear it. I'm coming up on the car now." Clancy landed on its roof and orientated herself so she could find the driver's window.

"Mia, I'm back. Can you show yourself to me, please?"

She angled her flashlight into the window. Mia's body was still floating against the roof. As Clancy continued to watch, Mia turned around and lowered herself to float toward the window. She didn't show Clancy a skeletal phase, instead her decaying body began piecing itself back together, regaining oxygen in its veins, along with life and vitality. Clancy spoke so that Jude knew what she was seeing.

"She's reanimating. Her skin is returning to a normal pallor. Her forehead has a wicked contusion, like she banged her head on something with force." Or someone smashed her head into a wall, Clancy thought, grimacing at how bad the wound appeared. "She has nail marks over her eyelids and down her cheeks. I'd make an educated guess and say someone tried to scratch her eyes out." Clancy could see the damage done to Mia's eyeballs. The gouging to the right one would have rendered her blind had she survived. Mia stared at her and started to open her mouth.

"Show me your true form," Clancy ordered before Mia could go any further. Clancy watched as all the damage that had been inflicted was wiped away and Mia was transformed. She floated before her in her radiance.

Clancy smiled at her. "Hello, Mia. You're safe now. You're free."

Mia tentatively put her hand to her mouth and slipped her fingers inside. Her eyes widened when she found what had been taken from her.

"I'm glad to see you got your tongue back. I've been desperately waiting to hear you speak to me."

Mia licked her lips, testing out her tongue. She smiled and Clancy thought she was beautiful.

"He cut my tongue out."

"Yes, he did. But you have it back now and we can talk. I'm here to take you out of the water."

Mia looked around her, her face losing its wariness as she began to process what had happened.

"That motherfucker drowned me?"

"Can you tell me the name of the motherfucker who did this to you?" Clancy heard Jude choke. She had a feeling Mia was well known for using that particular curse word.

"Grant Nichols, but that wasn't his real name. I heard his mother call him Steven."

"You met his mother?" Clancy repeated the names for Inez to start checking on.

"I saw her, but it wasn't her, it was him."

Clancy's brain began working overtime to decipher that revelation. "Okay, we're going to revisit that curious bombshell topside." She held her hand out. "Would you care to follow me, Mia? I have someone waiting for you above who has been searching for you since you disappeared."

"How long have I been gone?"

"A few months now."

"Smokey Joe?"

"He's okay. Jude has him. They're both here, above."

"Jude's here? Tell her she was right. I picked the wrong guy, and by the time I realized it he'd drugged me. I woke up choking on my own blood because that bastard cut my fucking tongue out to silence me. WELL, I WON'T BE SILENCED!"

Mia screamed her last sentence with all the power of a death knell ringing out. Her anger struck the water like an explosion. It surrounded the car, sending out a shock wave of fierce vibrations. Clancy held on tightly to the car's side mirror for fear of being washed away by the force of the tremors.

"What's happening down there?" Jude asked. "There are ripples coming up from the bottom of the river but you're not moving. It's rocking the boat like crazy. Are we having an earthquake?"

"Mia just screamed, Jude."

"Jude's here? Can she hear me? I need to talk to her."

"Then take my hand and follow me to the surface. She's in the boat above. She never stopped searching for you, Mia."

Mia put her hand out the window and Clancy held on tight.

"Who are you?"

"I'm Clancy."

"Are you gay? You're giving me a gayish vibe. I'm told my gaydar is impeccable. Are you single? My friend Jude needs someone to stop her from being so lonely. I worry about her so much."

Clancy smiled. No wonder Jude had been so desperate to find this woman, she was a sweetheart. Clancy really wished she was meeting her under better circumstances.

"We need to get your car out of the river. After I've done that, I'll come back and you can tell us everything that happened to you. Then you can talk with Jude, I promise."

Clancy swam them back to the surface. Mia got into the boat and exclaimed over seeing Jude. She hugged her, shouting her name in excitement.

Clancy saw Jude shiver but otherwise had no response. Mia sat down with a ghostly thump, disappointed.

"She can't feel me or hear me?"

"No, only I can see or hear you."

Jude gave Clancy a curious look. "Is she here with you now?"

"I'm here, Jude. Mia waved her hands in front of Jude's face, but Jude never acknowledged her. *Well, this sucks. How am I going to talk to her?"*

"I'll channel you so you two can speak." Clancy tapped the side of the boat. "Take us back to the pier, Jude."

"Aren't you getting in the boat?"

"Someone is in my seat," Clancy said, gesturing with her head to the empty seat beside Jude.

Jude squinted as if that would help her see. "What does she look like?" She shook her head when apparently nothing materialized before her and started the engine.

"She's resplendent in a white gown, kind of like the ones you see angels wearing in paintings." Clancy held on tight to the boat as Jude sedately steered them back down the river.

"Am I an angel now?" Mia looked down at herself and held her arms out to gaze at the material that draped her arms. *"Any chance I can wear my favorite shorts and get a blouse with less sleeve than this? I feel like I'm wearing curtains."*

Jude guided the boat along. "I bet she'd rather be in her shorts and one of those ridiculous blouses she'd wear."

Clancy smiled as Mia looked at Jude with a tender smile curving her lips.

"She knows me so well."

"I'm sure attire is something you can bring up with the angel waiting for you when we dock."

They rode for a while in silence then Clancy let go of the boat as Jude pulled up to the boat dock. She swam around it and hauled herself up onto the pier. Inez was waiting for them, along with the very familiar angel standing aside but watching over them all.

"Is he here for me?" Mia asked. *"He's very handsome."*

Clancy made a face. "I guess."

Mia laughed. *"I knew you were gay."* She eyed Clancy up and down as she started to remove her gear. *"Hmmm, I have to say you're handsome too."*

Clancy laughed and Jude looked over at her with a quizzical frown on her face.

"Mia is telling me I'm handsome."

Jude sighed. "Has she tried to set you up with me yet? That was her life's work to hook me up with someone."

"Shall I tell her we're already dating or do you…" Clancy shut up at the sound of Mia's jubilant cheering. "Okay, she took that very well." She spotted the angel coming toward them. "Mia, he's going to keep you company while Jude and I work on getting your car out of the river."

"My body is in that car."

"It will be taken by the coroner. We've got friends who are investigating your guy."

"He cut my tongue out and he slashed my wrists. Then the bastard left me to drown. I died in there, Clancy. Don't let Jude see me like that, please."

Clancy nodded. "I'll do my best. I cover the windows anyway, for protection."

The angel beckoned for Mia to join him.

"I'll see you later, right? You promised I could talk to Jude."

"Yes, you'll be brought back to us either later today or tomorrow, depending on how long it takes to get the car out. Time has no hold on you now. To you, you'll be back to me in no time."

Mia looked satisfied. She glanced over at Jude then whispered something to the angel. He gave her an indulgent look, then nodded and snapped his fingers.

Music started to play out of the boat's radio. Paul McCartney's voice rang out clear into the air, singing "Hey Jude".

Jude's face instantly crumpled. Her legs went out from under her and Clancy barely managed to catch her in time before Jude hit the splintered deck beneath them.

"I used to sing that to her every time I saw her. It used to drive her crazy. Now she knows it really is me here."

Jude's dam broke and she began sobbing her heart out. Clancy tightened her hold as Jude clung desperately to her. Clancy's own heart broke in the wake of Jude's inconsolable grief. Inez hurried over and cuddled into Clancy's side, leaving Jude her distance, but giving both her support.

The sound of The Beatles played out into the sunshine, drifting down the river, spreading its message far and wide. Mia left with the angel, but she kept looking back over her shoulder until they disappeared.

"I can't turn the radio off," Inez whispered to Clancy.

"I guess it has to play out until it's finished its purpose."

"She really was here," Jude mumbled into Clancy's shoulder.

"She's a character, Jude. She's giving your aunt Dolly a run for her money in the smartass stakes."

"I wish you could have known her when she was alive."

Clancy kissed Jude's fevered forehead. "I wish that too. But I'm glad I'm getting to know her now, and being the bridge between worlds to let you speak to her again."

"I don't want to say goodbye to her."

Clancy felt Jude's hot tears soak her neck. "No one ever does, lover. So, instead you'll say 'I'll see you soon.' To her, it will be no more than a blink in time when you walk through the veil to be welcomed back home by her."

"Do you believe that?"

"I have to. It's the peace I've been looking for all of my life."

Chapter Twenty-four

Clancy had meticulously wrapped a tarpaulin around the windows of Mia's car. It ensured that, if the glass shattered when the car was hauled out, no evidence would be lost. It also guaranteed that no one would be able to look in and see Mia's dead body. Jude had argued she'd seen dead bodies before. Clancy had argued back that *Mia* didn't want her to see her in that state and you didn't argue with the deceased. Jude had only been allowed in the water once Clancy had finished the wrap. Together, with Jude learning on the job, they rigged the car with floats and chains and left the rest for the tow truck to finish.

By midafternoon, Clancy and Jude sat in the boat, watching the car being slowly removed from the water. They remained, just in case rigging failed or they were needed to go back to the car. There was a small crowd that had formed, but they were being kept well back from the recovery site. Inez had informed them there was at least one news team filming.

Detective Chandler had arrived from New York with her team. They'd boarded a flight as soon as Inez had informed Chandler they'd found Mia. The DDU were running interference, telling people that it was just a routine salvage job. Their storyline was that the police had been tipped off about someone dumping stolen vehicles in the river. A car had been found and would be impounded to check if it was part of the ring they were prosecuting. There was no ring, but Clancy loved the deflection. She and Jude purposely kept out of the way of any cameras. They were too busy making sure the rigging held to get the car out in one piece.

"I've parked by that car ever since I moved into my apartment. Now, I'm sitting here watching it be pulled through the trees, knowing full well my friend's body is in it." Jude rubbed at her face. "It's so fucking surreal."

Clancy nudged her gently. "You did great out there today. You took to rigging a car like a natural."

"It's not much different from what I did as a diver. Though that was more to keep a vessel shipshape, not anything like uncovering a murder."

"I'm going to order us something to eat, then Chandler wants to sit in on the interrogation."

"Can't that wait until tomorrow? You were dragged out of the water this morning, knocked out by some mystic psychic stuff. We've just been mauled with cables, lines, and floats. Aren't you weary?"

Clancy shrugged. "To be honest, I'd rather get it all done and signed off on so that Chandler can take the investigation out of my hands. I'm just the gal who finds the lost. Chandler and her team have to figure out the who, what, why, and where of how they got lost."

"Do you think Mia can tell them what they need to know about the killer?" Jude wasn't looking at Clancy. Her attention was firmly fixed on the car being dragged through the foliage, inch by painful inch, to preserve every piece of evidence.

Clancy considered her answer for a moment. "I think she will tell them more than they know now concerning her own murder. Whether it fits in and expounds on the others, I guess we'll wait and see. I want this guy stopped. It would be cool if Mia was the one to bring his killing spree to an end."

"What happens to Mia's body now?" Jude asked quietly, as if afraid to know.

"Chandler and her crew will commandeer the coroner's office and perform the autopsy. They'll document every detail pertaining to Mia's death. See if there's anything definitive that can link it to the others."

"But *you* already know what happened to her," Jude said.

Clancy nodded. "But no court will just take my word for it so we do it by the book. Besides, they might find something I wasn't shown or I missed. I'm not infallible."

Jude turned her gaze to Clancy finally. "I think you're damn near perfect."

Clancy leaned in to rest her head on Jude's shoulder. "You're a sweet-talker and so good for my ego."

"Just stating the facts."

They watched a while longer, listening to the clank of the chains competing with the roar of the truck's engine pulling the car back to dry land.

"The crowd has been dispersed," Inez said over the radio. "Chandler doesn't want anyone getting footage of a body being removed. You just need to grab your floats and lines and we are good to go."

Clancy stretched and yawned. "You heard the lady. Take us home. I need to shower and make myself more presentable for the channeling."

"Are you apprehensive about what we'll hear tonight?"

"I've seen how Mia ended up. I'm interested in knowing all that happened before that. The previous victims said he just snapped. He went from the perfect date to a killer. I want to know more about that switch. I want to know what triggered him with Mia, because his cutting out her tongue was clearly a message."

Jude steered the boat back to the pier. "There's a part of me that feels like I'm going through these motions on autopilot. The other part can't believe my friend is dead."

Clancy rubbed Jude's arm in comfort.

"Can you do me a favor, Clancy?"

"Anything."

"Tell her not to play the song again. I don't think my heart can take another blow like that today. I know it's her. I recognize she's here. I don't need a sign. I have you."

"Consider it done." Clancy jumped out onto the pier and held out her hand to help Jude disembark. "I'll go retrieve our floats while you pack up the sonar." Clancy took a step then called back over her shoulder. "You in the mood for Red Lobster?"

Jude smiled and shook her head. "You and your bottomless pit of a stomach. Seafood sounds fine to me."

Clancy saluted her then started rattling off her regular order to Inez. She knew she needed to eat now because, after the channeling, she doubted she'd have the stomach to keep anything down.

❖

Detective Chandler entered the RV. Her keen eyes swept its length, missing nothing.

"I keep telling Blythe we need to get us an RV, get away from the city, go out and make new adventures." She sat in the seat Inez directed her to and readily accepted a drink.

Clancy was nervously pacing in the kitchen area, trying to make it look like she was busy storing the leftovers from their meal. Jude knew better. She watched Clancy's nervous energy all but spark and fly off her. Jude didn't stop her though, or try to quiet her. She knew Clancy had her own way of dealing with things and Jude wasn't going to interrupt her routine. She looked away to find Detective Chandler watching *her*. Jude raised an eyebrow at her boldness.

"How you enjoying the salvage business, Jude?" Chandler asked.

"Beats bartending any day," Jude said.

"I'm sorry it was Mia you found today and that her circumstances seem to fit our serial killer's MO. How you holding up?"

Jude appreciated Detective Chandler's sympathy. She wasn't just saying it because it was the polite thing to do.

"I'm really glad we found her because the not knowing was eating away at me. I just wish it hadn't been under the circumstances she apparently found herself in. I never expected her to be a murder victim."

Chandler nodded. "You know the details of her death already. Clancy was spot-on as always."

Jude felt Clancy move to her side.

"Did the autopsy reveal anything else?" Clancy rested her hand on Jude's shoulder and held on with enough pressure to make Jude look up at her. She could see Clancy was nervous.

"She was remarkably well preserved considering the length of time she'd been under water. Though decomposition had set in, the coroner could still make out a lot of the injuries she'd sustained."

"The water she was in was cooler than the rest of the river. The trees were thick and the shade had to have helped preserve her." Clancy squeezed Jude's shoulder. "She hung on for us."

Chandler took a sip from her mug. "She was the first to have a trophy taken."

"No sign of her tongue was found in the car?" Inez asked, scrolling down the screen on her laptop as she perused the coroner's report Chandler had given her.

"No. We can't rule out it was lost in the river though," Chandler said.

Clancy shook her head. "No, that car was sealed shut. The water got in, but I'd doubt anything got out. None of the windows were compromised."

"So, he took it as a keepsake?" Jude shook her head in disgust. "He keeps rising higher on the sick bastard chart."

Chandler set her mug down and reached for her video recorder. "Clancy, are you ready to get this show and tell started?"

Clancy moved around the chair to face Jude. "Remember, I am still in there." She leaned in, kissed Jude softly, then whispered, "I'm so sorry for what you're about to see and hear."

Jude swallowed hard and wished she'd asked for a bottle of something strong to be added to their restaurant order. She watched in trepidation as Clancy took her seat and shook herself out in preparation to be taken over. Chandler finished her preparations with the camera. She fixed a light on Clancy and pressed the record button. Chandler read off the date, time, and circumstances, then gave Clancy a thumbs up.

Clancy gave Jude one last look and then closed her eyes. Jude watched her intently, praying she wouldn't break down again. She knew this channeling was going to be brutal on her emotions.

"What? You mean I can really talk through you and everyone can hear me?"

The voice coming from Clancy was enough like Mia's that Jude bit down on her lips, hard enough to draw blood, to stop them from trembling. The conversation Mia was having was obviously with Clancy and they'd come in halfway through. Jude would never get used to how freaking weird all this was.

"JUDE!"

Jude jumped in her seat as Clancy's head turned to her and it was Mia's eyes Jude could see sparkling from Clancy's face.

"What the hell?" Clancy jerked a little in her seat but didn't move. "Why can't I go hug her? Well, that's just fucking unfair. What's the point of that?"

Jude tried not to smile at the whiny tone in Mia's voice as she argued, one-sidedly, with Clancy.

"Wait, I could really just run off with your body if you handed over the reins? Wow, that's freaky. I wouldn't do that to you. What? They're listening *now*? I thought we were still in your head." Clancy looked around at Chandler, Inez, and then back at Jude. "I guess this thing is switched on then! Sorry, folks, this is my first time being channeled. Still working out the kinks."

Loud meows came from another part of the RV and Smokey Joe came running down the hallway. He yowled and meowed and wrapped himself around Clancy's legs, rubbing and butting her roughly.

"Smokey Joe!" Mia called to him. "My baby!"

Smokey Joe jumped up into Clancy's lap and rubbed his face all over hers.

"Oh my God, this is going to be harder than I thought," Mia said as tears began to stream down Clancy's face. "I'm so sorry, baby, I never meant to leave you. I would never have left you behind. I'm sorry. I love you so much."

Smokey Joe rubbed himself against Clancy's hand that she had resting on her thigh.

"I can feel you!" Mia exclaimed. "Oh, thank you, Clancy, thank you for that. Who's mommy's best boy, eh? You are, yes, you are. I've missed you." Mia's eyes sought out Jude. "You have him?"

Jude nodded. "He's been with me since I couldn't contact you and realized something was wrong."

"Thank you, thank you. Is he being a good boy?"

"He's settled in well and he's found a second home here with Clancy and Inez. He's loved, Mia, and he's safe."

"Was he starving? I didn't mean to leave him. It wasn't my choice not to come home."

"He was hungry, but I fed him and he's okay now. He's happy, I think."

"You're the best friend I ever had, Jude. And I hate to admit it, but damn you, you were right. I swiped right and found a goddamned serial killer. He's killed before. I've seen them. They came to me when I was dying in the car. They stayed with me until I passed. They told me someone would find me. That they'd been found, one by one all in the Missouri River, and I would be next. So, I waited. I tried to go home to tell you where I was, but the walls moved in on me and no matter how hard I tried to push through them, I couldn't break through and the river pulled me right back. I tried, Jude, I tried so hard to come home."

Jude brushed roughly at her face to wipe away her escaping tears. "You have to tell them. You have to tell them everything so he can be stopped. You were the first friend I'd made in years, Mia. It's been hell without you. It will continue to *be* hell without you in my life. So, make it count. Help us stop him taking someone else's loved one."

Jude could see Clancy's hand petting Smokey Joe. She wondered how much of her protective wall she had to smash down to let Mia have that soothing connection with her cat. It only made Jude love her more. She'd fallen in love with a rakish butch. Someone who was exciting and sensual, submissive and dominant, kind and yet tortured. Someone who let the dead speak through her even though it pained her to do so. She watched the tears stream down Clancy's face and Jude moved before she could stop herself. She grabbed a tissue and wiped Clancy's face.

"I can *feel* you," Mia said, her voice soft and trembling.

Jude pressed a kiss to Clancy's cheek. "I miss you, my friend." She sat back down, wiped at her own eyes again, and cleared her throat. "Tell me what happened to you, Mia. Tell us everything you remember."

CHAPTER TWENTY-FIVE

"Y ou hear horror stories about dating but you never think it will happen to you. That there are monsters out there, hiding in plain sight." Mia sighed. "It's what he was, at the end. A monster. But, when we first met, I was certain he was going to be my Mr. Right."

"How *did* you meet him?" Jude asked. "Because you kept him awfully quiet from your friends."

"Through that dating app you constantly scoffed at." It was Clancy's face giving Jude a patented *Mia* look but all Mia's voice that added the directed dig.

"And you never once felt like he was hiding something from you?" Jude asked, not understanding how Mia could have been so blind.

"No, not even when he asked me to keep us on the downlow. Did I ever once think he was a serial killer? Hell, no. I just thought he was shy and still getting over the loss of his mother. We hadn't even slept together." Mia made an exasperated noise. "I was so stupid. I thought he was being a gentleman."

"Were all your previous dates in public places?" Chandler asked.

"Yes, so I was thrilled to be invited to his house. Something less formal, more intimate. I figured if he invited me to stay over, I could call Jude to chaperone Smokey Joe for the night." She looked down at the cat in Clancy's lap. "I would never have left him alone."

Jude couldn't mistake the grief behind her words. "So, you turned up on his doorstep?"

"Yes, a good hour earlier than we'd planned but I was excited. I wanted to see him. So, color me surprised when he answers the door looking like a new man. His blonde hair was now dark brown and he'd shaved off his moustache. In hindsight, he kind of looked like a deer in the headlights when he saw me." Mia said. "He kept complaining he had nothing prepared and I'd ruined the surprise by coming early. But he eventually let me in."

"I think you caught him unawares, without his carefully crafted disguise in place," Chandler said.

"I asked him if dark brown was his natural color. He said yes and that he liked to change it now and again. Said it made him feel like a new man, changing his look, growing a beard, seeing a new face in the mirror."

Jude's stomach dropped. He had shown a different face to each woman he had killed. Hearing Mia talk about it so matter-of-fact was terrifying.

"I was quite fond of his old face, the blonde hair with the dashing Travis Kelce moustache. But I was falling for the man, not the color of his hair. I changed the subject, asked if he'd give me a tour of his house."

"What was his answer?" Chandler asked.

"No!" The word sounded out sharp and harsh making Jude and Inez jump in their seats. "He scared me and then tried to smooth it over by saying something about a man needing to have some mystery, right? He'd never raised his voice before. In that moment, he sounded like my ex. I got triggered, so asked to use the bathroom. I just needed to step away for a moment."

"He let you walk around the house alone?" Chandler asked.

"No, he escorted me to the bathroom door as if I were incapable of finding it. He checked the room over as if expecting someone to be already occupying it. He was acting very strange. I tried to calm myself down as I refreshed my lipstick. Through the mirror, I see a cabinet door had popped open, just enough for me to see in. Inside was row after row of Styrofoam heads, each with a wig on or some elaborate false facial hair. I easily spotted Grant's familiar blonde hair laid out on a head along with his blonde moustache."

Clancy's body shuddered violently. Jude looked at her in alarm.

"It's okay, Jude," Mia said. "That was Clancy feeling my reaction. It really was like a moment from a scary movie. I went to take a closer look but noticed the bathroom door wasn't closed. Someone was staring at me through the gap. I lost it and yelled at Grant, asking what the fuck was wrong with him. I flung open the door but it wasn't his eyes I saw looking back at me."

Jude looked at Chandler who somehow didn't look as surprised as Jude was.

"In this scary, high voice, he said 'You really should have just come at the time you were supposed to.' Then his face started to contort as if something was crawling under his skin. Before I could freak out at that, he barged in and wrapped his hand around my neck. You'd have been proud of me, Jude. I fought that motherfucker just like you taught me. I dug my nails in him and drew blood, but he wouldn't let go. I couldn't breathe. He spun me around to face the mirror. I could see my eyes bulging and my face was going red as he choked me. Then he said, 'Did you really think you were worthy of him?' But the voice coming from Grant wasn't him at all."

Jude looked over at Chandler again and mouthed 'What the fuck?' Jude really wished she could speak to Clancy. She'd know exactly what Mia was on about.

"Grant got this really ugly smile on his face and said 'I'm the only woman he will ever need.' Then his face started to morph. I'd have dropped to the ground in a faint if he hadn't been holding me up. His face became an old woman's, her eyes black and evil-looking, her skin rotting off. I wanted to scream but Grant's hold was too tight. Then *his* voice said, 'But Mother, she's the one I really liked.'" Mia stopped for a moment, drawing a shaky breath. "I was so terrified by what I was seeing. I begged him to let me go but *she* just laughed at me from *inside* the mirror."

Jude saw Inez wrap her arms tightly about herself for comfort. Jude wanted to do the same. What Mia was talking about was pure fantasy. Yet Jude had no reason *not* to believe her. She was hearing it from her *ghost*, after all.

"They started arguing over me and his mother's arms shot through the mirror and grabbed me, screaming 'She's mine! Give her to me!' Grant argued that she'd had the last eight of them and failed. He begged her to let him keep me and to let him have his life back." Clancy's face twisted with Mia's obvious pain. "He was fighting her for me. In that moment, I thought he was my Grant again." Mia looked directly at Chandler. "She said she *needed* me. Grant said she needed my body to *return*. While he was distracted talking to me, she grabbed me, ripping me out of his hold. My head slammed into the mirror, shattering it to pieces." Mia paused then spoke quickly. "Inez, Clancy says she'd really appreciate some pain medication before she blacks out like I did."

Jude immediately went to Clancy's side. Mia started up her one-sided conversation again with Clancy.

"You're feeling everything I went through? Why the fuck didn't you say? We could have done automatic writing instead. Jude, come hold your lover a moment until the pain meds kick in."

Jude didn't need to be told twice. She wrapped her arms around Clancy, mindful not to wake Smokey Joe who was fast asleep on Clancy's lap. She held on tight, just how Clancy liked it. Mia spoke quietly in Jude's ear.

"This is only going to get worse, my friend. If you want to sit this next bit out, I'd understand."

Jude hugged harder. "I'm staying. For both of you."

"Clancy says you give the best hugs. I told her, you always did."

Mia's wistful tone tugged at Jude's heart. She tightened her hold a fraction more to keep them both safe in her arms.

When everyone was ready to continue, Chandler turned the video camera back on. "Mia, do you know how long they kept you captive?"

"I know I came to at some point, laid out on the kitchen table. I was lying on some mail Grant had brought in when I'd arrived. My eyes were unfocused but I managed to make out the name Steven Thorn on a piece of junk mail. I heard voices arguing about injecting me with something and felt the sting as it was stuck in me. Whatever it was, it knocked me right back out again. When I finally regained consciousness, I was outside. It was dark out, obviously night time, and so quiet."

"Were you already in the water?" Chandler asked.

"No, not yet. Grant sat beside me, in the passenger seat. He spun me a line about deceiving me as Grant because he didn't think I'd be interested in Steven."

Chandler smiled. "Confirmation of his name. Thank you."

"He said he wasn't the kind of guy you'd want to get involved with. Said he had mommy issues. For a moment, I'd swear he looked like his mother again. It was hard for me to pay attention to him. The more I came to, the more pain I was in. I could feel something trickling out of my mouth. Steven said they couldn't stop the bleeding. Something about his mother *really* not wanting me to talk him out of this. I put my fingers to my lips and got them covered in blood. I tried to talk but found I couldn't. My words wouldn't form. I put my fingers into my mouth and screamed when I couldn't find my tongue."

Clancy's body jerked. Jude wanted desperately to yank Mia out of her and let Clancy be free of the horrors she was experiencing second hand.

"Steven's eyes changed into his mother's but it was his hand I saw wield a huge knife that he tried to sever my hands with. I went hysterical, but even my screams no longer sounded like me. I heard his mother's voice saying 'Dump her.' That was the last I saw or heard from her."

"And Steven?" Chandler asked.

"He could barely look at me. He kept apologizing while he slipped the hand brake off. His last words to me, before he got out of the car, are seared into my memory. 'In another life, I could have seen myself burning bridges to be with you. I would have married you in a heartbeat. You made me feel like a hero.' He finally got the nerve to look at me and said, 'But, sometimes, you just have to put your family first.' Then that motherfucker locked the doors behind him and left me there, bleeding everywhere."

Jude clenched her fists tight to reign in her anger at what had been done to her best friend.

"He rammed into the back of my car. He pushed it through some bushes, and somehow got it through a space between two trees until the car dipped and started to teeter-totter over an edge."

"Could you see what type of vehicle he was pushing you with?" Chandler was quietly reviewing some notes on her iPad.

"No, I never looked back. I was too busy watching my car heading toward the river. He rammed me again and my car slid into the water. I freaked out as the water rose quickly up the sides of the car as it sank. I couldn't use my hands on anything. I couldn't call for help. I was still woozy from being drugged and was trapped by my seat belt. The water started filling up the car. It reached my chin then went over my head. I knew I was about to die. I thought about my family, my sister, Jude who would wonder where the fuck I was. I cried for Smokey Joe who was all alone, waiting for me to come home to him. But I wasn't going home ever again. I closed my eyes, frightened at what was to come next. And then I heard them."

"Them?" Jude said, hanging off Mia's every word.

"I heard voices saying 'It's okay, we're with you. You're not going to die alone.' I opened my eyes and saw eight women in the car with me. My friend Kelly Hu was one of them. I opened my mouth to speak but water rushed in and gagged me. They all reached out to touch me. They held my ruined hands in theirs, gripped my shoulders tight in solidarity. Kelly held my face in her hands and smiled at me. She told me I wouldn't stay here forever. That someone was searching the river for me. That they were finding us all, one by one. 'Your turn will come,' she said. I remember struggling against the water in my lungs until Kelly brushed her fingertips over my eyes to close them. She said 'Rest now. Your journey is over, your life contract fulfilled. Sleep until awakened.'"

"Oh, Mia," Jude whispered, tears filling her eyes.

"The waters of the Missouri River snatched away my final breath. And so, I slept. Until someone started calling my name."

CHAPTER TWENTY-SIX

Detective Chandler was already contacting her people to stake out one Steven Thorn at the address Mia had provided.

"This is intriguing," Chandler said, reading from her iPad. "Steven's a pharmaceutical rep, which goes a long way to explaining all his traveling to kill and the women being found in different states. Oh, and this is intriguing too, seems Steven had an NDE two years ago."

"An NDE like little Solomon Marshall?" Jude asked, still trying to get her head around all that Mia had told them. Her friend had suffered a terrible fate, but no one had time to mourn that. They had a name, his *real* name, and he had to be stopped.

"It just says he was in a car crash and died for two minutes before they resuscitated him," Chandler answered.

"Clancy wants to know how long his mother had been dead before then," Mia said.

Jude wondered how much longer Clancy could allow Mia to keep speaking through her. The interview was taking longer than Jude had expected and she could see signs of strain on Clancy's face.

Chandler checked her notes. "A month."

"Clancy bets ten dollars that she's a walk-in. She hadn't moved on, and when he died, she saw her chance to return and took over his body. When they resuscitated him, she was trapped inside and he became aware of her presence. He said she was after a body to return. She's piggybacking on Steven until they can find her a suitable body to shift into." Mia paused. "Clancy says, to be a walk-in, the host must be willing to let them in. Murdering someone doesn't make them a willing subject to hand over the keys." Mia began laughing. "You're funny, Clancy. I'm glad Jude has you to make her smile."

Jude was busy digesting Clancy's explanation. It oddly made sense, in a crazy supernatural way of thinking.

Mia looked over at her. "I can't believe you're sitting there, Jude, just taking all this paranormal shit in like it's normal. I couldn't even get you to watch *Friday the 13th* with me!"

"Let's just say I'm learning very quickly that there's a whole new world out there if I'm prepared to open my mind wider to experience it. Being with Clancy has been an eye-opener, in more ways than one," Jude said.

Mia went still then sighed. "I'm going to have to go."

Jude felt her heart drop like a stone in her chest.

"Clancy says just for now. She's reaching her time limit so I need to vacate her body. She says I can come back, Jude. And I've told the reaper angel I am not going into any light until that bastard is stopped so I'm going to be hanging around. Clancy has my number to call me any time."

Jude had to smile at Mia's playfulness. She was going to miss that so much. But she needed Clancy back. She could see her body trembling as the channeling took its toll on her.

"I'm still in the room if there are any more questions, Detective Chandler. Clancy can talk to me like usual." Mia petted Smokey Joe one last time. He was still curled up asleep in Clancy's lap. He was blissfully unaware of the horror story Mia had regaled them with. He'd just known his mama was close.

"I'll be back, Smokey Joe," Mia whispered.

Clancy's hand stilled in his fur and Jude watched as Mia gave her a wink before her eyes faded away and Clancy's returned. Clancy stayed motionless for a moment. Inez got a bottle of Mountain Dew from her little desk fridge and popped the top off it. Clancy slumped a little in the chair then seemed to snap to.

"God, that never stops being weird," Clancy muttered, reaching for the bottle and chugging it down without taking a breath.

Jude watched her intently as Clancy finished drinking and looked down at Smokey Joe on her lap. He woke up and looked up at her, meowing loudly.

"I know, boy, I know. Life sucks, and death sucks the most." Clancy picked him up and put him over her shoulder like a baby about to be burped. Jude was stunned into silence. That was a purely Mia-move with the large cat.

Clancy turned to Jude with a small smile. "How you holding up, lover?"

"I want to kill him a million different ways," Jude said, utterly sincere in her hatred of Mia's killer.

"In some ways, he's an innocent party too. He's possessed by his mother, so until we can separate the two, we won't know how involved he really is." Chandler was tapping away on her iPad. "Mia gave us the last pieces we needed. She was the only one he invited home. None of the other women had that experience."

Clancy looked like she was listening. Jude had a feeling Mia was right beside her, chatting her ear off.

"Mia thinks he was falling for her. They were well suited..." Clancy waited then laughed, "for a possessed mommy's boy and their next victim."

Inez reached over to hold Clancy's hand. "How are you doing? That was a brutal channel."

Clancy buried her face in Smokey Joe's fur. Jude had never seen her so hands-on with him before.

"I'm hurting a little. Mercifully, they cut her tongue out while she was unconscious, but the near severing of her hands is an ache I'll probably have for a few hours. And I know from experience what pain is like after just slitting a wrist. What they did was excruciating. Fortunately, Mia says she was so detached by then, with the drugs and the dying, that it didn't all register. Thank God for small mercies."

"Now we need to find physical evidence to tie all these things together." Chandler barely looked up from her tapping on her tablet. "I really hope Mia's tongue is still in the house." She paused then looked around, sheepishly. "Sorry, Mia."

"She says that's okay. She has no idea what they did with it." Clancy squeezed Inez's hand then let go. She handed Smokey Joe over to her. "I need to go lie down a minute, just to decompress." She kissed Jude as she headed back toward the bedrooms. "Thank you for not freaking out while I did all that." She played with Jude's hair a second. "You're really something special."

Jude watched her walk unsteadily to her room. She turned to Inez. "Is there anything I can do to help her?"

"She's psychically wide open now so she'll go play incredibly loud music in her headphones to drown out the voices that she'll hear scrambling for her attention. I usually leave her alone."

Jude didn't want to leave Clancy alone with what she'd just experienced channeling Mia. "Do you have any baby oil?"

Inez's eyebrows rose, as did Detective Chandler's. Jude smirked at them. "Minds out of the gutter, people. I know Shiatsu foot massage."

Chandler groaned. "That sounds so good right now."

Inez just pointed to the bathroom. "I'm sure there's something you can find in the cabinet. You really need to meet Uncle Toshiro. He's our resident bodywork master."

Jude shook her head in amazement. "Is there no one you don't have at your Wiccan commune?"

"A TV repairman," Inez answered immediately. "If our cable goes, the whole community mourns the loss of rewatching *Wednesday* on Netflix. We've had marathons of it since it was aired. Clancy painted the side of a barn and we use it as a projection screen."

Jude wasn't sure if Inez was teasing her, but Chandler was chuckling away to herself. Jude knew enough about electronics that she could probably work out what needed fixing. She'd save that information for later. She nodded to them both and went to ransack the bathroom for what she'd need.

❖

With a towel and a bottle of something that would do the job, Jude let herself into Clancy's bedroom.

The curtains were closed and Clancy lay with a pair of headphones on. Jude winced as she could hear the music from where she stood. She sat on the bed and began to peel Clancy's socks off. Clancy jolted but Jude rubbed a soothing hand on her leg. Clancy's knee-length shorts she favored gave Jude plenty of area to work with. Jude uncapped the bottle, squeezed out a sizeable amount, and began to spread it liberally on Clancy's left foot. She rubbed the oil in, pressing and testing Clancy's pressure points. Clancy moaned and sighed as Jude took care of her. She never opened her eyes, never said a word, as the music thumped away in her ears.

Jude loved the solid feel of Clancy's feet. The broadness of the sole, the blunt toes. These were not feet that had ever been squashed into high heels. These were feet meant for butt-kicking boots. Jude had never had a foot fetish but she had to admit, she loved everything about Clancy's body, feet included. She smoothed the oil over Clancy's ankles and up her shin, digging into her tight calf muscles. She repeated everything on Clancy's right side, and by the time she was finished as high as she could reach, Clancy was boneless beneath her.

Jude went back to the bathroom to wash her hands clean of the oil. She could hear Chandler and Inez talking at the front of the RV. She returned to Clancy's bedroom, closed the door, and locked it behind her. She stripped quickly, and piled her clothes in a heap on a chair. She watched Clancy for a moment, but Clancy still had her eyes closed.

Jude unfastened Clancy's shorts and began to ease them down her legs. Clancy opened an eye then both shot open when she saw Jude was naked.

"This isn't usually how I decompress," Clancy said, lifting her hips to help Jude remove her boxers.

"Should I stop?" Jude stilled her hands.

Clancy eased a headphone from her ear. "Sorry?"

"I asked if I should stop?" Jude waited patiently for her answer.

Clancy shook her head. "Something tells me you need the distraction as much as I do. I'm guessing playing loud music isn't going to cut it for you."

"I need you, Clancy. I need to lose myself in you before I lose myself in the horror I've just learned." Jude looked deep into Clancy's understanding eyes. "My head is being consumed by the darkness. I need you to keep me in the light."

Clancy sat up a little so that Jude could pull off her T-shirt, then they wrestled her sports bra off and Clancy was gloriously naked. She lay back down, gave Jude a wicked smile, and readjusted her headphones.

Jude tapped her on her chest and Clancy opened her eyes again in question. Jude put a finger to her lips as a warning. Clancy nodded and reached over into her bedside drawer. She pulled out a bandana, spun it around to lengthen it, then put it between her teeth to bite down on.

"Smart boi." Jude made sure Clancy could read her lips. Clancy's grin let her know she'd seen the praise.

Jude ran her hands up Clancy's thighs and she immediately opened them wider. "Always so eager," Jude muttered to herself. She brushed her hand over Clancy's belly, and up between her breasts. She held Clancy down a moment, making sure she knew Jude was in charge. Then Jude leaned over her, removed the gag, and kissed her. She left Clancy gasping for air and leaning up for more. Jude just pressed the bandana back between Clancy's lips and tightened it. She focused solely on Clancy's body beneath her. Jude leaned back, rubbed her palms over Clancy's broad shoulders, then down to encompass her breasts. She gently squeezed them, then rougher, and rubbed her thumbs over and around Clancy's nipples until the areolas pebbled and her nipples strained for more. Jude gave into her own desires and sucked on the taut nubs. She laid her body on top of Clancy's and kept her immobile while Jude drove her crazy with her mouth. Jude could feel Clancy's hips rocking, searching for any friction she could gain from Jude's flesh. Jude flicked her finger hard against Clancy's reddened nipple and watched as Clancy bit down onto the bandana to keep quiet.

Jude licked her nipple to soothe the ache, then ran her tongue down Clancy's chest to her stomach. Jude bit softly at the skin there, licking the bite to take away the sting. She shifted back on her haunches and positioned herself between Clancy's thighs. She grabbed for a pillow to raise Clancy a fraction then Jude shifted into position. She spread herself open and fitted her clit over Clancy's.

Clancy's eyes popped open to watch Jude at work. Jude knew Clancy liked this position. She'd told her how she loved watching Jude get herself off rubbing against Clancy's clit. Their arousal mixed together to provide all the lubricant they needed.

Clancy removed her gag. "Fuck, you look so damn good when you do this." She moaned as Jude thrust over her and quickly put the bandana back in her mouth.

Jude started at a steady pace. Their clits slipped and slid over each other and Jude could feel a jolt of electricity hitting her on every pass. Clancy's hips were erratic beneath her, chasing her own pleasure. Jude held her down more and deliberately directed their movements. The more she rocked, the more she could hear grunts escaping from Clancy's mouth. The harder she pressed; the more Clancy shook. Jude had never had a lover who gave herself over to receiving pleasure as much as she gave it. She looked down between them, at the strings of their wet desire forming every time Jude pulled back. She could feel her body tensing, readying itself for her climax. She wanted to make sure Clancy came first. Jude bucked harder and Clancy's teeth chomped down to stifle her reaction. Clancy began to shake and Jude felt her come, felt her release between them. Clancy's shudders brought Jude's orgasm closer to spilling. She rode Clancy rougher until she came with a harsh gasp. She kept her clit rubbing against Clancy until her body shuddered to a stop and the pleasure became too exquisite a pain. She lay down on Clancy and tried to catch her breath.

"You are so good at that," Clancy whispered after spitting out the bandana. She took off her headphones and wrapped her arms around Jude's trembling body. "No one usually comes near me after a channeling. I usually decompress alone."

"I wasn't going to leave you alone. And I needed you too." Jude rubbed her face against Clancy and kissed her damp skin.

"Are we needed back out there yet?" Clancy asked, her fingers tracing idle patterns over Jude's broad back.

"No, but we can't stay in here all night like I'd want to. I really want to just hide away and try to push everything I've learned today aside for another time. But Thorn needs to be caught, Mia needs to move on, and then I want us to get a moment to ourselves without any interruptions of the woo-woo spooky variety."

Clancy's body moved under Jude's as she laughed silently.

"That sounds good to me." Clancy sighed. "Want to streak out to the bathroom and see if we can fit in the shower in there?"

Jude lifted her head. "No funny business though."

Clancy agreed reluctantly. "Yeah, I guess. There's only so much hot water the RV will afford us after all. We'll save shower sex for your apartment."

"And maybe, with Mia found, no one will be trying to get through the walls to you while we're fucking," Jude said.

Clancy hugged Jude tighter to her. "I would appreciate the only ones in the room being you and I."

Jude helped Clancy up off the bed and held her close, reluctant to let go. "What am I going to do with all this devastating knowledge racing around in my head?"

"You're going to find a place for it, where you know it's safe, but where you won't keep returning to it. Her ending is just a small chapter in Mia's life story. You need to look back at the happier times, remembering her smile, and her humor. Remember her living, don't focus on her passing."

"Will it ever stop hurting?"

"No, but the pain will become more acceptable and you'll bear it like a scar that marks you deeply but fades over time."

Jude reached for Clancy's wrist and wrapped her hand around it. "Does your pain ever stop hurting?" she asked softly, seeking out Clancy's eyes, wanting to look deep into her soul.

"At times, yes. Like when I look at you and feel nothing but sunshine and warm hugs."

Jude huffed. "You make me sound like that chatty snowman in *Frozen*," she grumbled, enveloping Clancy in a hug, humbled by her reply.

"And how do you know about him?"

"Mia made me watch the movie," Jude admitted.

Clancy smiled. "And did you enjoy it?"

"Much more than I would have watching *Friday the 13th*."

Clancy chuckled at her. She reluctantly pulled away and opened her bedroom a fraction to peek outside. "Ready to make a break for it?"

"I'll be right behind you."

For always, if you'll have me, Jude thought as they streaked across the hall like naughty children.

CHAPTER TWENTY-SEVEN

The next morning, Clancy's RV was parked a few miles down the river from where Mia's car had been extracted. Inez had deliberately driven them away from the site. Clancy sat on the RV's steps, watching the sun shining across the slither of river she could see in the distance. She enjoyed the quiet, how the river continued flowing regardless of what they'd removed the day before. She had all her psychic walls up to just enjoy the tranquility, for however long it would last.

Her phone dinged with a message. Clancy grunted and hoped it was spam. It was a voice message from Detective Chandler.

"We staked out the Thorn residence last night. The place is empty. I bet they saw that damned news report I'd requested to be pulled from local TV. Someone's head is going to roll for that. I'm waiting on a warrant to get in the house to search it. I'll keep you updated."

Clancy blew out a disgruntled breath. Great. The killers were on the run. That was not how she wanted to start the day. She listened to the sound of Inez getting up and watched as Smokey Joe came wandering out of her room first.

"Did you enjoy your sleepover?" Clancy asked him and got a head butt in answer. "I hope you slept better than I did. Your mama left me with a head full of anguish that I couldn't sleep off." She petted him and listened to him purr. "We'd better feed you, eh? Your other mommy is fast asleep still so how about I do the honors? I reckon even I can whip up a bowl full of morning kibble for you."

Clancy lost herself in the normalcy of the moment, a quiet spot amid the madness.

Inez wandered in, stretching and yawning. "You're up early."

"Couldn't sleep."

"Not even with that hunkah hunk of burning butchness by your side?" Inez hip-checked Clancy as she reached for her cereal.

"Mia's death was on repeat in my head all night. I wasn't sleeping no matter how hot my bed partner is." She reached to pour Inez a mug of coffee from the freshly brewed batch. "I'm going to take a walk down by the river just to clear my head."

Inez nodded. "GoPro," she said.

Clancy dutifully fitted the camera onto her shirt. "You don't have to watch over me all the time, Inez. I'm a big girl now."

"You made the rules, Clancy. Anywhere near water it's cameras on."

"I did say that, didn't I? It's your mother's influence. She got me acting all responsible." She turned the camera on and wandered into the office space to turn on the monitor screen. "I won't be long. I just want to reconnect a little. Flex my toes in the grass, stare into the water and know it's clear. Well, as clear as the Big Muddy can get."

"Just keep focusing on the fact that the water at Disneyland will be clearer and way more relaxing." Inez sat where she could see the screen and sipped at her coffee with a contented smile.

"I'll probably be back well before Jude surfaces," Clancy said, slipping into her flip-flops and heading out the door.

"Find your peace, Clancy," Inez said and took another gulp of her coffee. "I have mine right here." Smokey Joe jumped into her lap. "And now it's doubly perfect."

Clancy laughed at her and closed the door behind her. The heat hit her and she raised her face to it, hoping it would permeate through her skull and the light would banish the darkness that resided in her mind. It hadn't yet, for all her wishing, but Jude had brought a new kind of light to her being and Clancy was basking in it.

The river was just a six-minute walk from where they were parked. Clancy was soon slipping out of her flip-flops and walking down to the edge of the water, keeping to the grass so as not to cut her feet on any of the loose gravel. She stared into the water for a moment, sipping her coffee, watching a lone fish swim its way downstream. She noticed there was a small, dilapidated pier. She gave in to the need to go sit on it, dangle her legs over the edge, and maybe meditate for a while. Rainbow had taught her how to center herself. To take some of the horrors she saw when channeling and reading, and release them out into the atmosphere. It was still a work in progress for Clancy. She had a hard time letting some things go.

Before she could move, she heard footsteps on the gravel. That was probably Jude. She turned, but it wasn't Jude at all.

"Hi, it's a beautiful morning, isn't it?" The man kept walking toward her. He was dark-haired and had a fashionable beard, trimmed close and shaped to his jaw.

"Yes, it is," Clancy said. "Can I help you?"

"I was just out walking. Heard there was a bit of excitement around here yesterday. Thought I'd come see for myself." He gestured back behind him. "You the Madsen Salvage gal?"

Clancy bit her tongue at being called a gal but she didn't bite at him. "Yes, sir, I am."

"Heard you found a car in the river."

"I did, yes."

"Heard the police were involved too."

You heard a lot, Clancy thought. She nodded. "They have to be called in if there's a vehicle. They have first dibs. I'm holding out for my salvage rights when they're finished with it."

"Is there a lot of money to be made doing what you do?"

"I get along. Sponsors keep me running," Clancy said, hoping he'd leave soon so she could continue with her day.

"Have you found many cars?"

"In deep enough water there's always something someone has thrown away. We're a race who would rather pollute the earth than keep it clean for the generations to follow."

He nodded sagely. "Did you see inside the car you pulled out yesterday?"

Clancy shook her head. "The river is so dirty you can hardly see your hand in front of your face."

"Why did you put covers over the windows then?"

Clancy noticed the small change in his tone. Sharp, biting, *accusing*. "To stop the windows from shedding glass into the water if they broke on the retrieval."

"How many bodies have you found, Madsen? Did the Missouri River hand all nine back or are you missing some?"

Clancy dropped her shields. Mia's voice screamed in her ear.

"HE'S HERE! THAT'S HIM!"

"CLANCY, RUN!"

Inez's scream woke Jude with a start. She quickly dragged yesterday's clothes on and hit the floor running. She pinballed off every wall in the RV to reach the office space.

"What the fuck, Inez?" she asked before she saw what was happening on the camera. "Oh my God." Jude didn't waste any more time, she slammed out of the RV without a second thought.

Chapter Twenty-eight

Clancy stared at the man before her. He didn't look like a killer, but she guessed that was the best disguise of all.

"Hi, Steven," she said and watched his face change from Mr. Average to a man perfectly capable of killing.

"So, you *do* know who I am. That's unfortunate. What gave me away?" Steven didn't look pleased.

"All the women you killed. Though you had different names for each one of them."

"All the better not to get caught by. I'm curious, how do *you* know my real name? Only one ever heard it."

Clancy tightened her grip on her mug. "Yeah, Mia says hi." She threw the burning coffee into his face.

He screamed as the liquid scalded him and began to peel the glued-on facial hair away from his skin. He barely had a chance to wipe at his eyes before Clancy smashed the cup into the side of his head and took off running. Blindly, he grabbed for her and managed to wrench her back by her T-shirt. Still blinking against the hot coffee burning his eyes, he slapped her hard across the cheek.

Clancy laughed, even though the hit had rattled her brain inside her skull and probably dislodged a tooth or two. "Oh my God, you even have to have your mommy fight your battles for you."

She punched him in a swift uppercut to the jaw, rocking him back on his heels. In retaliation, Steven charged at her. He pushed her off balance with considerable force, sending Clancy reeling down the bank. She felt the cold sting of the river water lap at her ankles when she slid to a halt.

Oh fuck, Clancy thought as she saw Steven's eyes change into something less than human as he pounded into the water after her.

"Really, two against one? Did your mother never teach you to fight fair?" She was shoved further into the water. His strength was unearthly and Clancy had nowhere to go. The water was up to her knees and she was struggling to stand against the current. And he just kept on coming. Fists flying, Steven knocked Clancy down and her head went under the water. She struggled to surface, but he waded out and grabbed her by the throat. Clancy dug her nails into his hands, tearing at his skin, but he apparently felt nothing. He appeared too far gone in rage and the possession. He tightened his hold, turned her around, and shoved her head back under the water.

Clancy fought desperately to hold her breath. She struggled against his bruising hold and realized he was dragging her out farther into deeper water. She couldn't stand up straight, the water was rushing past her, and she was quickly running out of air.

Steven yanked her head free of the water and Clancy gasped desperately for ragged breaths. She tried to clear her eyes of the filthy water and what she saw frightened her. His face had morphed and she saw the horrifying death mask of his mother staring back at her.

"You're going to die, bitch. Just like all the others. Who knows, maybe I'll take *your* body instead." The woman's voice had a purely demonic ring and Clancy prayed like she'd never prayed before. She sent out a mental plea for Jude to be kept safe and then she was pushed back under the water to drown.

It took Mia tapping at Clancy's face to get her to open her eyes. The water was lit with an eerie glow and everything was still and silent.

"You're not alone. We're all here."

Clancy looked around her and was astonished to see the faces of all the people she had recovered over the years. Starting with the most recent, the nine women from the Missouri River. There were the old folk from a nursing home who had all suffered with dementia. They had made a group pact to die before they lost who they truly were. Clancy remembered finding the five of them packed into a car, waiting patiently to be released. She remembered each and every one of the faces crowding around her. The teenagers who had been too drunk to fight against the water once they'd fallen in. Domestic abuse victims whose husbands, and a wife, all rotted in jail now. Innocents lost in all manner of vehicle accidents, all of them found by Clancy to be released into the light.

"How are all of you here?" Clancy was thankful they were able to converse telepathically. Her eyesight was clear. She felt no pain.

I'm dying, she realized with a finality that was oddly comforting. Fate was finally giving her what she'd desired for so long. For the voices to stop. For her to rest. To find her own peace.

But Clancy didn't want that now. She'd found Jude. Being with her was worth all the pain that living with the dead pressed upon her. She had Inez and Rainbow, people who were her found family. She had reasons to stay now.

Mia smiled at her. *"We're here for you, like you were for us."*

"I'm not ready to go. I have Jude. I don't want to leave her. I love her."

"Then fight, Clancy. Fight!"

Clancy stared into the face of her grandma. "He's too strong." She saw a light appear behind them all. She knew exactly what it was. "No! I am not going into the fucking light!"

"Then fight, for her sake!" Mia screamed at her.

All the dead joined in. They crowded around her, lifted her and with one voice they all screamed *"FIGHT!"*

The force of it pushed Clancy's body through the water and out of Steven's grip. She saw him stumble and disappear under the water from the forceful wave that hit them both. Her head was barely above the surface but she was no longer watching from her physical body.

Clancy walked out of the water and looked back at her lifeless form floating.

"NO!"

Jude's roar startled Clancy. She watched Jude run straight into the water to drag Steven away from her body as he tried to pull Clancy back out into the depths. Jude punched him with all her force, purposely raining blows aimed at his face and throat, then she pushed him back into the water, leaving him bloodied and dazed.

Clancy watched Jude pull her body out. Jude was calling to her. Clancy heeded it. She stood beside Jude while she began to perform CPR. Clancy knew Jude had been trained for this. Her unflappable lover was doing the compressions with military precision. Then she breathed into her mouth twice, the kiss of life from her lover. The compressions started again.

Clancy watched her unresponsive body and how hard Jude was fighting to bring her back. She tried to put a steadying hand on Jude's shoulder to let her know she was near. Her hand passed right through her. Then she heard it, Jude's breath coming out in frantic sobs as she counted off the compressions.

"Don't. You. Leave. Me."

Clancy looked up as Mia and her grandma joined her to stand watch over her body.

"Do you truly love her?" her grandma asked.

Clancy nodded. *"With all my heart."*

"Then the choice is yours. Don't waste it."

Clancy saw the bright light appear behind her and the familiar angel who stood beside it. He raised his eyebrow at her and held his hand out in an invitation for her to leave.

Clancy looked down at Jude, looked at her lifeless body that Jude was pounding on, then back to the angel.

She wagged her finger at him.

"Not yet."

Intense pain flooded through Clancy's whole being. Pain, fierce as a lightning bolt strike, forced her back into her body with a bang from Jude's hands on her chest. She drew in a gulp of air, but water still lay in her throat and she gagged. Jude quickly flipped her onto her side and Clancy coughed up the water in deep, wracking hacks. She finally flopped back over and winced at the feel of gravel pressing like knives into her back. All her senses were dialed up beyond what she could cope with. She felt raw and exposed to this harsh reality she'd very nearly left behind.

Jude gathered her up into her arms. "Thank God, thank God," she whispered.

Inez rushed to their sides and grabbed Clancy's hand. She sobbed uncontrollably, barely getting her words out. "Detective Chandler's coming. There's an ambulance on its way too."

"I'm okay, I'm okay," Clancy told them over and over, her body shaking uncontrollably. "Everything's okay now."

There was a loud commotion from the water. Clancy looked over to see all nine of the women Steven had killed forming a circle around him. They had kept him trapped in the river while Jude resuscitated Clancy. He was struggling to keep his head above the surface. His pitiful calls for help were ignored as he splashed frantically to stay afloat.

"What are you seeing?" Jude asked while they watched him flail. Absolute terror was visible on his battered face.

"Justice of the nine prevailing," Clancy said as she watched the women pull him under the water, dragging him down to the depths.

Before Clancy could even blink, a dreadful roar sounded out. A fathomless dark hole appeared out of thin air, hovering directly above the water. Steven's mother's spirit popped up on the water's surface, flailing yet floating, freed from his body while he, no doubt, was breathing his earthly last. Two forms stepped out of the darkness. They were shrouded in long black cloaks. Their hoods were raised, obscuring any features. Clancy tried to see if they even had faces visible, but the hood was filled with as black a space as that which they'd arrived in. The portal hissed and crackled with electricity, like it was a dreadful tear in the very fabric of existence. One of them reached out a pale skeletal hand that held a ball of black onyx. It transformed into a lethal-looking spear and the hooded form ran her spirit through with it. It dragged her through the water like a fish ensnared. It pulled her up, still impaled and wailing like a banshee, and tossed her back through the hole as if discarding rubbish.

Clancy was stunned into silence. She'd never seen a spirit be taken by anything other than an angel. Had her nearly dying given her something new to bring back with her? It was a darker, more sinister, new sight but an upgrade nevertheless to her psychic armory.

Its purpose complete, the black hole disappeared with a nails-on-a-chalkboard screech that made Clancy flinch at its ear-piercing pitch. Its disappearance returned daylight and sunshine to the world. Clancy looked up at Jude who was watching her, obviously sensing something else was happening that she couldn't see.

"Show's over. They're both gone. Someone came to take out the trash," Clancy said, still in a state of awe.

"And you're here, thank God. I thought I'd lost you there, for a moment." Jude brushed Clancy's hair back from her face and was gazing at her with such blatant adoration Clancy was almost blinded by it. "I love you, Clancy Madsen. You died, and I nearly lost my chance to tell you."

"But I came back," Clancy cupped Jude's cheek and tried to soothe away the anguish in Jude's eyes.

"Why though? I know it's something that's plagued you all your life. That need to let go of all the voices. You had the chance to go." Jude clung on tighter to Clancy, making it very clear she wasn't going to let Clancy go anywhere now she had her back.

"Because I love you, Jude. Your voice was the one I heard calling me home."

Jude's eyes welled with tears. "I don't ever want to go through that again. I can't imagine my life without you in it." Jude shifted Clancy in her arms to make a space for Inez to fit in between them. Inez sobbed uncontrollably against Clancy's chest, not caring how soaked Clancy was.

Clancy lifted her hand that felt like a ton weight to rub at Inez's back to try to reassure her.

"I'm still here, kid. I'm okay. I'm gonna need a stomach pump to clear my insides of all the Big Muddy shit I've swallowed, but I'm going to be fine."

Clancy looked up to see her grandma standing nearby, watching them all with a wistful look on her face. "Hey, Grandma. Thanks for bringing the cavalry." She felt Jude and Inez go very still at who she was talking to.

"Your family is beautiful. Their love will light your way from now on. Follow their lead and remember, you're not alone now."

Clancy smiled at her. "Thank everyone for me, Grandma. I rescued all of them, and today they saved *me*."

Her grandma nodded then directed her gaze to Jude. *"You finally found your soulmate. She'll be good for you. Love her til your last breath."* She narrowed her eyes and Clancy braced herself for a scolding. *"This is the second time I've had to drag your sorry ass out of the water. Don't make me have to come back for a third."* She shook her head in exasperation then her demeanor changed again in a flash. *"I'm so very proud of you. I love you, sweetie."* She blew Clancy a kiss and faded away.

"You okay there, Clancy?" Jude asked as the silence grew.

"Yeah. Just realizing I have more people in my corner than I could ever have imagined." She gazed into Jude's eyes. "And the woman I love told me she loved me. This could be the best day ever, minus the out-of-body experience and me smelling like wet cat." She hugged Inez more and deliberately wiped her wet arms on Inez's shirt. Inez giggled through her tears and struggled to break free. "Chandler can deal with it all now. Our job is done."

CHAPTER TWENTY-NINE

The ambulance crew had been fantastic. Clancy was wrapped in a foil blanket that she had every intention of keeping. She'd been checked over but was expected to have an overnight stay in the hospital just for observation. Clancy had vehemently argued against that, but Detective Chandler had promised she would personally bring Clancy in later.

For now, they were waiting. All eyes were fixed on the river, waiting for it to release its dead.

"They could just keep him down there as fish food," Jude said, her arms wrapped around Clancy as they sat with their legs dangling over the edge of the chipped and worn wood of the old pier.

"I don't think they want to leave him there. There's a harsher judgment awaiting him." Clancy knew the deceased women had given him payback for what they'd been subjected to. As he'd died, he would have seen all their faces around him as they held him down to drown.

"I thought I'd killed him," Jude said. "I'd have made my peace with that if I had."

"You didn't though, so your conscience is clear. You did however, punch the fuck out of the bastard that killed Mia and that's something to brag about."

"He nearly killed you too." Jude shuddered behind her and tightened her hold.

Clancy twisted in Jude's arms to look back at her. "But you saved me. I'm bragging the hell out of that fact at Gentleman Jackie's as soon as I'm given the all clear."

Jude grimaced. "I've used up all my vacation. I'm due back at work next Monday."

"Do you want to go back?" Clancy asked, curious as to what Jude wanted to do next.

"No. I want to stay with you. I want to chart the waters with you wherever the job takes us. That first night we were together I knew I wanted more time with you. I'll never have enough time with you. Eternity wouldn't be long enough."

Clancy smiled at Jude's ardent tone. "I do love a woman with a romantic soul..." She leaned in to whisper for Jude alone, "and a dominant side with a penchant for tying up good bois with their belts." She kissed Jude's reddening cheek.

"What do you want, Clancy?" Jude's eyes were serious as she gazed upon Clancy's face as if memorizing every inch of her. Clancy had a feeling she wouldn't be let out of Jude's sight for a while. She had no problem with that.

"I'd like for you to come home with me, back to the commune. I know everyone will love you, and you'll find I'm not the biggest weirdo there. I'd like you to leave the bar and come sail with me on every adventure. If that's what you really want."

"You've told me what you'd like me to do. What do you *want*, Clancy?" Jude deepened her tone and not even the foil blanket stopped the shiver than ran through Clancy.

"I want to wake up every morning in your arms. I want to close my eyes every night knowing you've just fucked me into oblivion. I want a home with you in it, with us sharing our lives together, helping others as we go. I want to love you for eternity, because I know angels who have friends in high places. I think I could get them to put a good word in for us to get a happy ever after for all time."

"I love the sound of that." Jude nuzzled into Clancy's neck. "You're going to have to adopt Smokey Joe."

"You're a packaged deal; I can live with that. I can channel your family back three generations. Think you can cope with that?"

Jude hummed against Clancy's ear. "I get to choose who I talk to."

"I'll put up a 'No Cold Callers' sign." Clancy looked out over the river, watching the calm water flow. "So, we're really going to do this, right? You and me? A relationship?"

"You and me, exclusive. No more fucking in bathroom stalls for you."

Clancy smiled. "I only ever did that with you, lover."

Jude stilled. "Seriously?"

"Yep. Was I *your* first bathroom tryst?" Clancy grinned at her over her shoulder.

"You were. I was the only member of staff who hadn't gotten involved with a customer. Until you walked in, all butch swagger and sweet-talk."

Clancy planted a kiss on Jude's lips. "We'll have to come back every year on our anniversary and lock ourselves in the staff bathroom to celebrate. When you leave, don't give them the key back."

Jude shook her head at her indulgently and kissed her back.

"Hey, lovebirds, how much longer do we have to wait?" Detective Chandler called over from where she and Inez sat in deck chairs, drinking coffee, and comparing notes. Chandler's team were sitting in their vehicles at the top of the road, waiting for her call. Chandler had already documented Clancy's injuries, taken scrapings from under her fingernails in one of their mobile forensic vans, and then had interviewed her and Jude. Inez had promised copies of the recording of the attack from the GoPro. Chandler was now waiting for one last thing.

"I haven't heard anything yet," Clancy called back. "They were probably waiting until the ambulance left."

"That was twenty minutes ago," Chandler complained.

"Forgive me, I've been distracted. I had a near-death experience and a declaration of love to swoon over. Give a butch a break!" Clancy kissed Jude again just for show. Jude grinned at her, equally unrepentant.

Clancy looked around to make sure no one else was in earshot. "Hey, Mia, the coast is clear," she called.

The river began to ripple and bubble. Steven Thorn's dead body popped up, floating on the surface, buoyed by ghostly hands.

"You can have him back." Mia appeared beside Clancy and Jude. She sat down next to them and gently swung her legs back and forth off the pier.

"How'd it go?" Clancy asked.

"You should have seen his face when we all appeared before him. We switched to our death guises and he freaked out. He definitely pooped his pants. It was totally worth it. I only wish he'd taken longer to drown but at least, in the end, he knew how it felt for each and every one of us receiving that end.

"How are you feeling, though? You were so nearly number ten."

"I'm okay. I'm having to spend the night in the hospital in case of complications or something. Chandler has snagged me a private room and I've been promised unlimited Jell-O so what's one night in a hospital bed when I could have been laid out on a mortuary slab instead?" Clancy felt Jude stiffen at her unthinking words. "Sorry, Jude. My bad. It's probably not the most appropriate time for me to be using dark humor as a coping method."

Clancy watched Chandler waiting at the side of the river as Steven's body was directed toward her by invisible aides. His pale body was washed up onto the bank. Chandler called for her people and a coroner's van drove for the retrieval.

"Can you see him?" Jude was watching Chandler's people deal with the body quickly and efficiently.

Clancy shook her head. "I'm guessing he's already been taken elsewhere by reapers until they can interrogate him."

"Are you going to be expected to do that?" Jude bristled. "Because I really don't want you..."

Clancy laid a restraining hand on Jude's chest. "Whoa your ponies, Jude. I don't interrogate killers. It's enough of a strain to work with the victims. But those I *can* help. There's no helping a murderer. Chandler has someone else who does that dirty work for her."

"So, what happens now?"

"Well, for you, Mia, we need to go visit your family so you can say your goodbyes to them. They were informed last night that you'd been found. They'll need a day or two to process that before I can go in and speak for you. I'm just glad your family are open-minded. Not every family agrees to meet with me."

"I was told I can talk to you whenever I want to. Until I sign a new soul contract and return to Earth to live a new life.

"If I choose to return."

"The choice is always yours. Who knows, maybe you'll come back as someone who grows up to be mine and Jude's apprentice and you'll take over our work. Perhaps you'll fulfil your karma by being the one who seeks and finds that time around."

"Will you recognize me?"

"I might spiritually, but you'll be a new soul. A whole new you. Jude might recognize traits she sees that remind her of you. Either way, you get the choice; to come back, or to move on."

"And what's there if I move on?"

"I don't know, but I'm told it's something unique to each soul."

"Damn, I have never wanted to hear the dead more than I do now, to work out just what the hell you two are philosophizing over," Jude said.

"Just talking shop," Clancy teased her.

The angel appeared in Clancy's eyeline. She saw Mia look too.

"I have to go."

Mia got up from the pier and dusted off her gown out of habit. She stared down at Clancy and Jude with a small smile.

"All I ever wanted was to find love. How ironic that you two found it because of me."

"You brought us together, Mia. We're both eternally grateful for that."

"Yes, totally," Jude said, agreeing to the one side of the conversation she could hear.

"Then, if nothing else, something beautiful came from my death.
She waved to the angel, acknowledging he was waiting. *"Clancy, go to the hospital and do as you're told. Don't make me haunt you."*

"Yes, ma'am," Clancy saluted her. "We'll see you soon."

"Tell Jude I love her and that her girlfriend is hot."

"She'll never believe me that you said that!" Clancy said, side-eyeing Jude.

"She said you were hot, didn't she?" Jude rested her chin on Clancy's shoulder. "Even in death, she doesn't change. Is she leaving?"

Clancy nodded.

"Love you, Mia." Jude's voice wavered just a fraction on her name.

Mia's beatific smile made Clancy's heart ache for them. For the friends whose reunion was to be short-lived. Uncharacteristically silent, Mia rested her hand on her heart and nodded. She walked away, back to the light with an angel as companion.

Clancy leaned back in Jude's arms. "She loves you too. She's gone now."

"If someone had told me a few months ago that I'd be holding conversations with my dead neighbor after I'd fought with her serial killer boyfriend? I'd have checked how potent the alcohol level was that I was serving." She shook her head with disbelief. "And you watched the nine of them drown him. Then you saw his mother be carted away by monsters." Jude tightened her grip around Clancy. "How the fuck am I supposed to sleep tonight after all this while medical staff keep *you* under observation because you damn well died?"

"Chandler got me a room where they'll set up a spare bed for you to stay with me. Inez too because I can't leave her alone after today. Chandler is going to sleep in the RV tonight and watch over Smokey Joe. I think she just wants to check out van life. I'm pretty damn certain she covets my RV."

Jude breathed a heavy sigh of relief. "Thank fuck for that. Is there anything that woman can't do?"

"Oh, lover, we're just barely scratching the surface of what power the DDU has. You being able to sleep beside me in the hospital tonight is mere child's play to them."

"I think I should be frightened by that, but I'm too weary." Jude rubbed at her face.

"Remind me to ask Chandler about Rafe and that angel being linked to her partner. Ever since I started rescuing people, he's been appearing to ferry them to the other side. I never really thought about it, but now I'm wondering if he's the one who told the DDU about me. I never understood how they came to hear about me. I wasn't exactly high profile. I was just skipping around the country, living in my pickup, and scouring message boards where people posted about their loved ones being lost."

Jude nodded. "We'll ask her later, I promise. For now, you need a shower to get the Missouri River off you. Do you think you can eat?"

Clancy gave her a look.

"Silly question. Okay, a shower, clean clothes, and a decent meal inside you before we all go to the hospital where they'll monitor you to make sure you don't have any problems after swallowing whatever is in this godforsaken river."

"Then I can be given a clean bill of health and we can go home."

"That RV of yours has felt more like a home to me than my apartment ever has," Jude said, surprised by her own admission.

"So, you won't be averse to moving in with us once you've quit your job and started the salvage business full time?"

"I'd love to." Jude kissed Clancy sweetly then licked at her lips. She stuck out her tongue with a grimace. "Shower time, for both of us."

"You gonna join me?"

"I'm not leaving you under the water alone, for a multitude of reasons." Jude got to her feet and helped Clancy up. "Do you want me to carry you? We both know I can."

Clancy smiled at her. "No, I'm more than capable of walking. Just don't make it too obvious if I stumble and you have to hold me up. I have a reputation to uphold." Clancy tugged her blanket around her and started to walk over to where all the DDU minions were working on the scene. Farther up the road, they had Steven's car and were tearing it apart for evidence.

"Chandler. I'm heading back for a shower, then ordering food in so bring everyone back to the RV when you're done here," Clancy called over to her.

"*Then* you're going to the hospital." Chandler's tone brooked no arguments.

"Yes, Detective, then we can all go to the hospital and prove I'm here to stay."

Inez hurried to her side and looped her arm through Clancy's. Jude had her arm firmly around Clancy's waist.

"We'll catch up with you all later," Chandler said, waving them off and getting back to work.

"Let's go home," Clancy said, loving how that sounded. She was determined never to take it for granted again.

The church was a glorious display of faith and wealth. Numerous stained-glass windows lined the walls of the nave, depicting stories from scripture in bright colored glass. The ceiling was painted as a starry night, a deep blue adorned with white lights shining down on the congregation.

Jude hadn't stepped foot in a church for years. She'd been brought up to be deathly afraid of everything connected to true faith. To be afraid of God, to fear his wrath, to be terrified of sinning. Her grandma had deliberately left out the brighter side of having a belief that got you through life. She looked around at the statues and finery, the people praying, the soft piped music filling the huge room. She remembered her grandma's words, spoken through Clancy's channeling.

I learned none of it matters.

None of the grandeur and ceremony, the tall hats and the gilded robes, the pompous words and the collection plate passed around from pew to pew. Yet, Jude had found herself needing to find a place to just sit and think about the last few weeks.

Clancy had died. She'd drowned and Jude had fought to bring her back. Clancy was fine now. She had moved on surprisingly quickly. Jude had noticed the weight Clancy always carried on her shoulders seemed lighter now. She'd asked Clancy if she felt different. Clancy had joked she felt like Eeyore's dark cloud had been removed from over her head. The crazy thing was, Jude believed that. Clancy had been saved by the spirits of those who had been lost and she had found.

They had come back for her when she had needed them the most. It was miraculous and altogether freaky as fuck, but Jude had sat with Inez and Clancy and learned all of their names and the circumstances of their deaths. Now she sat near the altar where candles were lit for loved ones and she'd lit a candle for each and every one of those people.

She'd also lit candles for each of the first eight victims of the Missouri River Killer. Their stories were now being told. The press, however, only ever mentioned Steven Thorn in their news reports. They had no idea he'd had an accomplice. He was branded a weird loner, the mommy's boy who used fake names and elaborate disguises to lure women in off dating apps, only to kill them and sink their cars into the river. His mother, Janice Thorn, had been revealed only as the "overly devoted" mother who had physically and mentally abused her son throughout his life. Yet, even after her death, he couldn't escape her. Steven and Janice's interrogations at the DDU left them with no doubts she was a cruel and sadistic murderess, using her son for her own means. Steven, though possessed, was just as culpable. He never sought out an exorcist. He didn't turn himself in after that first kill. He could have saved them all, drove *himself* into the river, and trapped his mother there with him for eternity. But he didn't, and nine women died because of them.

Lastly, Jude had lit a candle for Mia. She sat watching it flicker and burn so brightly in its ornate tealight cradle. She'd heard Mia's voice again a week ago. She'd sat in with Mia's family, listening to her tell her parents and sister she was so sorry and say her goodbyes to them with Clancy's help. Inez had been on hand to support them in their grief. Detective Chandler had told them what she felt they could handle to hear and then prepared to draw the investigation to a close.

It had been a draining day for all but, back at the RV, Clancy had found the baby oil Jude had used on her and asked for a lesson in Shiatsu foot massage. She'd proved to be a most excellent student.

Jude's lips quirked just a fraction as she recalled how diligent Clancy had been to learn every pressure point. Jude knew she was doing it to distract Jude from the gut-wrenching sorrow that had permeated the Murray household. It also distracted Clancy without bursting her eardrums.

Mia's funeral had been heart-wrenching. It had been held in a small church, a closed casket affair, and Jude had hated every minute of it. Her only solace had been side-eyeing Clancy who was watching the ghost of Mia wander around the congregation. The only bright spot had been Mia's mother coming to ask Clancy if Mia had been in attendance.

"Yes, she's here. She loves the flowers but she wants to know who invited Uncle Ben? She says he still smells of mothballs."

Watching Mia's mother smile at that had been a blessing. Mia spent that evening in their RV, cuddled close to Smokey Joe who seemed to know she was there. Clancy had mediated the long overdue conversation between Jude and Mia.

But Mia still hadn't moved on.

Jude stared at the statues of deities adorning the walls. She wasn't sure what she believed in anymore. Clancy and Inez had some interesting beliefs of their own that she knew came from Rainbow's way of life. Jude didn't believe she was too old to learn new things. She was moving to the Wiccan commune with Clancy. She found herself intrigued and oddly excited to see what that entailed. Inez had already gifted her a crystal. An amethyst, the 'stone of the soul.' Inez had informed her that amethyst helped restore your inner tranquility and emotional balance in times of mourning. Clancy called it the "spikey purple grief gem." Smokey Joe just kept rubbing his face all over it.

Jude took one last look around the nave and rose to light one more candle.

"Whoever is out there watching over us, thank you for returning Clancy to where she is most needed."

Jude gathered up her backpack and sauntered back up the aisle. A few people gave her disapproving looks, but Jude just continued walking. Those people would learn, just like her grandma had, that their bigoted opinions matter little in the grand scheme of things.

❖

Jude came out of the church to find Clancy, Inez, and Smokey Joe in his carrier, sitting on the grass eating an impromptu picnic.

Other people sat on the benches to enjoy the afternoon sun, but Clancy and Inez were doing their own thing. Clancy had obviously been to Subway given that they were eating what appeared to be foot-long sandwiches.

"You all finished with the hallelujahs?" Clancy asked around a mouthful of garlic cheese steak, her latest obsession.

"We got you your All-Star Chicken." Inez held up a wrapped sandwich with its paper slightly torn. She grimaced a little in apology. "I may have opened it to give Smokey Joe a little snack."

Jude could see him still licking his lips. "He needs to buy his own damn supper." She joined them on the grass, opened up her sandwich and went to take a bite, but a plaintive meow stopped her. She sighed, pulled out a piece of meat, and fed it to him. "Mia will haunt me for the rest of my life with his new eating habits."

"It's chicken, it's healthy," Clancy said.

"It's covered in garlic and herb sauce." Jude watched him gobble it up.

"I'm still not cleaning his litter tray so give him what he wants."

Jude poked Clancy's ribs in retaliation, enjoying the grunt she emitted, then settled in to eat.

"When we get back home, we'll show you our way of honoring the dead," Inez said.

"And we won't expect you to pay for it either," Clancy muttered.

"Do you think it was dumb, me coming here?" Jude took a bite from her meal and waited for Clancy's answer.

Clancy looked up from her sandwich. "You know the dead hear our prayers. They hear us every time we think about them. How they are remembered by us is never dumb. And you remembering all those we've been touched by is pretty fucking awesome." Clancy leaned over and kissed her.

Jude licked at her lips when they parted. "Hmm, garlic."

Clancy sat back. "Don't worry, it will be gone once I've dampened it down with ice cream."

Jude shook her head at her. "Are we still charting the river tomorrow?"

Clancy nodded. "Yeah, then I think we can call it quits. I know we're going to come up empty on anything now, but it seemed crazy to come this far only to stop when there's just a bit more to clear. Besides, you're on the last week of your two weeks' notice. We're nearly done here. It didn't take much to get your stuff mailed ahead and the rest packed in the RV. We are ready to roll."

"Home," Inez said, doing a little happy wiggle. "I can't wait to see my mom in person and not just on FaceTime."

"We've just got to detour to see Jude's folks first. I'm looking forward to meeting your mom and dad," Clancy said.

"We're going to have to roll you back to the RV after she's fed you. Mom cooks for an army and you eat like one."

Clancy grinned at her and pointed to Jude's half-eaten sandwich. "Speaking of which, you eating all that?"

"I swear you buy me too big a sandwich just so you can finish it off," Jude muttered, handing half of it over.

"You love that about me." Clancy gave her a winning smile.

"I love everything about you." Jude stared at her intently.

Inez sighed dramatically. "We're in public, guys."

"Hey, we're still dressed, what more do you want?" Clancy said, picking out another choice piece of meat for Smokey Joe and then taking a big bite for herself.

Jude looked around at the family she'd found for herself. Out of sorrow, love had grown. That was truly something to hold onto and believe in.

CHAPTER THIRTY

There was something almost decadent about waking up in her own bed, in her own home, with her girlfriend being the big spoon holding Clancy close. For a moment she kept her eyes closed and just savored it. The clean sheets beneath her and covering her, thanks to Rainbow. The warmth from Jude's naked skin pressed firmly into Clancy's back. Jude's arm wrapped tightly around her and her hand clasping Clancy's breast. Clancy loved that Jude was so tactile, and that she loved it when Clancy's hands were all over her too. Clancy remembered her grandma calling Jude her soulmate. Her grandma was never wrong.

From the comfort of her large bed, Clancy imagined she could hear the river that flowed north of the commune. It was her favorite place. She wanted to take Jude on a boat ride on it, show off the area they lived in. She hoped Jude would grow to love it as much as Clancy did and want to make it her forever home.

They'd been welcomed back joyously by everyone yesterday. Jude had just taken it in stride and already had a name to put to every face. Rainbow had welcomed her into the family as if Jude had always been there. Rainbow *knew* if someone was sincere and genuine. Jude was all that and more.

Clancy distantly heard a door open and close. She was feeling too lazy to pay it any attention until she startled at the feel of something crawling up the bedsheet that was draped over her. She knew Smokey Joe's weight and heavy paws when he jumped on the bed with them. This was not Smokey Joe.

Clancy cracked open an eye just as a small furry body slipped over her shoulder and fell on the bed before her. A tiny meow announced himself, and a small cream-and-white cat with chocolate brown markings around his eyes head-butted Clancy's chin and snuggled in beside her.

"Salem, how the fuck did you get in here?"

Salem, Inez's new kitten, lifted his head at his name. He batted at the hair that fell over Clancy's face.

"Clancy, are you awake?" Inez's voice called softly from outside the bedroom door.

"I am now that you've sent your hellcat in after me," Clancy muttered. She felt Jude shift behind her.

"We're awake," Jude replied.

"There's a welcome back breakfast barbeque in half an hour with your names on it," Inez said.

Clancy perked up. "Half an hour?"

"First come, first served," Inez singsonged cheerfully.

Clancy turned a little to look over her shoulder. "Are we decent?" she asked Jude who nodded but tugged the sheet a little higher. "Come get this four-pawed menace of yours who is trying to tangle himself in my hair."

Inez stepped in, not sparing them a glance. She only had eyes for her cat. She scooped up the kitten. "Isn't he precious?" she said, crooning at the little cat who basked in all the attention while still not letting go of Clancy.

"For someone whose name means 'peace' he's already disturbing mine." Clancy tried to get her hair untangled from determined kitty claws.

"I named him after the sassy cat from *Sabrina the Teenage Witch* so he's living up to his namesake. I thought you'd stand a better chance of acknowledging his early morning wakeup call seeing as you've been ignoring my texts for the last hour. You're going to miss out on the feast Mom and everyone are preparing for our welcome home."

"Clancy will never miss out on a meal," Jude said, yawning and preparing to stretch. Clancy felt her stop abruptly, realizing their predicament.

"To be honest, I expected you two to be up by now. I guess being back at home means you get to sleep in more. Also, you might want to break the norm around here and start locking your door so you don't have your neighbors walking in on you unannounced."

"Like you just did?" Clancy said.

"I announced my intentions seven texts ago. You have twenty-seven minutes." Inez walked out of the room, cradling her cat. "Bring your appetites!"

Clancy listened to Inez going down the stairs and letting herself out.

"So, you don't lock your doors here?" Jude said.

"We might want to revise that in case of further kitty invasions while you have your fingers in my pus—" Clancy's comment was lost under Jude's urgent lips. "I'll start locking the door," Clancy said when Jude finally pulled back.

"Is that even safe here? Not locking up at night?"

Clancy raised an eyebrow at her. "It's a Wiccan commune. Would you risk getting hexed just to steal something from here?"

"*Can* they hex someone?" Jude looked intrigued.

"The fear of it is what keeps us safe and sound."

"That didn't answer my question."

"Let's just say some of our residents have amazing talents for mixing potions and some might have other talents should the need arise." Clancy loved watching Jude's face when it dropped the stoic look. This time she looked comically astounded.

"You brought me to live with witches? *Real* witches?" Jude whispered.

"You don't have to whisper. Most of the witches are old and can't hear very well so you're safe."

"Are you fucking with me?" Jude's eyes narrowed at her.

"No, because we've only got thirty minutes before the breakfast buffet and I never fuck around before food." Clancy wriggled out of Jude's hold. "We have time for a fast shower then I'm first in line at the table. You are going to eat like a king here!"

"*Are* there real witches here?" Jude jumped out of bed to chase Clancy into the bathroom. She caught Clancy and pinned her against a wall.

Clancy stared into Jude's serious eyes. "Yes. Real, honest to goodness, spell casting witches, who welcomed you into their circle last night."

Jude contemplated Clancy's revelation for a moment. "Will you make sure I don't say anything stupid like I did when you first told me you were psychic? I don't want to fuck up a second time."

Clancy hugged Jude to her. "I love you so much."

Jude hugged her back. "This world you're showing me, full of psychics, witches, angels, and demons. It's not the world I'm used to. But with you? I want to experience it all."

Clancy snuggled into Jude. "Aunt Lily, the old crone you met last night? She told me, if she could bottle up the love she could see between us, she'd make a fortune."

"I like the sound of that." Jude cupped Clancy's face in her hands. "You walked into my bar and turned my world on its head. I can't wait to see what our life together brings."

Clancy nuzzled into Jude's neck and groaned. "No, don't say sweet things like that to me when we have people waiting and our door's unlocked!"

"Have I told you how much I love your house?" Jude switched on the shower and they waited for the water to warm up.

"It's our house now. Our refuge to come back to after all our adventures."

"Where the bed is bigger than what we share in the RV and we don't have to worry about how loud we are." Jude stepped in under the spray. "I want to fuck you in every room."

Clancy quickly stepped in behind her and reached for the soap. "This is where I applaud myself for picking the plot of land farthest away from everyone else."

"You're my smart boi."

Clancy groaned and lathered up her hands. "If we had more time, I'd help you tick the bathroom off your list. But I refuse to sit around the firepit with every maiden, mother, and crone knowing why we were late to breakfast."

"We'll take Smokey Joe with us, get him used to socializing with the other animals who live here."

"Judging by how well he and Salem got on last night I'd say he's going to fit right in too." Clancy pulled Jude down for a tender kiss. "Welcome home, lover."

The smile Jude gifted Clancy with only made her fall more in love with her. She wanted that smile directed at her for the rest of her life and Clancy intended to live a very long life with Jude by her side.

❖

"She looks happy here."

Clancy looked up from her contemplation of the crackling flames burning in the firepit. Mia was watching Jude as she talked with Rainbow and Inez. They'd all come out that evening to chat, then to chart the stars as they shone bright in the night sky. Jude was walking them back to their homes nearby while Clancy had lost herself to the quiet of the night.

"I'm hoping she'll come to love it as much as I do. This place and its people have saved me more times than I care to admit."

"I've come to say goodbye."

Clancy's heart sank before she could stop it. She'd spent so many weeks with Mia as a ghostly companion that she was going to miss her dreadfully. She'd seen for herself why Jude had appreciated having her as a friend.

But Mia had been anchorless since her death. She'd watched her family struggling to cope with the aftermath of her murder. She'd seen them dealing with all the news coverage once the truth came out and the victims' stories were told over and over again. The press camped out at their door, desperate for any detail that hadn't already been dug up. The harrowing details were repeated every night, the photos of their faces paraded out online for armchair sleuths to pick over like vultures until the next sensational story broke and they got brushed aside by the newest awful act.

Mia had spoken to Clancy about it, complaining that the angel had pointed out that *this* was why souls passed on. They weren't meant to stay and relive their demise, weren't meant to see their families crumple and mourn.

"What's made you decide?" Clancy was curious as to why now, after weeks of Mia haunting them all.

"My sister is pregnant. She's worried about telling my parents."

"But that's good news, right?"

"But I'm still dead."

"Nothing can change that, Mia. Whether it's two weeks, ten months, or thirty years, life is destined to continue without you."

"I wanted what she has. A husband, a family, a life."

"But in this life, you weren't destined to have that. Maybe in your next life you *will.* It's too late to change what happened here and now."

"It's not fair."

"No, it's not. It's not fair your parents lost their wonderful daughter, or your sister lost an enthusiastic birthing coach, or your niece or nephew will only know of you through photos and memories. We can't turn back time, we can't stop what happened, and we can't give you your life back. But you left your mark here, your story has been told. It's time for you to embark on a new one."

"Will you miss me?"

"You know I will. And Jude especially will, but we'll understand your decision. It's not been fair to you, having just me who can see and hold a conversation with you. And I can only let you possess me for so long so you can let your voice be heard."

"I had unfinished business where Jude was concerned. I hated the idea of her being alone in her apartment without me living next door. She was so lonely before she met you, Clancy. Now she's smiling and seems content. I think I can rest now, knowing my friend has found her home. Her home with you."

"We're good for each other. She's my everything."

"You'll take care of her for me?"

"Every day of my life with her."

"Can I say goodbye to her, please. One last time?"

Clancy nodded and stood up to see if Jude was coming back. She found her, keeping her distance while no doubt seeing Clancy was occupied. Smokey Joe sat beside her. Clancy beckoned her forward.

"Is it Mia?" Jude asked as she reached the fire pit. Smokey Joe jumped into Clancy's lap.

Clancy petted him, her eyes starting to tear up as she prepared to help Mia say her final goodbyes. Jude tensed and sat down beside her with a thump.

"She's finally leaving, I take it?" Jude looked around as if trying to see Mia standing before her.

Clancy nodded.

"Jeez, Mia, you always were a procrastinator, but you elevated it to an art form not stepping into the light every time it's been ready for you." Jude's voice was teasing but the tightness in her tone was noticeable to Clancy's ears.

Clancy closed her eyes and invited Mia in. She let down her psychic walls so that Mia could feel Smokey Joe and pet him. He sensed the difference and began to purr and trill at her.

"I couldn't go until I knew you were all settled here," Mia said, her eyes shining from Clancy's face. "Jude, there's a *witch* living next door to you! A real one, not a crunchy granola one."

Jude laughed. "I know."

"I really hope you'll be happy here."

"I will be. Mrs. Baker's coming next week for a visit. Her sister just died and though she's still got her nephew and his family she says it's not going to be the same. Clancy invited her to stay here for a while. There's a woman who has a spare room she's been welcomed to stay in."

Mia was quiet for a moment. "She won't go back once she's here."

Jude nodded. "Yeah, I have that feeling too. Good neighbors are in short supply and I've missed her. Mrs. Baker was good to both of us."

"Yes, she was. Please, if she's open to it, give her my love and thanks for being such a treasure."

Jude nodded then took a deep breath that came out shaky when she exhaled. "Oh, I'm going to miss you and Clancy's one-sided conversations. But you have places to be that don't include us. I really hope you find your happiness through that light."

"I'm frightened, Jude. I'm scared to see what is next. I wanted so much in this life and, in my search, I found a serial killer who gaslit me to the very end, talking about burning all his bridges for me while leaving me bound and helpless in that damned car. He'd better not be the one I see as I walk through the light!"

"I doubt very much he's going to be in the same place you're going."

"I'd stay if I could, but I've come to realize this isn't where I belong any more. But I will miss you desperately, Jude. You were and have continued to be, even in death, the best friend I could ever have hoped for. Be happy in your life here, please. Love this woman with all your heart and soul. Find your peace, Jude, and live every day as if it's your last."

Jude shifted to kneel beside Clancy. She took her hand, knowing Mia could feel her. "God bless you, Mia. I hope you find your happiness too."

Clancy leaned forward and Mia gave Jude a kiss on her cheek. Then Mia ran Clancy's fingers through Smokey Joe's fur for the last time.

"You be a good boy for your mommy Jude, now. I love you so much, Smokey Joe. You were always my very good boy." She looked up at Jude and said with finality, "Goodbye, my dearest friend."

Clancy felt Mia leave and she opened her eyes to find Jude clinging to her hand in desperation.

"Has the light appeared for her?" Jude asked, shaking like a leaf.

"Not yet," Clancy said, wiping at her eyes after receiving Mia's final goodbye to herself.

"We would have been the best of friends, you and I. I wish I could have gotten to grow old with you and Jude. Maybe in another life we'll get that chance. I'll be waiting for you both. Come find me."

"It isn't dawn already, is it? There's a weird light..." Jude shut up and stared incredulously as the light got brighter and bigger.

Clancy watched Jude squinting at the bright light that had appeared. "You can *see* that?" She whipped her head back and forth between *the light* and Jude's awestruck face.

"Is it what I think it is?"

"Yes, that's the light to welcome you home and I have no idea why you're seeing it." Clancy saw the angel appear and beckon Mia forward. Instead, contrary to the end, Mia turned back to look at them.

"Oh my God, I can see her!" Jude exclaimed. Her hand flew to cover her mouth as she laughed and cried at the same time. "She looks beautiful. Just like she always did."

Mia lifted her hand and waved to them both. She took one last look up at the stars, then she blew them a kiss and stepped into the light. The angel nodded graciously to Clancy, mouthing her a *thank you*, then he followed after Mia and the light disappeared in a flash.

Jude was crushing Clancy's hand but she didn't care. The angel had just given Jude the most beautiful parting gift. The gift of seeing her friend whole and smiling, embarking on her next journey, instead of the remembrance of her lost and lifeless at the bottom of the river.

Clancy sent out a heartfelt prayer to all those lost who finally found their way home.

"Merry we meet, and merry we part; and merry we meet again."

The End

About the Author

Lesley Davis lives in the West Midlands of England. She is a die-hard science-fiction/fantasy fan in all its forms and an extremely passionate gamer. When her games controller is out of her grasp, Lesley can be found seated at her laptop, writing. Her book *Dark Wings Descending* was a Lambda Literary award finalist for Best Lesbian Romance. Visit her online on Twitter @author_lesley or email at lesley_j_davis@yahoo.com.

Books Available from Bold Strokes Books

Anywhere with You by Margo Glynn. On a road trip through the Great American Southwest, two friends discover nature, hope, and each other. (978-1-63679-907-0)

Burning Bridges by Lesley Davis. Can Clancy and Jude crack the case of nine missing women—and the secrets of their own hearts? (978-1-63679-872-1)

Dreams Entangled by Sophia Kell Hagin. Amid self-doubt, secrets, a pandemic, fear of attack and attempted murder, Pirin and Gracie's attraction turns to love and their lives will never be the same. (978-1-63679-892-9)

Echoes of Love by Catherine Lane. As Hazel's and Jo's paths intertwine, they're swept up in a whirlwind of long-buried secrets, sizzling chemistry, and memories that won't be denied. (978-1-63679-835-6)

Moonlight Obsession by Sheri Lewis Wohl. All it takes to stop a clever killer is moonlight, love, and a silver bullet. (978-1-63679-831-8)

My Boyfriend's Wife by Joy Argento. Amid betrayal and heartbreak, can two women discover a love that could heal their pasts and rewrite their futures? (978-1-63679-866-0)

Tapout by Nicole Disney. A struggling MMA fighter finds her edge in an underground ring, but as she falls for the magnetic and ambitious promoter behind the matches, their dangerous world threatens to destroy everything they've fought to rebuild. (978-1-63679-924-7)

The Fame Game by Ronica Black. Wild child Hollywood actress Luna Kirkman begins dating Hollywood's leading man, only to fall for his straitlaced sister instead. (978-1-63679-858-5)

An Extraordinary Passion by Kit Meredith. An autistic podcaster must decide whether to take a chance on her polyamorous guest and indulge their shared passion, despite her history. (978-1-63679-679-6)

That's Amore! by Georgia Beers. The romantic city of Rome should inspire Lily's passion for writing, if she can look away from Marina Troiani, her witty, smart, and unassumingly beautiful Italian tour guide. (978-1-63679-841-7)

The Unexpected Heiress by Cassidy Crane. When a cynical opportunist meets a shy but spirited heiress, the last thing she plans is for her heart to get involved. (978-1-63679-833-2)

Through Sky and Stars by Tessa Croft. Can Val and Nicole's love cross space and time to change the fate of humanity? (978-1-63679-862-2)

Uncomplicate It by Kel McCord. When an office attraction threatens her career, Hollis Reed's carefully laid plans demand revision. (978-1-63679-864-6)

Vanguard by Gun Brooke. Beth Wild, Subterranean freedom fighter, is in the crosshairs when she fights for her people and risks her heart for loving the exacting Celestial dissident leader, LaSierra Delmonte. (978-1-63679-818-9)

Wild Night Rising by Barbara Ann Wright. Riding Harleys instead of horses, the Wild Hunt of myth is once again unleashed upon the world. Their ousted leader and a fey cop must join forces to rein in the ride of terror. (978-1-63679-749-6)

Heart's Appraisal by Jo Hemmingwood. Andy and Hazel can't deny their attraction, but they'll never agree on the place they call home. (978-1-63679-856-1)

Behold My Heart by Ronica Black. Alora Anders is a highly successful artist who's losing her vision. Devastated, she hires Bodie Banks, a young struggling sculptor as a live-in assistant. Can Alora open her mind and her heart to accept Bodie into her life? (978-1-63679-810-3)

Fearless Hearts by Radclyffe. One wounded woman, one determined to protect her—and a summertime of risk, danger, and desire. (978-1-63679-837-0)

Forever Family by L.M. Rose. Two friends come together after tragedy to raise a baby, finding love along the way. (978-1-63679-868-4)

Stranger in the Sand by Renee Roman. Grace Langley is haunted by guilt. Fagan Shaw wishes she could remember her past. Will finding each other bring the closure they're looking for in order to have a brighter future? (978-1-63679-802-8)

The Nursing Home Hoax by Shelley Thrasher and Ann Faulkner. In this fresh take for grown-ups on the classic Nancy Drew series, crime-solving duo Taylor and Marilee investigate suspicious activity at a small East Texas nursing home. (978-1-63679-806-6)

The Rise and Fall of Conner Cody by Chelsey Lynford. A successful yet lonely Hollywood starlet must decide if she can let go of old wounds and accept a chance at family, friendship, and the love of a lifetime. (978-1-63679-739-7)

A Conflict of Interest by Morgan Adams. Tensions rise when a one-night stand becomes a major conflict of interest between an up-and-coming senior associate and a dedicated cardiac surgeon. (978-1-63679-870-7)

A Magnificent Disturbance by Lee Lynch. These everyday dykes and their friends will stop at nothing to see the women's clinic thrive and, in the process, their ideals, their wounds, and a steadfast allegiance to one another make them heroes. (978-1-63679-031-2)

A Marvelous Murder by David S. Pederson. When a hated director is found dead in his locked study, movie star Victor Marvel, his boyfriend Griff, and friend Eve seek to uncover what really happened to Orland Orcott. (978-1-63679-798-4)

Big Corpse on Campus by Karis Walsh. When University Police Officer Cappy Flannery investigates what looks like a clear-cut suicide, she discovers that the case—and her feelings for librarian Jazz—are more complicated than she expected. (978-1-63679-852-3)

Charity Case by Jean Copeland. Bad girl Lindsay Chase came home to Connecticut for a fresh start, but an old, risky habit provides the chance to save the day for her new love, Ellie. (978-1-63679-593-5)

Moments to Treasure by Ali Vali. Levi Montbard and Yasmine Hassani have found a vast Templar treasure, but there is much more to the story—and what is left to be found. (978-1-63679-473-0)

The Stolen Girl by Cari Hunter. Detective Inspector Jo Shaw is determined to prove she's fit for work after an injury that almost killed her, but a new case brings her up against people who will do anything to preserve their own interests, putting Jo—and those closest to her—directly in the line of fire. (978-1-63679-822-6)

www.ingramcontent.com/pod-product-compliance
Lightning Source LLC
Chambersburg PA
CBHW022006010726
47494CB00003B/913